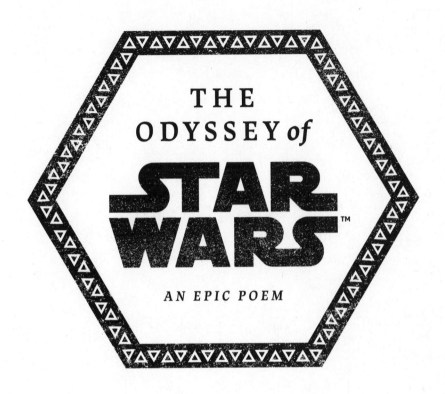

THE
ODYSSEY *of*
STAR WARS™

AN EPIC POEM

THE ODYSSEY *of* STAR WARS™

AN EPIC POEM

JACK MITCHELL

Abrams Image, New York

Editor: Connor Leonard
Managing Editor: Annalea Manalili
Designer: Diane Shaw
Design Manager: Shawn Dahl, dahlimama inc
Production Manager: Rachael Marks

Library of Congress Control Number: 2021932638

ISBN: 978-1-4197-5628-3

Printed and bound in the Unites States
1 3 5 7 9 10 8 6 4 2

Abrams Image books are available at special discounts when purchased in
quantity for premiums and promotions as well as fundraising or educational
use. Special editions can also be created to specification. For details, contact
specialsales@abramsbooks.com or the address below.

ABRAMS The Art of Books
195 Broadway, New York, NY 10007
abramsbooks.com

Lubae

uxori carissimae

Caio Silvanoque

filiis optimis

do dedico

CONTENTS

BOOK I: TATOOINE   1

BOOK II: THE DEATH STAR   29

BOOK III: YAVIN   47

BOOK IV: HOTH   69

BOOK V: DAGOBAH   89

BOOK VI: THE PURSUIT OF THE *Falcon*   109

BOOK VII: CLOUD CITY   127

BOOK VIII: THE RESCUE OF HAN SOLO   149

BOOK IX: ENDOR   169

BOOK X: THE CHOICE OF VADER   193

ACKNOWLEDGMENTS   216

TATOOINE

T he choice of Vader, who forsook the way
    And knelt before the throne, and wore the mask,
    Slayer and slain, betrayer and betrayed,
More god than mortal, more machine than man –
Sing of it, Muse, who linger on the rim
Of one lost galaxy, far, far away,
Recalling how it was that, long ago,
The paths of son and father first converged
Above the wastes of Tatooine, compelled
And doomed by that indwelling power that binds
All living things and balances our fate:
What brought those two together, long apart,

INVOCATION

10

And kindled savage war among the stars?
The Death Star's readouts, secret diagrams
That built a battle station like a moon,
A planet-killer, poised in every sky,
The Emperor's implement of terror: soon,
The Senate crushed, the Council dissolute,
The proud Republic's remnants swept away,
20   Illimitable cruelty, matchless power
Would crown at last the malice of the Sith.
        Yet new hope beckoned: from the lofty vaults
Atop the soaring spire of Scarif's base
Jyn Erso stole the secret, slipping down,
Daring with her indomitable band
JYN ERSO   To infiltrate, encircle, and assault
The Empire's archive: so it was Jyn claimed
Her birthright, since that Death Star was devised
By Galen Erso's genius, from the day
30   The Empire stripped the father of his child.
Far had the orphan wandered, seeking fate,
At first in Saw Gerrera's stubborn ranks
But soon forsaken, while her father toiled
Over his plans and prints, willing to bear
The names of slave and tool of war machines
If only he might chisel, at its core,
A fissure, imperceptible to all,
So that the Death Star, perfect and immense,
Might shatter at the prickle of a pin.
40   Alas that you, poor Galen, never saw
Its end, as, bombed and broken in the rain
Of Eadu, you, with dying breath, bequeathed
The secret to your daughter, whose fierce tears
Vowed more than mourning; she'd have made you proud:
Rebel among the rebels, now Jyn flinched
From nothing, launching on a rogue attack,
BATTLE OF   Daring with that indomitable band
SCARIF   To pluck and beam the readouts to the fleet
That rushed to save her; but all perished there,
50   On Scarif or in Scarif's crystal sky,
Commandos, frigates, starfighters, corvettes,
Except a few who, lancing past the stars,

Fled safe to Yavin and the hidden base:
For Vader came, and, like a fortress door
That falls to trap attackers in the gate,
There to be scalded, crushed, shrinking to face
Extinction, so his Star Destroyer blocked
The path to safety: Raddus' flagship rolled
Disabled as the troopers stormed aboard
60   To seize the stolen plans, Lord Vader first,
His saber flashing, though a sleek corvette,
Detaching at the last, escaped. Meanwhile,
Arriving like an omen tolling doom,
The Death Star struck the Scarif base below:
Then troopers, rebels, battlements, and ships,
And Jyn herself, with Cassian, came to naught
Beneath the bright, apocalyptic fire.
      Yet so it was the secret readouts slid
Through Vader's fingers as he clenched his grip:
70   For Bail Organa's daughter, brave and bold,
Aboard that sleek corvette, received them safe,
And to Antilles now she turned her gaze:
      "Captain, fear lies behind us, fear ahead,
But hope within. Steer for the Outer Rim
And not for Alderaan; seek those twin suns
Not distant, circled by the world of sand."
      So Leia spoke; Antilles shifted course,
And through the constellations picked his way,
Adhering to no line, but doubling back,
80   To Ukio the bountiful, then Roon,
Then damp Kowak, then out to Hypori;
FLIGHT OF
THE Tantive   But there was Vader, waiting, since the Force
Was with him; *Devastator* was that ship,
A mighty Star Destroyer; with a scream
The turbolasers' livid salvo struck
The *Tantive*, although the hyperdrive
Was spared, Antilles with his own hard hand
Engaged it, and they shot to Iskalon.
Yet like a bird of prey that twilight sends
90   Aloft to circle far above the dew
'Til from its trembling den the hapless hare
Scampers and feels sharp talons pluck its flesh,

So Vader tracked them, matching course for course,
From Iskalon to Vuzsa and at last
From Vuzsa to the skies of Tatooine.

How shall I do you justice, desert world?
Little of life you have, but that most stark

TATOOINE Amid the lifelessness; little of fate
But that so fateful as to shift the stars.

100 O realm of solitude, your brutal cliffs
Chiseled by oceans none can now conceive,
Your canyons dug by demiurges, caves
Known only to the wind, your scorching plains
And rippling dunes see little of my race:
Rather the gaffi-bearing Tusken roams
Your wastes atop the bantha, single file,
Between the farms which from the arid air
Distill a golden dew. Gritty the man
Who settled first your bitter dust, relieved

110 To lift his gaze to Chenini at dusk,
To Ghomrassen and Guermessa the bright.
Into that sky the *Tantive* flashed forth,
Hurtling from hyperspace; the hot pursuit
Of *Devastator* followed, Vader's ship,
Whose turrets crackled, smashing through the shields,
Striking the main reactor. So the chase
Concluded: soon the dogged tractor beam
Will seize and roughly haul them back and up
Into the hangar. Princess Leia sees

120 The seconds ticking down before the storm;
She sprints across the reeling ship to call

LEIA'S
PLAN A loyal droid, R2: in robes of snow
She stands before his camera, fingers clasped,
Making the speech the astromech records:
"General Kenobi, years ago you served
My father in the Clone Wars. Now he begs
Your help against the Empire too. Alas,
I cannot plead in person, since my ship
Has been attacked, and I shall not succeed

130 In ferrying you hence. This astromech
Bears information that the rebel cause

Must have or die, and which my father knows
How to recover. Please, bring this droid safe
To Alderaan: the last, most desperate hour
Hastens upon us. Help me now, I beg:
In Obi-Wan Kenobi lies my hope."
  Just so she spoke, and slipped the secret disc
Into the good droid's memory, whispering words
Of clear command, then veiled her braided head
140 And fled to hide away; the shuddering ship
Is clasped; before the airlock brave marines
Level their blasters for the final fight.
  Meanwhile the smoky starship's battered halls
Echo the droid's name, echo R2's name
As brass C-3PO pursues his friend,
Vociferously fretting, filled with dread,
R2-D2 AND But soon enough relieved to reunite.
C-3PO Then through the roiling battle they proceed,
Around the sprawl and agony of death,
150 With R2 leading, wheeling right, now left,
Now right again, along that corridor
Where the escape pods wait; there, ducking in,
They drop unseen into the breathless void.
As when autumnal seeds of wroshyr twirl,
Borne by a crisp wind to the clammy ground
Along a route no watcher could predict,
Just so the capsule crossed the stratosphere,
Plummeting, 'til the jerky chute deployed
High in the dry bright sky: the Jundland Wastes
160 Receive it, like a stone upon the sea.
  Across a dune they're dragged, and from the pod
With many a groan and whistle they emerge
To gaze on nothing, only endless sand;
Though R2's scanners buzz: he chirps and purls.
Alas, dissension soon divides the friends,
Whether to try the gorge or scale the ridge,
And thus the brass interpreter declares:
  "Oh, dreadful hour of desolation, why
Did I, the darling of adversity, agree
170 To follow you down here? My gears freeze up
For lack of oil, my joints for lack of rest.

C-3PO'S
LAMENT

This secret mission, from which these fond bleeps
Give me no peace, serves rather to raise doubt
Of your poor circuitry, which in this heat
Perhaps malfunctions. No, enough's enough:
Follow the gorge, but I shall try the ridge;
Now pester me no more, I'll help you not."
        Thus Threepio, who turned his metal back;
So each companion picked a separate path,
180   The one annoyed, the other duty-bent,
But both regretful and foreboding ill.

        Thus on the planet; meanwhile in the sky
Vader commands they tear the ship apart
Until the plans be found; in disbelief
He heard Antilles' diplomatic claim,

VADER
AND LEIA

Wringing his neck with more than human strength.
They dropped the captain's corpse into the void
To freeze among the mummies of his crew,
Floating forever. Then from deck to deck
190   The troopers, blasters set to stun, pursue
The passengers, soon captive; they parade
The Princess to the presence of their lord.
        Fearless she stares up at that awful mask
Before which Jedi quailed, when through the stars
He hunted them at Palpatine's behest
'Til all their fire had left the universe
And he remained alone: that mask he'd worn
Since she for whom he'd picked the path of wrath
Had judged that death was better than the dark;
200   Terror as black as starless space itself
Haunted the polished mouth and eyes, its breath
The rasp and suffocation of despair.
Yet Leia dared to face him and to feign
Amazement, outrage; but Lord Vader thus:
        "Ah, Princess, check your shock: only a fool
Could think compassion brought you here: myself
I stalked this ship at Scarif: rebel spies
Transmitted you those plans. Senate, you say?
Traitor twice over, since you have rebelled
210   Against that order of the galaxy

Which ought to be your care! Yet have no fear:
Your insolence, and your Rebellion's, reach
The preappointed end. Take her away!"
 So Vader spoke; just as the awful mask
Concealed him from her, neither could he see
In her the eyes familiar to his dreams.
 Some troopers drag her off, others report
How the escape pod, seeming lifeless, fell;
He charges them to seek it: soon a squad
220 Aboard a shuttle passes far aloft
Over the planet's surface, scanning swift,
With no success before the break of day.
Landing, the troopers occupy the town,
Mos Eisley, wretched hive, procuring beasts
Toughened to desert travel: soon they reach
The pod and note the telltale track of droids.

 Meanwhile interpreter and astromech
Pursued their separate routes across the sand;
Yet danger lurks among the dunes and crags:
230 A lonely walker seldom walks alone.
 Strange are the forms of life and manifold,
Peopling the habitable spheres: on some
Myriad fauna, flora, humanoids
Bicker and thrive in their diversity;
THE JAWAS But Tatooine had few: the crafty worrt,
The slippery womp rat, and the tasty gorg,
The dewlap and the bantha and the krayt,
Th' immortal Sarlacc, whose perpetual feast
Would torture Fett; yet of these denizens
240 Two only had evolved the power of speech,
The brutal Tusken Raiders and that race
Of canny Jawas, whom the dragons drove
For refuge to the mines of silicax;
But soon the miners left, and soon those tribes
Took up the old equipment, plied the plains,
Peddling their stock in sandcrawlers, tall towers
Of mobile metal grinding over rock.
These now, with eyes like glowing coals recessed
Beneath their hoods, take aim: for R2 glides

250 Within the ambush, and their ion blast
Fells him. Four seize the poor insentient droid,
Sucking him up into the cargo cage,
A purgatory of relics, droids too smashed,

DROIDS
REUNITED Too rusty, mangy, antiquated, marred
For labor: all the outcasts, all the scrapped,
The desert chattel. In that cage R2
Detects, in his despair, to his delight,
His fussy dear companion, seized himself
By that same Jawa crew. Then through the dark
260 The friends, interpreter and astromech,
Rumble and rock toward the closest farm.

There was a youth, a farmer's son, a boy;
He loved Beru, who 'round the wide Dune Sea
Was called the desert rose, a girl most dear
To Shmi, the youth's stepmother, who advised:
"Owen, why do you hesitate? Speak now
And let Beru have all her heart's desire."

BERU AND
OWEN So they were married. Often, at the hearth,
Beru heard tales of how Shmi's only son,
270 By birth a slave and fatherless, but schooled
To battle evil and maintain the right,
Roamed through the stars, a Jedi Knight, her son!
But when Beru would ask, Shmi would not say
Where he was living, why he kept apart.
Yours was a bitter fate, poor Shmi: too late
To stop the torture of a Tusken blade
Your son came home, pursuing them too late,
Holding you as you died, 'til hatred swelled
Within: all of them, all the Tuskens, all,
280 He sabered, slaughtering, hacking, 'til that camp
Was strewn with limbs of old and young alike.
Beside your grave he buckled; there Beru
Shivered to watch him weep, as love and hate
Fought back and forth across that still fair face,
And Owen said, "My brother is accursed."
Never again they saw him, 'til one eve
A peddler wandered past, a humble man,

Bearded and cloaked, and Owen looked askance;
And somber was the news the peddler brought:
290   "Beru and Owen, though you know me not,
To me you are familiar from his tales,
Anakin's, who upon the ashy pyre
Has left this world, your brother and my friend.
I am Kenobi, lately of that creed
Of ancient Jedi, whom now fear and grief

OBI-WAN   Have exiled, grief for Anakin, and fear
KENOBI   Of him who claimed him, whom myself I fought
On Mustafar, that world of shade and flame:
The Emperor's apprentice: then the hand
300   Of Anakin was severed by a trick,
But up I snatched the weapon of my friend.
The Emperor hunts the Jedi, but in vain:
For in a newborn babe the Jedi live:
Behold, I bring the son of Anakin,
A baby whom the mother, as she died,
Named Luke, for whom nor kith nor kin remains
Except for you. I cannot raise the child:
A warrior is no parent; in my grief
I seek seclusion and a silent spot
310   To contemplate the purpose of the stars.
Here is your nephew; will he be your son?
This only I request, that when he grows
And comes of age this lightsaber be his,
A token of the father he'll know not."
    So Obi-Wan declared, and in one hand
He showed the weapon, while the other clasped
The bundled babe, asleep beneath his cloak,
Whom bright Beru with softest fingers took.
She had no child, no child but this; her heart
320   Filled with affection. So her sober spouse,
Seeing her bliss, agreed, but with a frown
To Obi-Wan thus grimly he replied:
    "We take the boy, and for Beru and me
He'll be both son and nephew, though my heart
Is heavy as I guess my brother's heir
Shall know still greater grief. Alas the day

He followed your ideals, getting involved
In some crusade! Such is the bitter wage
Of reckless courage. Yes, we take the boy,
330   But at this price, that he must never learn
His father's wizardry and yours, old man.
We take the boy, but that fey saber keep
Yourself, to sell or cast away: his task
Shall be the chores of farmers, patient arts
Of toil and husbandry, the lot of man."
    So Owen spoke, and so amid the crops

And vaporators Luke from infancy
To boyhood and the cusp of manliness
Advanced, aiding his uncle, learning much
340   About the taste of earth, the weight of air,
The language of condensers; yet his heart
Was fixed beyond the circle of the sky.
When duty left him leisure, he would speed
His uncle's old skyhopper down the gorge,
Or bull's-eye womp rats in that T-16
Up Beggar's Canyon; irresponsible
Some termed him, others asinine, some few
Adventuresome, though none could well deny
No better pilot winged the desert bush
350   Except for Biggs, three years gone, Biggs who'd left
To practice at that pilot school. His friends
Would look away and mutter, "Patience, Luke,"
But patience seems no virtue to the bold.

    Filled with such thoughts atop the breezy slope,
Young Skywalker at daybreak first descried
The rusty transport jostling on its way
Toward the silent farm. So down Luke jogs
To call his uncle, who with folded arms
Awaits the sandcrawler already; soon
360   The transport halts, the Jawas tumble out,
Flaunting their ragged stock, and then R2
And Threepio together pass to Luke,
Whom Owen bids prepare them for the work.
    Only a droid, thick with the grime and grease
Of thankless labor, knows the salving bliss

Of bathing oil from which a gritty limb
Emerges fresh anointed; thither Luke
Guides the interpreter, turning to chip
The crud off R2. Soon the talk ascends
370   To worlds beyond the dunes, the clash of war,
The resolute Rebellion; unforeseen
THE   A hologram, R2's projection, flits,
HOLOGRAM   Showing a woman wrapped in robes of snow,
Fair as the dusk, her single utterance looped:
"In Obi-Wan Kenobi lies my hope":
No more can Luke recover from the droid,
Nor learn her name, nor whence the message comes,
But ever and again she speaks the same:
"In Obi-Wan Kenobi lies my hope."
380   Then R2-D2, clever to the core,
With many a beep to Threepio, affects
That the restraining bolt, voltaic chain,
Obstructs his circuits, so Luke sets him free;
Yet nothing more the wily droid displays,
Nor even what he'd shown; baffled, they blame
His rusty innards, even his good faith.
Yet Luke, the woman etched upon his eye,
Ponders anew; he recollects old Ben,
That hermit whose abode lay past the dunes:
390   He bore the name Kenobi. Soon Beru
Calls him to supper, where his uncle frowns,
Reporting Obi-Wan as long-since dead,
Deaf to the boy's ambitions, which again
Turn to the pilot school. Unhappy home
In which the future wrestles with the past,
Where sons despair of parents, they of sons,
And each restricts the other's destiny!

Meanwhile the good R2, as down the sky
Those rosy discs, eternal partners, slipped,
400   Snuck from the farm unhindered, rolling off
Into the rocky maze of silent shade.
R2-D2   As when, across the gulf of space, a stone
SETS FORTH   Hurtles alone from star to distant star,
Rebounding through the nets of nebula,

Just so the astromech sought him whom once
He'd saved above Naboo, and then again
High in the war-torn sky of Coruscant,
When General Grievous, striking from afar,
Gambled his whole huge fleet in one grand raid.
410 What visions haunt the dreams of droids? By night,
The only balm, oblivion, softly falls
On brains and marrow, like a blanket tucked
By mother's hands around a dozy child;
Yet droids do not forget, save if we wipe
Their memory: thus could R2 recollect
Kenobi's whiskers ere the frost of care
Had grazed them, even ere he'd shed the braid
Of Padawan, when like a sudden brook
That rattles boulders off the mountainside
420 He overpowered Maul and took revenge
For his dear master. This and all that flowed
From those dire days now occupied the droid,
Who pushed ahead in darkness. When the dawn
Restored the hue and measure of all things,
Luke woke to find him gone; without a word

LUKE'S PURSUIT To aunt or uncle, Threepio in back,
He leaps into the speeder: swift as pods
That used to race on Malastare, they fly,
Skimming the outstretched desert. Soon the scan
430 Detects the quarry, whom they overtake
Among the crumbling crags of rusty flint.
C-3PO delivers this rebuke:
    "What shame is mine to find my friend has none!
What faith misplaced in utter faithlessness!
That's quite enough of missions, quite enough
Of Obi-Wan Kenobi gibberish: cease!
Here is your master, here your place – What's this?"
        For like a kettle kept upon the flame
R2 is whistling, whirling: from the east,
440 He urges, several living things approach.
Then Luke, with hapless Threepio in tow,
Daring or reckless, dauntless or unwise,
Ascends the ridge to scout; his scope discerns

THE
SAND PEOPLE

Two brooding banthas, yet no Sand People:
For those, with stout gaderffii sticks, were first
Upon that ridge, the Tuskens: Tusken howls
Of ambush, triumph, tear the dusty air:
Poor Threepio is broken, limbs askew;
The farmer lad is struck and knows no more.

450

    Your tale then, Luke, was nearly at an end
In wretched death or slavery; nonetheless
The Force was with you: through the hollow gorge
Uncanny echoes of a beast enraged,
The cruel krayt dragon, universal foe,

THE
HERMIT

Dispersed in dread those raiders of the waste;
Yet R2-D2, hidden close, beholds
No monster stoop beside his master's form;
No, some old fellow, nameless 'neath a hood,
Is kneeling there: his beneficial touch

460

Brushes the boy's cold brow, who soon awakes.
The joyful astromech emerges; Luke
In grateful wonder greets the old man thus:
    "O stranger, do I live, and do I breathe?
My thanks, if you have found me; triple thanks
If you have saved me. Where's the droid, Artoo?
Ah, here he comes: in quest of him, old man,

LUKE'S
ACCOUNT

Too lightly traveling through the Jundland Wastes,
Another droid and I have come to grief;
Artoo alone, intent upon a task

470

Set by a woman clad in white, snuck off
To seek an Obi-Wan Kenobi, whom
The lady named: she said her only hope
In Obi-Wan Kenobi lay; alas,
This Obi-Wan is dead; instead we seek
Old Ben, the hermit, some relation, who
In contemplation dwells among these crags,
For he may know the droid. Good stranger, tell,
Where is his door? Is Ben Kenobi far?"
    So spoke young Skywalker, to whom in turn,

480

With quiet laughter, casting back his hood,
The fellow spoke, helping him to his feet:

"My lad, your Ben's not far, however old,
For here he stands before you, though in truth
We ought to seek that door without delay:
The Sand People who scatter soon return.

But Ben knows not your droid, and never owned
An astromech, though hundreds have I seen.
Perhaps in my adventures we once met.
Yet here's some comfort: Obi-Wan still lives

490

In me, for I am Obi-Wan, a name
Unspoken through the years since you were born,
So how your lady knows it I know not.
Homeward, therefore; but bring your other droid."

So spoke Kenobi, and Luke climbed ahead
To where in pieces lay poor Threepio,
Soon reassembled; then the speeder hastes
Along the hidden route to Ben's abode.

Deep in the desert, blended with its dust,
Rubbed by the rolling sandstorms rose those walls,

500

Cheerless without but comforting within,
Cool as a cup of water, soft as wool,
With couches, tables, tea, an antique stove,
Lit by a hollow window and a lamp;

There Ben gives Skywalker a seat, provides
A snack of fruit, a basin and a towel,
Refills the glistening waterpipe of chrome,
And lets the guest repose. Upon the walls
Strange items dangle, which, awaiting Ben,
Sipping his tea, young Skywalker admires:

510

A tiny painting most of all, well daubed,
That showed a setting sun and, spread beneath,
A sprawling city, infinite, that ringed
A temple topped with five ascendant towers,
Four guarding one, which in tranquility,
Ageless and deathless, scraped the flaming sky;
A costly work, but framed in scraps of wood.
Enchanted by the picture, with a sigh
Luke wistfully exclaims to Obi-Wan:

"What treasures hang here, symbols of bold deeds,
520 Or so I guess, feats such as I, in time,
LUKE'S After the harvest, may myself achieve.
AMBITION If only he, my father, like yourself,
Had bravely gone to war, not risked his life
For profit as a navigator – risked
And lost it – on some freighter: thus, perhaps,
Such relics might be mine, and I the heir
Of glory, bearing more than just a name."
    Thus Luke; the hermit entered and replied:
    "Forgive my sigh, my smile; your name, o Luke,
530 O son of Anakin, is more than fame.
Ah, how your words seem echoes, even now,
LUKE'S Of that fair comrade, best of friends, with whom
FATHER I battled in the Clone Wars, side by side.
Your uncle's fooled you. Navigator, eh,
On freighters? Nay, a fighter was his ship,
And none could match him. Jedi Knights were we,
Guardians of peace and justice, sworn to serve
The proud Republic. Here, if treasures hold
Some interest, take this relic for your own:
540 A lightsaber, your father's, such a blade
As Jedi wielded ere the darkness fell,
A piece of history: with this very sword
Your father slew Count Dooku the accursed."
    So speaking, from the dusty chest he lifts
That wondrous weapon, which the boy receives:
Standing, Luke flicks a button; from the hilt
THE The dazzling edge, a flame of blue, extends,
LIGHTSABER Like fire infused with sky, or stars with sea,
Crackling with kyber, cleaving through the gloom.
550 As when a fisherman, whose patient rod
At last provides a supper, whirls it quick
To left, to right, uniting wrist and wit,
So Luke first swung that incandescent brand,
Exulting in its elegance, and spoke:
    "Alas that I can never meet him, nor
Know more than stories: such a tool as this

Is worthy of a champion. Oh, alas,

LUKE'S
QUESTIONS
If he was such as you describe, good Ben,
A Jedi Knight (whatever that may be),

560
A famous fighter pilot (oh, what fame!),
How could death overtake a man so great?"
  To which at length old Obi-Wan replied:
  "Now there, my lad, I am not blameless. Once
I took a pupil, named myself a sage,
Though he was old, and I perhaps too young,
And seldom what I taught was learned; too late

OBI-WAN'S
PUPIL
I saw him slip and stumble from the path,
Seduced toward the dark side of the Force,
And take the name of Vader; by his hand

570
The Jedi fell; betrayed and murdered too
Your father with them. Yet to die is sweet
Beside poor Vader's fate, whose madness sought
To overthrow the tyranny of death."
  Then Skywalker, amazed, had this to ask:
  "But what could ever counter death? What too
Is this strange Force? How came it to be dark?"
  At this the hermit softly made reply:
  "My answer will seem easy to a youth;
For me, who stand so close, the breath of death

580
Is cold; yet knowledge steadies me the more.
For death is nothing but the form of fate
Toward the end: we sense in its embrace
A love of what must be, must ever be,
Surrounding us and penetrating us,

THE FORCE
The timeless Force, which breaks and binds all things,
In which all things arise and fall away.
Ah, but the Force is hard to understand,
A mystery wherein Jedi knit their will
With destiny itself, and so with death.

590
Alas, death fascinates us: some are drawn
To dominate and make a slave of fate,
Exchanging what must be for what cannot,
Acceptance for ambition, joy for hate,
Order for rage, contentment for despair,
And peace for ceaseless battle; thence it flows,

The dark side of the Force, which chooses power
Not over self but over all the world.
That dark side triumphs now, since through the stars
The Jedi fled from Vader's fell pursuit,
600   And he remains alone. Yet hope is found
In strange occasions: with these withered lips
I prophesy the Jedi must return."
        Such was the word of Obi-Wan, but Luke
Could give no answer: straightaway R2
Projects the Princess' hologram: at last
She stands before them, flickering, fingers clasped:
        "General Kenobi, years ago you served
LEIA'S   My father in the Clone Wars. Now he begs
MESSAGE   Your help against the Empire too. Alas,
610   I cannot plead in person, since my ship
Has been attacked, and I shall not succeed
In ferrying you hence. This astromech
Bears information that the rebel cause
Must have or die, and which my father knows
How to recover. Please, bring this droid safe
To Alderaan: the last, most desperate hour
Hastens upon us. Help me now, I beg:
In Obi-Wan Kenobi lies my hope."
        So spoke the woman clad in robes of snow;
620   Amazed, the listeners rise, as though inspired
By flutes or trumpets. Like a knight of old
Kenobi girds himself, his aching spine
Shrugs off the decades and the hoary beard
Juts out, his breathing slows, his eyes perceive
The present and the future and the past.
He turns to Luke and speaks these wingèd words:
        "You ask about the Force, young Skywalker,
BEN'S   But you yourself are stepping on the path.
PROPOSAL   To learn the way, come now to Alderaan
630   With me, for her Rebellion and for her.
Was ever duty clearer? No, not when
Windu decrypted Depa's signal, beamed
From the grim pirates' ship, and with his blade
Of amethyst delivered her, who soon

Would counsel Jedi. But Organa's child –
For such is she, a princess of the stars –
Shall never summon Obi-Wan in vain."
　　　Yet Luke, like one who hesitates to plunge
Into a frigid stream, though foes approach,

640　Mentions his uncle, duties on the farm,

**LUKE
DECLINES**

The distance. Wisely then old Obi-Wan
Accepts a lift to Anchorhead instead.
They climb aboard the speeder, droids in back;
Across the gusty plain they wing their way.

　　　Vader meanwhile had quitted Tatooine
To seek the Death Star, taking Leia too;
Three squads upon the planet, steady troops
Detached to hunt the fleeing droids, now tracked
The sandcrawler. From farm to farm that day

650　They plod its dusty furrows; as they go
They seize two banthas; these, in Tusken guise,
They use to lure the Jawas, who, alas,
Fall to the troopers' skillful blasts; their chief

**DEATHS OF
OWEN AND BERU**

In dying points the way to Lars's farm.
Thus even as Luke gazed upon the walls
Of Ben's abode, the walls of home were burned,
For Owen spat defiance, and Beru,
Who rushed to save him, perished at his side.
　　　Across the plain the pillars of those fires

660　Were seen by Luke and Ben; no bantha tracks
Could trick a Jedi; horrified, Luke speeds
From the dead Jawas to those moisture towers
Familiar as the sky, but now destroyed:
A scene of devastation shocks the eye,
The drifting soot, the scars of blasters, wrecks
Of other droids, the shattered T-16,
And there before the door, like broken glass,
Two skeletons still smoking. Then Luke's heart
Was crushed with horror, crushed as though to burst;

670　Yet even so a whisper in his thought
Invited him to sorrow and to life,

To shed the shackle of uncertainty,
To reach beyond the circle of the sky.
Listening, he wept and spoke a last farewell:
　　"For this, it seems, Beru, you took me in;
Uncle, for this you taught me all I know,
That here before your doorway, cruelly killed,

LUKE'S LAMENT

You'd lie unburied. Someday I'll come back
To raise a double tomb upon the plain

680 Beside my father's mother; through the stars
I'll seek my father's own, roaming with Ben,
To lose my life or learn the Jedi way;
My love of Tatooine will rest with you."
　　Just so Luke spoke, and shook away the tears,
Rejoining old Kenobi and the droids
Beside the smolder of the Jawas' pyre.

　　Soon they were skimming off toward the port,
Past Anchorhead, the farmers' depot, down
The canyon from the mesa, 'til they reached

690 Mos Eisley, wretched hive of villainy,
Swept by the sandstorms, thirsty with neglect,
A maze of alleys, faceless doors, dead ends,
A city filled with moaning, muttered deals,
And cryptic hints of profit in the sand.
Here the limp law could little hinder greed;

MOS EISLEY

Hither the smugglers of the Outer Rim
Would scuttle past the tariffs; here the Hutt
Had slapped his seal upon the hyperlanes
That linked Arkanis, Ryloth, Molavar;

700 The outlaw here was king, here life was cheap,
Here murder seldom noted, ever feared.
　　Into the foul metropolis they cruised,
And many a cautious word old Ben bestowed
With eloquent examples; yet the troops
Were there before them, armor smudged with smoke:

A JEDI MIND TRICK

A checkpoint blocks their path: the droids are eyed
By stormtroopers' white helmets. Subtle Ben
Deflects their questions, turns their cold commands

To blessings: these were not the droids they sought;
710   The testy captain waves them past the guns.
In answer to Luke's wonder, Ben remarks:
    "My boy, the Force lies not in swords alone:
It may be wielded like a club or cloth
That steers the feeble-minded back and forth.
But more of this in time: behold, we've reached
The old cantina. Aye, in this rough place
Most of the slickest freighter pilots drink.
Follow me now; the droids must wait outside."
    So spoke the Jedi; through the narrow door
720   He steps into the gloom, and Luke attends.
Ah, what a throng of patrons meets his eye!
Freebooters, scoundrels, pirates, renegades,

THE CANTINA   Madmen, marauders, mercenaries, moles,
All came to Chalmun's, species numberless:
The furry Gotal and the Pacithhip,
The Snivvian sour, the Saurin jagged-toothed,
The lipless Duros, eyes a bulbous red,
The wily Devaronian and the Talz,
Pointy Arcona, thirsty Chadra-Fans,
730   The hammerhead Ithorian, double-mouthed,
The Wookiee, all too easily enraged,
The fickle Stennes Shifter, the Ranat,
And countless more besides: gamblers and quacks,
Pickpockets, hustlers, desperados, scum.
The drink was flowing, music swinging free:
That band of black-eyed Bith had seized the stage,
The Modal Nodes, and Figrin D'an had dropped
His horn to sing of Windu, how he slew
Bold Jango Fett, the father of the clones,
740   On Geonosis when, like some vast wave,
The battle droids descended, Jedi fought
Against an army, how poor Jango's head
Was cut from those thick shoulders, tumbling back
Into his son's small hands, who vowed revenge:
Such was the song; the band was swinging free,
The drink was flowing. Trailing Obi-Wan,
Young Skywalker takes station at the bar.

Yet even as Kenobi seeks a ship,

A QUARREL   Two wanted men browbeat the farmer lad,

750   Picking a quarrel: Dr. Evazan

And Baba drew their blasters, but in vain,

For Baba's arm was severed by the blade

Of Obi-Wan Kenobi, flashing forth

Like ice aflame; then with a slender smile

The Jedi lifts the fallen Luke unhurt,

Leading him, with the Wookiee, to a booth.

Now who is unfamiliar with the skill,

The bowcaster, the growl, the towering wrath

Of proud Chewbacca? Bountiful Kashyyyk

760   Had been his home, 'til Wookiees felt the chain

CHEWBACCA   Of slavery, forced to hew the wroshyr tree,

AND SOLO   Wood better whittled into spears to spit

Imperial occupiers; yet good luck

Appointed him a buccaneer's first mate,

Solo's, with oaths unbreakable. To him

He guided now the Jedi and the boy,

For there Han sat, rejoicing in his wit,

Han Solo, who'd once made the Kessel Run

In fourteen parsecs (or, some say, just twelve),

770   A prince of rogues. The Wookiee briefs his chief,

Who skeptically addresses Obi-Wan:

"Old man, to Alderaan, as Chewie says,

You seek quick passage, dodging, shall we say,

Imperial entanglements? For that

You'll surely need a ship as quick as light

And (what is rather rarer) expert hands

SOLO   To steer her. The *Millennium Falcon*'s yours,

NEGOTIATES   Swiftest of ships, not much to look at, though

She's got it where it counts, since I myself

780   Have tinkered somewhat here and there: she'll make

Point five past light speed, easy, and she boasts

Quad cannons on three hundred sixty turrets, skids

As neat as any fighter. Aye, she'll do,

But at a cost: ten thousand in advance

And safely you'll reach peaceful Alderaan."

Such was the smuggler's bargain, but to this
Sly Obi-Wan responded with a smile:
"Desperate indeed would be the man who paid
Ten thousand in advance, yet not more so
790 Than he who asked it. Such a ship we seek
And such a pilot also: we can pay
Only two thousand now – the boy must sell
His speeder, I give all I have in store –
But Alderaan shall grant you fifteen more.
Thus seventeen, once, upon Alderaan,
We're satisfied and drink each other's health."

Now those who live by luck know every creak
A BARGAIN Of fortune's wheel, its lurches, its ascents:
But even Solo, swashbuckler supreme,
800 Had seldom met such random luck as this,
Nor half so timely, since that day his neck
Was in the noose: he'd dumped his smuggled spice
And owed the mighty Jabba, who, enraged,
Had bade the bounty hunters trail him; so
With joy Han seals the deal, and Chewie leaves
To prep the *Falcon* at Bay 94.

Yet luck had other tricks to play. In stealth
Luke and Kenobi leave as troops approach.
Han Solo follows slowly, sunk in thought;
810 But who confronts him, blaster pistol drawn,
But Greedo, bounty hunter, Jabba's tool,
GREEDO The sneering Rodian? Bulbous eyes alight,
He motions Han to sit, and so they sit,
The pistol pointed at the smuggler's eye,
And then the Rodian, coldly chuckling, speaks:
 "Ah, Solo, have we not been here before?
And this is where you promise to repent?
No, no, that touching chapter's finished now,
For Jabba's set a bounty on your hide
820 That half the stars are hunting. Would you care
To meet the Hutt yourself? He's not far off,
Surly, impatient, out beside your ship,
And maybe he'll take that instead of cash.
Go on, go see him; I'll be right behind."

So Greedo spoke. Han Solo, grinning still,
Pondered two courses in his teeming brain,
Whether to trust his enemy and seek
The mercy of the Hutt, and beg for life,
Or risk the Rodian's pistol, shooting first
830 With surreptitious aim, since Greedo's tale
Of Jabba lumbering through Mos Eisley's streets
Was hard to credit – nothing but a ruse.
Pondering all this, but loathe to shoot him first,
Han steered the talk astutely to the risks
That crafty smugglers run; yet all the while
He touched his blaster; cocking it, he pulls

**DEATH OF
GREEDO**

The trigger 'neath the table: Greedo's chest
Explodes; sizzling he slumps, his prior shot
Bent far astray, rehearsed so often, now
840 As futile as his gloating and his glee.
Flipping the barman some small coin, Han strides
Across the smoldering corpse into the street.
        Meanwhile the droids, R2 and Threepio,
Skulked from the passing stormtrooper patrols,
Not spotted in the slum; but Luke and Ben,
The speeder sold, are shadowed by a spy
Who watches them rejoin the droids and jog
Toward Bay 94; there Chewie's growl
Salutes the passengers. Yet right behind,
850 Summoned by secret watchers, trot the troops,
Who charge the bay with E-11s cocked,
Bidding the *Falcon* stop; instead Han sprints
The gangplank, shouts to Chewie to take off.
The stormtroopers' bright lasers split the air
Like streaks of softest chalk a painter swabs
Along fresh parchment, scratching, hissing quick,
Faster and faster still, until he's sketched
The shimmer of a glistening solar wind:
Such was the laser rifles' fusillade;
860 But from the *Falcon* came a sterner blast,
Its cannon answering back at Chewie's touch
As Solo throws himself to the controls,
The others strapping seatbelts: up aloft

Into the dusky purple sky they launch,
Ascending through the jostling atmosphere

ESCAPE OF
THE *FALCON*

To space. The planet, scene of Luke's whole life,
Still bends below; above, the Empire's ships,
Imperial cruisers, three of them, inbound,
Like sharks possessed by ceaseless hunger, glide

870 To trap them, turrets blasting: Chewie points
The rear deflector shield as Solo crams
The nav computer; to Luke's petty taunt
About the *Falcon*'s speed Han answers thus:
        "No doubt three cruisers – seems you're no small fry –
Three cruisers often stalk you on the farm.
Of course they're gaining! No one but a fool
Would blindly jump to light speed; short's the trip
Through supernovas, asteroids, stars – aha!
Here's what we need, the course: we're all strapped in?"

880   Thus Han and, even as the cruisers lunged
With turrets blasting and the battered shield
Was failing, Chewie punched it and they fled.
As when a battlefield of lush Naboo
Resounded with the twang of catapults
That flung the boomas, potent balls of blue
Whirling aloft into the sapphire sky,
Just so the *Falcon*, ere the cruisers struck,
Broke through to hyperspace: the smudging stars
Yield to the velvet of that wrinkled zone

890 In which existence folds, whereby all worlds
Are reached across the infinite abyss;
Therein they hurtled, bound for Alderaan.

        Meanwhile Darth Vader with the Princess came
Unto the Death Star; she is marched away
For questioning about the rebel base.
But Vader meets the bickering officers,

DEATH STAR
MEETING

Whom rank had shorn of mercy, though enhanced
Their jealousy: one doubts the Death Star's strength,
Should rebels gain its secrets, striking swift;

900 Another, with a frothing recklessness,
Extols it as a universal power,

Displacing superstitious Jedi ways –
Poor fool, whom Vader coldly answers thus:
   "What pride is this, that flows from mere machine?
The power to liquidate, explode, or rend,
To smash a planet or to break a seed,
Is nothing next the power of the Force
Which may crush death itself. Knowledge alone
Reveals the future, wherein present deeds
910   Are judged. Therefore have faith, for faithless men
Must learn the lesson of a sorcerer."
   So speaking, Vader lifts an iron hand,
Twitching his fingers; at the other's throat
A grip as cold as ice constricts, a grip

VADER'S GRIP Unseen, unwavering, and unbendable,
Though nothing but the press of flesh itself;
But Tarkin enters, bidding Vader cease,
Rebuking the dispute between the fleet
And Death Star captains, since the stolen plans
920   Would soon be claimed from sandy Tatooine,
While Leia to th' interrogation droids
Would name the hidden sanctum of the foe.
Lord Vader contradicts him: though the plans
Be found, the Princess cannot be compelled
By some mere tool; yet Tarkin has a ploy.

TARKIN'S PLOY He bids the Death Star pilots set a course
For Alderaan, then Leia to be brought
Before himself and Vader. Straightaway
They make it so, and Leia stands unbowed
930   Before them, fearless-eyed, her white robe bright
Among the drab and dreary uniforms,

ALDERAAN Like Alderaan itself, which hung in space
Upon the screen, a circle green and blue,
Loveliest world of all the Core, its seas
Surging with boundless life, its forests thick,
Its cities rich, its snowy mountains sheer;
There, smooth and shapely, 'neath a peak, was built
The regal palace, where Queen Breha dwelt
With noble Bail Organa, ruling well
940   That peaceful people, weaponless and true:

Those were the Princess' parents, that her home,
Those were her cities, those her mountaintops,
Her seas; for love of Alderaan she'd joined
The brave Rebellion, since no beauty counts
If it shall be enslaved to evil men.
Then Grand Moff Tarkin of the Empire speaks:
   "Indeed, o Princess, nothing can compare
To peerless Alderaan, that gave you life;
Gratefully you may give it life in turn.
What glory, to be ranked among the saints

950

Who saved their worlds! Observe the cross-hairs' drift
Across its snug equator: though the blast
Of this destructive station cannot miss,
It may still be deflected or delayed.
Choose now: shall peaceful Alderaan be lost
Through one girl's stubbornness, or shall I pick
A military target? One that hides
The hidden rebel base, from which your fleet
Is wont to prick us? Make the choice yourself."

TARKIN'S THREAT

   So Tarkin spoke, and Leia, frightened pale,
Pondered two courses in her teeming brain,
Whether to give them Yavin, where the base
Was nestled on a jungle moon, in hope
Of saving precious Alderaan, or name
The rebels' vacant base on Dantooine.
Pondering all this, she gave them Dantooine;
To which grim Tarkin, with a slender smile:
   "Now there I do believe you; yet my aim
Is twofold: stamp a rash rebellion out

960

And also bring the restive Core to heel.
Twice have I seen this battle station's blast
Carve pieces from a planet: Jedha lies
In utter ruin, Scarif's seas are boiled;
Single-ignition blasts were those, but here
The full strength shall be tested: let the Core
Observe the fate of Alderaan and crawl."
   So speaking, Tarkin gave the cold command
To fire when ready; Leia, gasping, fought
Against the iron vice of Vader's grip.

970

As slow but sure as mud, which ceaseless rains

Have fed for weeks, will scrape the mountainside,
Colliding with a forest, churning through
The village, so the operation went
Of using that great weapon: target lock,
The final pause, the final safety check,
Ignition of the kyber cores, which yield
Eight hypermatter beams, a livid green
As lucid as a pulsar, whining through
Eight tributaries, 'til the focal point

990 Perfects the bright, apocalyptic ray.

As when a skillful prince of yore let fly
His bronze-tipped spear, when through the battle line
The chariots burst like thunder and afar
The stricken foe crashed backward to the earth,
Yielding his angry spirit with a shout,
Just so the Death Star blasted Alderaan,
Burrowing through the surface: like an egg
Is cracked in careless hands, the vital yolk
Blending with white, the shell in bits that hang

1000 Together with no purpose, so the crust
Of Alderaan now ceased to cup its core,
Here sinking, tipped into the molten depths,
And there blown into orbit, scattered far;
The mass diffused, its gravity unhinged,
The atmosphere is mixed and dissipates,
The mantle scribbled red against black space;
The solid core is ruptured and explodes.
Then, on the screaming surface, oceans drain,
Mountains are dust, the cities ripped to bits,

1010 Palaces, cabins, nurseries, monuments:
A single moment stops the course of time.
All life at once is suffocated, burnt,
Quartered and flayed, depressurised and crushed,
All mammals and all birds, all reptiles, fish,
All insects, down to microscopic cells,
Call out in terror, silenced instantly
And little mourned, for who shall sing laments
When all the mourners perish with the dead?

Poor planet, since your system first took shape,
1020   You'd circled your bright star, the eons etched
Upon your surface, unbeholden, fair;
Better it were that life had never walked
Your fields nor swum your oceans than that now
Its destiny should draw the Death Star near;
For life brings death: the very elements
Diffuse, and what was once a noble globe
Shatters for ever into nameless rocks
Colliding in the quiet of the void.

BOOK II

THE DEATH STAR

INVOCATION

S pirit of learning, angel of the Force,
  In grief, in longing for your tender touch,
  I call you to my side: let sorrow cease,
Let not my singing stagger in despair:
For Alderaan is lost, but we remain
To learn from loss. Instead provoke my thought
With tales of reckless daring, how Luke came
To search the Death Star, how the Princess fought,
How both beheld your servant's sacrifice.

10   Past constellations now the *Falcon* flashed
At lightspeed; far in back the cruisers lagged,

Like slugs behind a cricket; soon the droids
Face Chewie at the bright dejarik board,
Prudently losing; Solo steers the ship;
But Luke and Ben talk idly of the Force,
Its methods and its mysteries and its reach.
Yet even as they speak, Ben winces, groans,
Clutching his side and faltering to a seat.
As when an agèd Duros, rough with toil,

20   Hauls groceries home, and from the temple top
Discerns the funeral bell, and drops his sack,
Pulls off his gloves, enumerates the years,
So now a great disturbance in the Force
Rippled within the Jedi: even then
Poor Alderaan with its two billion souls

THE FORCE   Had slid into th' abyss. Ben winces, groans,
DISTURBED   And Skywalker, perceiving, helps him sit.
Kenobi pauses, patiently explains:
    "Some awful thing, I sense, has come to pass:

30   Disorder in the Force, Luke, voices gripped
By terror, millions suddenly extinct.
Thus knowledge must be paid for: such despair
Afflicts the wisest, even as he raves
That only what must be shall ever be.
Aye, there lies cool serenity and calm,
The ceaseless click of causes and effects,
Parabolas of comets, pulsing stars,
Which, unobserved and unobservable,
Inhuman, like an endless spool, unfurls.

40   Could but the Jedi step beyond himself,
The form of man, but insubstantial, pale,

BEN   Forsaking love and hate, and so align
REFLECTS   With only nature, like a dog that trots
Upon the leash beside a rumbling cart,
And neither drags it nor is dragged, why, then
Disaster and success, evil and good,
The ruin or the triumph of a world
Would all be much alike, and give no grief."
    So spoke Kenobi; with a trembling hand

50   He smoothed the creases of his sandy robe.
But Skywalker was young, and youth is bored

By sorrow: snatching at philosophy,
Luke asks how will could ever be abjured;
To which the teacher, glad to turn his thoughts
Away from ruin and despair, responds:
     "These things are hidden: only deeds avail
To prove the truth; yet someday what I say
May echo what you've learned, and so resound.
First this: the part can never leave the whole,
60   Nor can the whole reject its parts; our will
Belongs to us, as we belong to all.
The rushing river lifts the solid rocks,
In choking ash a sacred peak erupts:
That is the continuity of change,
The peace of violence: a fighter learns

**BEN
REVEALS
A SECRET**

By losing; wrung with longing lovers wait,
Savoring absence; grieving parents purge
Their anguish: so the flinty will of man
Scrapes against fate, makes sparks, and kindles thus
70   Affection, loathing, passion, hope, despair;
Which all, thereby, are fated. Eager boy,
Do not disdain your will, but let it move
In step with life to music of the spheres.
Just as the will within us points our flesh,
A will aligned with fate may even rule
Events, and so make miracles. You ask
How human and inhuman could be one?
Only in this, in certain knowledge, earned
By inspiration and unceasing toil:
80   Before the seer's eye the future flows,
Like ancient deeds when sages reminisce,
And each is incomplete; but seek the whole,
Whose secret only Jedi can perceive:
There is no present, no today, no now,
Only the past, the future, which unite
Where what has been becomes what soon must be.
There stands the Jedi, learning each from each,
His wisdom action and his action wise,
His words and deeds as one within the Force."
90   At that Kenobi rises; from a nook
He takes a small gray sphere, a toy remote,

THE
REMOTE
And bids Luke draw his saber: up it floats
Into the cabin, hurling tiny streaks
That sting the flesh, flitting this way and that.
Skywalker stands on guard, and boldly glares,
And bravely seeks to parry, all in vain:
At once it pricks his leg. Han Solo laughs
To see it as he enters, settling in.
Grinning, the smuggler teases Skywalker:

100   "Why, are you spies or theologians? Ha,
That antique sword! Perhaps I'll plot a course
To a museum? Boy, it seems you dream
Of ancient days when, some declare, the Force
Secured a settled world. No more of that:
If it's just myth, I'll take the gritty truth;
If it's the truth, it's better as a myth.
For, though you change yourself, you cannot change
Your time, and ours is – as you see it. Kid,
I've flown the length and breadth of heaven's realm,

110 From Abregado-rae to Kal'shebbol,
From Bonadan to where th' Imyni dwell,
Along the Trade Spine, up the Axis, through
The Core itself, where stars are thick as snow,
As Chewie often warned me – far I've roamed,
Seen endless marvels, creatures passing strange,
But somehow missed the mystic energy
Which, strung from star to star, selects my fate.

SOLO'S
ADVICE
Don't fumble with religion: seize the day;
Pick up the blaster, not some holy sword;

120 Unlucky men soon find a lonely grave,
The wise, the foolish; those whom luck selects
For sudden, inexplicable success
Die old and rich – there's my philosophy!"

    So Solo, grinning, spoke; Skywalker frowns,
To whom, with quiet merriment, old Ben
Presents a helmet with the blast shield down:
Placing it on Luke's head, he bids him fight
The coy remote without the use of eyes,
Since oft the eyes deceive: instead, he says,

130 The soul must stretch beyond the passing hour.
Again Luke stands on guard, but now the blade,

LUKE'S
SUCCESS

His father's saber, matches stroke for stroke,
Safely deflecting every bolt; amazed,
Luke lifts the sightless helmet; Ben applauds,
And Solo starts to talk of luck; but then
A signal and a klaxon interrupt
To show they're coming up on Alderaan.

Now Solo joins the Wookiee at the helm,
The sublight engines at his fingertips;
140 The boy and agèd Jedi sit behind.
As when a hawk that picks upon a gull
In striking must untuck its noble wings
Lest predator and prey together fall,
So out from hyperspace the *Falcon* braked
At Alderaan's position. Yet no globe

ALDERAAN
IS GONE

Floats there to greet them: silent, they behold
The splinters and the wreckage of a world.
Then Chewie moans, and to Luke's baffled gaze
The worried voice of Obi-Wan responds:
150 "It's been destroyed. This was the tremor felt
Across the heavens, this the Emperor's blow;
Though how he struck I wonder – not the fleet.
But, captain, look, what's blinking on the scan?"
Yet even as he spoke, the sensor screeched:
A speedy TIE fighter swooped past, to port,

THEY
CHASE A
FIGHTER

As delicate and nimble as a kite
That twists and dances in the freshest air.
Perplexed – since no TIE fighter roams alone
Far from the sheltering hangar – Han gives chase
160 Lest it report them; Chewie jams its comms.
But, even as they gained and Han got set
To blast it, from afar they guessed its goal:
Beyond the jagged rubble hung a sphere,
A moon without a planet: sunlight glared
Across its glassy, smooth meridian,
As though on pristine glaciers. Mesmerized,
They tremble as before an omen, rapt
In awful silence. It was Obi-Wan
Who first perceived it was an evil thing,
170 A work of man. The gritty freighter shook:

They'd flown too close: a dogged tractor beam
Had seized the *Falcon*, stretching from that sphere
(The Death Star, though they'd not yet learned its name),

A TRACTOR
BEAM

Reeling them in; Han Solo struggles, kicks,
Locks in the extra power, and begs the ship
To ditch it; tall Chewbacca gives a groan.
As when a summer gnat, a petty pest,
Coasts to a candle from the evening air,
Seduced too close in longing for the heat

180 And soon incinerated, so that ship
Floats ever closer to its doom, ensnared:
The moon becomes a battle station: lights
Of frontier towns across the barren waste
Prove but the portholes of its garrison,
Its peaks but turrets, oceans only plates,
Its canyons trenches etched across the sprawl
Of hangars, engines, depots, barracks, towers;
What seemed a noble crater, leagues in breadth,
Is rather (they perceive) a mammoth dish.

190 Then Solo, like a hero, made to fight,
But gently old Kenobi stayed his hand:
    "Trust not to luck this time; the winding path
To victory often takes us through the shade.

KENOBI'S
PLAN

If smuggling is your talent, smuggle us
As contraband across this grim frontier;
And you, Chewbacca, falsify the logs
To say we fled the ship at Tatooine.
But come, be quick, we drift within its maw."
    So spoke Kenobi truly: as a drop

200 Of water moves in zero gravity,
Suspended, down a horizontal line,
So the *Millennium Falcon*, helpless, slid
Past the invisible magnetic shield
To Bay 327; countless eyes
Of clerks and troops inspect its rigid course.

THE *FALCON*
A PRISONER

Above the pad it floats, 'til droids pry down
The landing gear, on which the vessel rests.
At once the bay commander checks its marks
Against the latest database, alarmed

210 To find they match a recent fugitive's;

Reports are made, salutes received, and soon
Lord Vader learns the news. At once he rounds
On nearby Tarkin, and he would have smiled:
"Behold the subtle power of the Force!

VADER IS
INTRIGUED

The plans we seek have sought us out instead.
Doubtless these are the droids of Tatooine
Which traitors have dispatched to Alderaan.
Indeed your anger kindled at the trick
The Princess played, when Dantooine was found

220 So long abandoned; but delay your wrath:
It seems we may yet trace the rebel base."

So speaking, Vader, turning on his heel,
Swept from the room toward the *Falcon*'s bay.
As when a tempest gathers in the clouds,
Scattering the leaves, foreboding bitter rain,
And dusk descends at noon, so, in the bay
Where squads of troopers hurry to their ranks,
The air, as Vader came, grew thick with fear.
He takes the curt reports: nor crew nor droids

230 Have yet been found, the logs record they fled.
But Vader, who of all the Jedi felt
The Force most keenly, save for that small sage
Who once had trained his teacher, stretches out,

VADER
SENSES BEN

Sensing the potent presence of the past,
Roaming in recollection, seeing still
The sun, the lowly streets of Coruscant,
The war against the ranks of anarchy,
The end without a death, the endless death,
On Mustafar. Quickly he quits the bay

240 For baleful meditation, bids the troops
Check every inch and send a scanning team.
These soon appear as ordered, trunk in tow,
The scanning team doomed never to return:
For ere they'd shuffled carelessly aboard

UPON THE
FaLcon

The *Falcon*, from compartments in the deck
Chewie and Solo, Luke, the droids, and Ben
Had long emerged: a quiet ambush clouts
The startled scanning team, then summons aid
From one poor trooper, TK-421,

250 On guard beside the gangplank with his peer.

Too late the soldiers, climbing, spot the trap:
Three muffled shots from Solo fell them, who,
Unconscious, soon lie safely stowed and bound
In those compartments. Chewie strips their gear
And armor, which the younger men put on.
    Now everything depends on sudden speed:
Kenobi, Solo, Chewie, and the droids,
Sprinting the gangplank, seek the lift, while Luke
Hangs back, 'til from the gantry overhead
260   A testy captain gestures to rebuke
The absent guards; Luke waves him down for help.

THEY SEIZE THE GANTRY
Poor captain, who unluckily unlocked
That gantry gate to meet a Wookiee fist!
Han shoots another, and the gantry's theirs,
As Luke rejoins and swiftly bolts the door,
Distressed at Solo's blasting, Han himself
Displeased at all the sneaking. Obi-Wan
Ignores their quarrel and instructs R2,
That droid of faultless cryptographic skill,
270   To find the beam that blocked the *Falcon*'s flight.
The buoyant astromech, with many a bleep,
Extends an arm to access and display
The whole Imperial network, slicing past
Its petty protocols. His counterpart

R2-D2 LOCATES THE BEAM
Reports success: the tractor beam controls
Lie not far distant, by a black abyss.
Kenobi ponders the location, hoists
His dusky cloak, and vows to go alone,
With many courses weighing in his brain:
280   The Force, he knew, was with him: to what end
He would discover. Skywalker protests:
    "So I'll be left to tend the ship? Revenge
For dearest aunt and uncle be delayed?
Glory elude me! Ben, you saw my skill,
With this, my father's blade, how I stretched out.
Let me come with you; Chewie, Han can stay."
    So spoke the eager youth; but Ben replied:
    "Ah, Luke, you've stepped into a larger world;
But now have patience, since the best revenge

290   Is often indirect. Shall Alderaan
Be just the first of countless planets crushed?
The droids are all, the rebels' final hope.
There lies our duty, though our paths diverge.
Fear not: the Force stands ever at your side."
    So spoke Kenobi; with a careful glance
He raised the gate and hastened on his way.

BEN SEEKS
THE BEAM
Not distant lay the goal: to lesser men
The Death Star seemed a puzzling maze of steel:
To navigate its intricacies, troops

300   Obeyed their guides, the whimpering rodent droids;
But at Ben's feet the path is plainly spread,
To whom the Council, ere the Council fell,
Had oft entrusted its most desperate quests,
As when upon Kamino, where the storm
Washed 'round the sea-girt cradle of the clones,
He coaxed its secrets and confronted Fett;
With tact he now explores the maze: like blood
That draws the ravening monsters of the deep,
Just so the Force, his compass and his means

310   Of evanescence, guides him to the goal:
For where he creeps the sentries look aside,
Their senses baffled, seeing marks of rank
Instead of sandy robes, which they salute.
    So through the station Obi-Wan advanced;
Yet though none saw him, Vader felt his power,

VADER
NOTES BEN
For friendship, more than love, will leave a scar
If once forsworn: of Jedi two alone
Had fled (he thought) the vengeance of the Sith:
The little master and tall Qui-Gon's heir;

320   For Windu fell, first victim of the plot;
And Plo, the mighty pilot, blown apart;
Secura, cruelly murdered by her troops;
And countless knights and harmless Padawans,
Upon that day of infamy, or soon
Inquisitors' and legionaries' prey,
'Til Tano fell at last amid the wrack.
Kenobi, though, was never dragged to death
Nor touted as a trophy; close at hand

Darth Vader unmistakeably discerns
330 His former master. Straightaway he seeks
Grim Tarkin and imposingly reports:
  "A tremor in the Force, as I divined,
Reveals Kenobi. No, he is not dead:
Preserved, perhaps, so that upon the hour
That our new order dawns the old may set.
My blade shall draw him: he seeks no escape;
And so the incomplete will be complete."
  Thus Vader spoke, turning upon his heel
To find the ancient foe, his breath like surf
340 That grinds the boulders on a battered shore.

  Meanwhile the good R2, devoted droid,
As Luke and Han debate the dignity
R2-D2 LOCATES Of old Kenobi, starts to sift the files,
LEIA As loyal as proficient, since he seeks
Some sign of her, the last of Alderaan.
Then with a symphony of beeps and swoops
He trumpets his discovery: she is there,
Detention level AA-23 –
The Princess, as C-3PO explains;
350 But Han protests, foreboding some new scheme:
  "A princess? What is this? Our trip has brought
More trouble than our bargain! Kid, your look
Means some fresh folly. She's a prisoner here?
Oh, aye, our metal friend will name her cell,
And we'll – what? Blunder in (though your old man
Commanded us to linger), bust her out?
Talk sense, we're only three, and one a boy."
  So spoke Han Solo; Luke with tact replies:
  "Don't worry, Han, I won't make some appeal
360 To conscience – no, though few would leave a girl
To lonely death, as like as not you're one,
And who will lecture otherwise? But look:
This princess is no pauper: none but she
First sent these droids: it's Bail Organa's child,
A rebel leader's; are the rebels poor?
LUKE'S Just picture the reward: it's more, still more
PLAN Than smugglers dream, with every debt discharged.

Aye, so, we'll do it? Good! Now here's a plan
To infiltrate the dark detention block:
370   We'll both be stormtroopers, Chewbacca bound
Our prisoner, while the droids await us here."
        So spoke the farmer lad; a pair of cuffs
Lay handy, which he rashly tries to fix
Upon the Wookiee's wrists; but Chewie's pique
Is soothed by Han: he'll tolerate the shame.
C-3PO alone is doubtful, lest
The Empire seize them, though he must obey;
He takes one comlink, Luke the other. Soon
The rescue party stalks the gleaming halls.
380   Skywalker's plan, so artless, seems to work:
Even in binders Chewie daunts the foe;
None dare distract his guards; they reach the lift,

DETENTION
LEVEL AA-23

Hurtling aloft at numb velocity.
If doubt afflicts them, doubt must step aside:
The lift has stopped at AA-23
Whose commandant abruptly asks their aim.
Luke's bluffing buys them seconds, 'til the guards
Step into Chewie's reach: then with a roar
The Wookiee sends them soaring, Han spins 'round
390   And fries the commandant: then blaster bolts
Fly thick as Ewok fireworks at dusk
When rival tribes, beneath the bursting sky,
Combine to sing their paeans, arm in arm:
Luke nails another guard, then dashes down
The cell bay, Chewie finishes the rest:
Soon all the cameras, lasers, and alarms
Are stumps of wire. Luke stops before the cage
That holds the Princess, lifts the heavy door,
And first encounters Leia, like a dream
400   Of silent beauty, resting on her side.
        Black was that cell, where prisoners pondered death,
But white her garment, white her regal cheeks,

LUKE FREES
LEIA

Save where the tears, which trickled as she slept
And dreamt of happy Alderaan, had run:
Asleep, the fiercest lack ferocity.
No hologram is she, and yet unreal.
Waking, she wryly notes a stormtrooper,

Shorter than most, and soon bareheaded, who
Hastily says he's Skywalker, he's come
410 To rescue her – a youth, perhaps her age,
Fresh and unpolished. Babbling of a droid,
He then adds this: he's here with Obi-Wan.
At that the Princess, leaping to her feet:
　　"What, Obi-Wan Kenobi? That same man
Who served my father? Aye, to him I sent
A droid, a trusty astromech, for there
He dwelt apart, on sandy Tatooine,
Though once, my mother said, a Jedi Knight
Who saved Naboo, a warrior and a sage;
420 That was a forlorn hope. Kenobi's here?
I won't ask how – hurry, we go to him!"
　　So Leia spoke and, like a lioness
That spots a weak gazelle upon the flats,
Plucking herself from drowsiness and shade,
Soon coursing, muscles rippling, for the meat,
So Leia bounded to the corridor
Alongside Luke: but there the plan's adrift:
A pirate is no diplomat, and Han,
When puzzled questions crackled on the comm,
430 Had fried it with his blaster: now a squad
Of troopers blows the elevator door;
The firefight erupts as through the breach

BATTLE
IN THE
PRISON They struggle, shots like drops upon the roof
When summer tears the thunderclouds; few live
Whom Chewie targets, few escape Han's aim,
Yet numbers tell: far back the pair is forced
Into the cell bay, whence there's no escape.
Then, though the rest despair, the Princess scoffs
And, snatching up Luke's weapon, she exclaims:
440 　　"Is this my rescue? Better freedom lay
Inside my cell. What plan for getting out?
We cannot linger: Obi-Wan awaits
And surely someone's got to save our skins!"
　　So Leia spoke, and turned the laser gun
Upon the garbage chute, which splinters: down

DOWN THE
CHUTE She climbs into the dark; Han Solo grins,
Admiring and exasperated, kicks

Chewbacca after, not without a howl,
Whom Luke next follows, Solo after him.
450 The troopers, none the wiser, still sustain
Their salvos as the rebels slip away.

Elsewhere, the droids, R2 and Threepio,
Still patient in the gantry, face a test:
For soon upon the gate there came a knock

C-3PO'S
BLUFF
And cold command to open. Now the hour
Had come, C-3PO, to take your place
In deathless memory, wielding protocol:
The gantry's gate is lifted with a hiss
And yet the clumsy troopers find it bare,
460 Though from the closet comes a frantic tap:
Freed, the companions reel into the room,
And then, C-3PO, you deftly spoke:
"Saviors! Is this the lot of loyal droids,
To be confined by madmen? Rebel scum,
Violent, lawless, and discourteous,
Who thought to kidnap us, to aid their plot
Upon the prison level; 'Nay,' said I,
'Deactivate, disintegrate me first,
I'll not desert the Empire,' and much more.
470 Alas, so much excitement's overrun
The circuits in my counterpart, who needs
Some care of maintenance. May I take him there?"
At this, the startled officer commands
A swift pursuit; but with a hasty nod
He liberates the droids: they seek a nook
Facing the *Falcon*; there Imperial crews
Are busy still. In vain R2 plugs in,
For though all Death Star systems are alert
For rebel spies, no spies have yet been seized;
480 R2 suggests the comlink, which his friend
Switches back on: Luke's livid shriek is heard:
"Threepio! Threepio! You're there at last?
Listen! Shut up! Just tell Artoo to halt

LUKE'S
PLEA
The garbage mashers – every single one –
On the detention level. Do you hear?
Oh, every masher! Artoo, do it now!"

Such was Luke's shriek, and to his master's need
R2 responds as swiftly as a spark
That zips, unreally quick, within a chip:

490   The garbage mashers rumble to a halt,
The comlink scatters whoops of pure delight,

THE CHUTE
CONTINUED   Which Threepio, poor fellow, hears amiss
As evidence of gruesome ends. But Luke,
The horror passed, recounts the grim ordeal,
How first the refuse, into which they'd plunged
In fleeing from the furious firefight,
Had proved the den of some malicious beast,
Slithering and serpentine, immensely foul,
Which slunk beneath the slippery filth and seized

500   On Luke, submerging, choking, gluttonous,
Whom, in the soggy dreck and murky slop,
In vain the others desperately pursued;
But soon the beast released him, once the gears,
Obedient to their hours, began to grind,
To press and clench the unrelenting walls,
Mashing the slimy scraps and heroes too,
All effort useless to resist the push,
All supplication hopeless, death at hand,
'Til R2 stopped it; for which many thanks.

510   So Luke explains, while he and Solo shed
Their trooper uniforms, keeping the belts.
With Threepio they plan a rendezvous
And back toward the *Falcon* pick their way.

Meanwhile Kenobi, not without his sword,
Guided by destiny, had reached the source
Of th' unseen beam that checked the *Falcon*'s flight.

KENOBI'S
MISSION   Upon the lip of an immense abyss
It perched, lit dimly by its own array.
Just as a tightrope walker calmly steps

520   Along the wire, and watchers hold their breath,
Though she herself thinks little of the risk,
For knowledge guides her sinew and her soul,
Just so Kenobi stepped along its rim;
He lifts a handle, twists the power offline,

Restores the handle, stepping swiftly back,
The *Falcon* freed. Though stormtroopers stand guard
At every exit, Obi-Wan can trick
Their minds with idle gossip, turn their heads
To phony echoes and uncanny clangs,
530 And so the Jedi vanishes, a breath,
A shadow; yet escape was not his plan.
For just as Vader felt him in his thought,
So Obi-Wan Kenobi felt the Sith,
Whom he himself, in bygone days, had met
On windy Tatooine, for whom he'd vouched,
The boy he'd trained and mentored: like a scar
That throbs before a winter storm, its pain
A rusty relic of the wars of youth,
So now the master's agèd spirit ached
540 To sense Darth Vader's anger drawing near.
      Close to the hangar where the *Falcon* sat
There stretched an empty corridor, its floor
As smooth as ebony, its walls bedecked
With lights unblinking, hemmed at either end
With blast doors such as none could penetrate;
These now stood open: on the hither side,
Etched stark against the hangar's light, he stood,
Taller than man, his black cape like a mist,
His armor gleaming and his helmet proud,
550 Apprentice to the Emperor, cold in rage,
Darth Vader. Just as when the rumbling earth,

BEN FACES VADER Seething below with vast commotion, gorged
On molten rock and gasses, passes up
Its scalding plumes of steam, so Vader's breath
Rasped in the echoing corridor. Old Ben
Went softly forward, shrugging off his hood,
And as he went he lit his glowing sword,
That blade of sapphire, work of his own hand,
The same as he had whirled on Mustafar.
560 In answer Vader's saber, blazing red,
Halts the old man's advance, and Vader speaks:
      "At last my expectation is achieved.
The circle, Obi-Wan, is now complete.

VADER'S
BOAST

My strength still waxes, though your beard is gray
And folly saps your power. Are those the lips
That used to mutter precepts in my ears?
Now I shall teach you; from the dark side learn
How those who conquer death feel no regret."

     So Vader spoke, and struck a savage blow;

570

But like a dog that, snarling, baits a bear,
Cheered on by crowds, the favorite of the ring,
So Obi-Wan abruptly leapt aside,
Belying Vader's taunts, slashing in turn,

DUEL OF BEN
AND VADER

Parried: their luminous lightsabers collide,
Crackling like ice and scattering steely flame,
As once and twice and thrice they counter-cut
And answer lunge for lunge and feint for feint
At feverish pace, until both disengage.
Then softly subtle Obi-Wan responds:

580

     "You conquer what I ceded long ago
And claim the prize a Jedi would disdain.
Control the present, since you have nor past
Nor future – so I stand and prophesy:

KENOBI'S
ANSWER

Ascendant evil, universal power,
Must plunge into the emptiness at last;
But he who strikes me down propels me hence
To paths of power and glory unforeseen."

     So Ben Kenobi spoke, and, with a cry,
Renewed the fight, which teeters to and fro,

590

'Til all the hangar echoes with the blades
Which simple troopers contemplate with awe.

     Meanwhile the rebels in the Death Star's halls

BATTLING
TROOPERS

Split up: for as they reached the *Falcon*'s bay
Around the corner marched a sudden squad,
Whom Solo, roaring, blasted, giving chase
To buy more time, Chewbacca at his heels;
At which the Princess, with a grin, exclaims:

     "Your pirate's brave indeed; but is he sane?
What hand but his can pilot such a ship?

600

If he and that great carpet – Chewie, yes? –
Should fall, how shall the astromech be saved?

Within its memory lies our final hope.
But what? Oh, here's more coming – flee with me!"
　　　So Leia spoke, and none too soon they fled
Before more stormtroopers, who dog their steps,
Blasting at random. Soon they reach a gap,
A pit without a bottom, whence the bridge
Has been retracted. Crossfire pins them down,
A streaking web of livid blaster fire,

610 But Leia answers shot for shot as Luke
Finds (for the Force was with him) on his belt

THE BRIDGE A grappling hook. The hero, pitching hard,
Tosses it and secures it, grabs the girl,
Who, with a kiss for luck, bids him prevail,
And so they swing across the vast abyss.
No bolt can touch them: from the farther side
They dash back to the hangar, seeking Han.
　　　Meanwhile the Wookiee and the smuggler fought
Ambush and counter-ambush, charge for charge,

620 Through closing blast doors, into cul-de-sacs,
Across the shocks of ceaseless fusillade.
At last they face the *Falcon*, swiftly met

REUNION AT By Luke and Leia, both the droids nearby,
THE *FALCON* The *Falcon* fenced behind a ring of foes.
But then, to Han, it seemed a miracle:
The spacious hangar echoes with the clash
Of lightnings, searing red and blazing blue;
The sentries at the *Falcon* turn aside
To stare in awe. Han hauls the others up,

630 Bidding them sprint toward the empty ship;
Chewie, the boy, the girl, the droids converge
Upon the *Falcon*. As they dash ahead,

LUKE SEES Luke's eye is caught: he sees old Ben, alone,
VADER Ragged as some poor scarecrow in a storm,
Whipped by the wind, lit by the flashing sky,
And soon to blow away. Beside Ben looms
A fearsome figure, black from head to foot,
No Jedi, though he held a Jedi's blade,
Crushing all comfort. Horror fills the lad,

640 The hangar seems to shudder as he sees

One dancing saber fall, the other whirl,
Parry and thrust again; Luke shouts Ben's name.
    At that the Jedi Master flicked an eye
Toward the *Falcon*, where he saw them both,
A nimble princess and a handsome youth,
Leia and Luke, now dashing arm in arm
Together. As a captain on the deep
Whose ship has waited ages for a breeze
Will sniff the dawning air, scenting a shift,
650   Calling his crew to wake, to rise, to work,
So Obi-Wan perceived it, stretching out:
The future and the past, theirs and his own
And Vader's. Then the world of human grief,
Of hope forever ending and renewed,
Seemed to dissolve; and, like he used to heed
Old Qui-Gon's lessons, so he now obeyed
A whisper of th' indwelling power that binds
All living things and balances our fate,
And so renounced his will and raised his blade.
660   Darth Vader struck, a devastating blow
Not parried or eluded: on the side

VADER STRIKES BEN

The crackling saber struck, but met no flesh,
For even as Luke screamed to see Ben die
The body vanished and the robes fell free.
Amazed, Lord Vader stamps the empty cloth,
Then rounds upon the *Falcon*; troopers turn,
Their blasters barking, Chewie answering back,
But Skywalker, through flowing tears, takes aim,
Frying the blast door panel, locking out
670   The Sith's advance. Solo and Leia flee
Into the rising ship, droids safe, Luke last,
And Solo's subtle hand guides their escape.

BOOK III

YAVIN

INVOCATION

Keeper of memory, who in ages past
    Endowed the blind with second sight, reveal
    No more of mysteries that surpass this flesh,
No more than what the living brain can bear:
With no eternity but ceaseless fame
My song shall crown the son of Skywalker,
Who dared to trade his shovel for a sword,
His tunic for a flight suit and to don
The helmet of Red Five, when X-wings raced
10   To meet the Death Star's overwhelming might.

    From Bay 327, unpursued,
Soared the superb *Millennium Falcon*, free

Before the turrets could revolve or roar.
As when the dart, blown from a stony pipe,
Tipped with a secret poison, hisses quick
To prick the malia, prey of the Ragoon,
Just so that ship shot past the unseen shield.
Around the dim dejarik board, the droids
In mournful silence study Leia's face,

20   Shaken at first, but soon composed afresh,

MOURNING
FOR BEN

As gently she admonishes the boy:
    "Brave fellow, come, do not accuse yourself.
Think rather that we witnessed Obi-Wan
Defying an indomitable foe:
That other was Darth Vader, who, they say,
Destroyed the Jedi, and whose power defers
To nothing but the horror on the throne.
Is such a death unworthy of a sage?
Why do you stare so hollow-eyed, so mute,

30   As if your grief could overturn the past?"
    To this young Skywalker has no reply.
Bewilderment as much as grief assails
His spirit, like a puzzle in a dream:
Furiously he ponders how, before they'd fled,
He'd aimed his blaster at the troopers, yet
Discerned – or was it true? – Kenobi's voice
Calling, "Now run, Luke, run!"; he'd heard, he'd run.
But was he crazy? How could even Ben
First vanish, then be heard beyond the grave?

40   Such were Luke's brooding thoughts; but even then
Han Solo entered, summoning him to fight:

TIE FIGHTER
ATTACK

The *Falcon*'s course had brushed the sentry ships
That ringed the Death Star: with a tearing screech
TIE fighters overtake them; Chewie tilts
The frail deflectors as the captain sprints
To arm the double cannon, guiding Luke.
    Now the *Millennium Falcon* had this shape:
Round as a disc, but tapering to the rim,
Its cockpit, well to starboard, pushed ahead

50   Like a snake's head that fixes on a mouse,
While to the fore twin elongated bows
Projected half its length again; for war

It bore concussion missiles, now in want;
A pair of turrets too: the one atop
The central hull, the other at the base,
From which all arcs were covered by the guns.
    Below Luke hastens, Han ascends, to sit
In twisting seats, four targets on their screens,
As past them shriek their foes. Velvety space
60   Is split by stark green lasers, orange too
As Luke and Han spin blasting back, but wide:
Those pilots were no rookies: right and left
They twitch and tumble perilously tight
In delicate and deadly craft: too quick
They make their runs, whom neither gun can touch,
Strafing the heat exhaust; then Chewie banks
To dodge them – no, the laterals won't respond;
The *Falcon* shudders, toppling both the droids
Who hurry round the decks; smoke billows thick;
70   But R2-D2 saves them once again,
Dousing the blaze, extinguishing the fire:
The roaring Wookiee at the helm pulls free
To shake the fighters; Leia scans the stars;
In turn the TIE formation scatters wide.
    Then Solo was the first to claim a prize,
Catching one as it rolled, shearing the wing,
Its ion engine bursting in a ball;
Luke wrestles his controls, as though to bend
The targeting computer to his will,
80   And misses, aims again, and nails his own;

THE TIES
DESTROYED

But Leia, as they celebrate, points out
The two surviving TIEs, which wheel and blast
The *Falcon*'s engine, desperate to delay
That freighter 'til more squadrons can appear.
But Chewie dove, dipping the *Falcon*'s nose,
And square before him Skywalker perceived
A perfect target, which he blew away;
The last in fury raced against Han's gun,
With which the smuggler finished the dispute.
90   Wookiee and princess, rogue and farmer lad
Clasp in the flush of victory and relief,
While R2 whirls, retrieving Threepio

Where his poor counterpart had tumbled; soon
They take their seats for hyperspace and launch,
Course set for Yavin and the hidden base.

Behind them, from the Death Star, Vader's gaze
TARKIN
FRETS Observes their progress, Tarkin at his side.
Biting his lip, the agèd governor speaks:
"Now even as the hour of triumph strikes
100 We stake the gains of twenty years and more.
'Twas I who, while the Emperor's strength was new,
Championed the Geonosians' first design.
Alas that ever Krennic, clumsy fool,
Was tasked to build it, trusting renegades
Like Erso; but now Erso rots unmourned
On rainy Eadu, Krennic in the wreck
Of Scarif, and our battle station looms
In every trembling sky: yet at this price:
Organa's child is free: Kenobi's ship
110 Ferries her with this battle station's plans.
You're sure the homing beacon cannot fail?
The risk is great to win the rebel base."
So Tarkin spoke, and Vader made reply:
"Fear not: these hours are pregnant with events,
VADER'S
PLAN And, though the details still be indistinct,
Our destiny is nigh: the very day
That saw Kenobi fall reveals the fate
Of all the rebels' rash imaginings:
A thousand years shall contemplate our deeds."
120 Just so Lord Vader spoke, and truly: soon
The homing beacon beckoned on the screen,
Showing the *Falcon* quitting hyperspace,
Restored at Yavin. Tarkin names the course
And soon that battle station, lithe and sleek
Despite its bulk, begins the grim pursuit.

At Yavin, meanwhile, where the glowing arc
Of glorious crimson cut across the skies
Of four and twenty satellites, the base
Detects the *Falcon*: Leia sends a code,
130 And like a dove upon the rising air

ARRIVAL AT
YAVIN

Along the fourth moon's atmosphere they glide.
Green forests greet them, home, in ancient days,
To mystical Massassi, architects
Of mossy temples, which amid the leaves
Still towered, converted to the rebel cause.
Now, as they seek the landing pad, Han smiles,
Boasting to Leia in the cockpit thus:
    "To scoundrel, ruffian, rogue, and buccaneer
I'll add another title: rescuer

140

Of royalty most worshipful. To think
We sprang you from that dungeon! Cash in hand,
Chewie and I will celebrate afar
Whatever you and your revolt achieve."
    To which the Princess hotly made reply:
    "One thing, it seems, no princess could achieve,
To make you love what's greater than such spoils,
A galaxy not shackled, or the ones
Who'll break those shackles. Reap your rich reward,
But have a care: this ship, however swift,

150

Could never have eluded Vader's grip
Were we not tracked and followed even now.

LEIA'S
REBUKE

With cash, therefore, depart, so farmer lads
May win the glory mercenaries scorn."
    So Leia spoke, and left the cockpit; Luke
Passes her at the door and gets a smile.

    Yet at the base, meanwhile, the rebels' mood
Was bleak, for most had flown to Scarif, shamed
To wait while Erso's daughter and her band
Set forth to sure destruction. Few had lived:

160

Of six corvettes, a trio had returned;

AFTERMATH
OF SCARIF

Just one among the frigates, brittle ships,
Nebulon-Bs, survived; the transports now
Were only two, where seven flew before;
The *Ghost*, at least, remained, but of the rest
Where were the Dorneans, where was Raddus' own,
That Calamari cruiser, huge and smooth,
The tall *Profundity*, wherein lay hid
The *Tantive*, that slipperiest corvette?
Alas, the fighters also stood reduced:

170   Blue Squadron, plunging through the closing gate
To Scarif's surface, never reappeared,
Except for one, who, slipping from the storm
That tore the very planet, brought report
Of how they'd fought like dogs around the tower
With swarms of fell TIE Strikers, swooping down,
Strafing the AT-AT walkers on the beach,
While Jyn's commandos, battling to the last,
Defied the legions' wrath; Rogue One itself
He'd seen, the famous shuttle, short-lived prize

180   Of Eadu; even, at the pinnacle,
Three figures wrestling by the tilting dish

REPORTS OF
THE BATTLE   Just as the plans were sent. Then, like a ray
Of daylight bent and focused through a lens
With which an idle child torments a bug,
There'd come a beam as bright as twenty suns,
Whereat the whole horizon had dissolved,
Engulfing all. Red Squadron's X-wings too
Had followed Garven Dreis against the TIEs
Of two huge Star Destroyers, twisting in,

190   Picking them off and twisting out afresh,
While bold Gold Squadron's Y-wings bombed the gate.
These last recount how Raddus gave the word
To lame th' *Intimidator*, calling up
The *Lightmaker*, a hammerhead corvette,
To shove the crippled hulk into its peer,
The *Persecutor*, so that each huge ship
Impacted on the other and the gate,
Crushing the whole, uncovering one last chance
To rescue Erso's daughter. Then it came,

200   That terror like an artificial moon,
The Death Star, real as ever Jyn declared,
Immeasurably vast, whose dish disgorged
A beam into the surface: as a flower
Pushes its petals at the eastern glow,
Yellow without, but bloody red within,
So the colossal cloud of rock and fire
Had blossomed on the surface, killing all.
Then Raddus bade them flee before such might;

But as they prepped for lightspeed, pulling back
210   (So those report who made the latest jump),
A different Star Destroyer had appeared,
Wielding, perhaps, an interdiction field
To hinder all escape; there knowledge stops:
What never fled they reckon as destroyed,
Even the proud *Profundity*; no word
Had come about the precious secret plans
For which they'd fought and died in Scarif's sky.
       Then even as they'd mourned for Merrick, burned
Upon the sand; for Oquoné the brave
220   Who'd plunged into the gate; for poor Red Five,

DESPAIR ON YAVIN IV

Young Pedrin Gaul, whom four TIE fighters stalked;
For fearless Raddus too; and countless more,
The news had come of Alderaan, not maimed
Like Jedha or like Scarif, but expunged
From every map, its peaceful people lost,
The nightmare of the Emperor's final power
Made real: they seem a galaxy of slaves.
Mon Mothma then, the pillar of the cause,
Convened the council, called for sober calm,
230   Though panic, in the shadows, paced the room:
Some blame Jyn Erso and her rash attempt,
Some blame themselves for doubting Jyn's good faith
And so attacking piecemeal; all agree
The Empire and its weapon rule the stars
Unchecked, uncheckable, and doom is nigh.
At last they choose the counsel of defeat:
The three corvettes, the frigate, and the *Ghost*,
Dispersing, General Draven in command,
Shall seek new harbors, though the Yavin base
240   Shall guard the thirty fighters that survive;
Before Mon Mothma's dignity, none dare
To utter, yet, the universal thought.

      So they debated; meanwhile at his post
Upon the temple roof the lonely guard

THE *Falcon* ARRIVES

Detects a single freighter slipping low
Across the treetops: aye, that was the one,

The YT-1300 with the code.
Pointing his scanner, he directs its course
To Platform 4, where soon it settles, scarred

250 (The baffled rebels note) with many blasts;
And old Dodonna meets it there himself.
Then down the gangplank lowers, down there steps
A towering Wookiee with a swashbuckler,
Both ill at ease, and next a gawking boy,
Whose eager glance is fixed upon the foils
Of nearby X-wings. These Dodonna greets,
Asking their names and purpose; ere they speak,
A fourth descends, wrapped in a robe of snow,
Fair as a summer evening, flashing-eyed,

260 The princess, Leia, Bail Organa's child,
Youngest of all the captains of their cause,
Who clasps his hand, and instantly declares:
    "Indeed, dear general, I'm alive; my tale

LEIA'S
GREETINGS
Itself must wait: I bring an astromech
Whose memory now contains our final hope,
The Death Star's secret readouts, last bequest
Of Erso's daughter, whom I saw destroyed
On Scarif: victory shall avenge them all."
    As when the breath of summer crests the peak,

270 Flowing to soothe the plains below, when girls
Let loose their hair to whip along the wind
And brothers hurry to the grav-ball field,
So Leia melted old Dodonna's dread
In laughing tears; he clasps her in his hands
And, shucking off the years, retrieves the droid
And sprints to his computer; Leia turns
To see Mon Mothma, graceful in her joy,
Approaching, who from infancy and youth
Had been her gentle mentor and her friend,

280 Senator once, the voice of Chandrila
Before the days of shadow. Stoically
The lady smiles serenely at the girl:
    "No word, dear Leia, can express the loss
Of Alderaan. At least we need not mourn
For you, whose fire oft reignites our own.
Who are these other comrades of your ship?"

To Mothma Princess Leia then responds:
"My rescuers: the *Tantive* was seized
At sandy Tatooine; Antilles too
290   Was killed; upon the Death Star I was kept
And watched my planet die; Kenobi came,

LEIA'S
FRIENDS
The very Jedi whom my father knew,
With these strange heroes, saving Erso's plans,
Though Ben himself, alas, alas, is gone.
This Wookiee, like the others, knew Kashyyyk
Before its day of slavery, roams the stars
With Solo here, who's earned a rich reward,
A peerless pilot, if a reckless rogue;
The boy, like me in age, is brave indeed,
300   A skillful flyer too, he says, who bears
A Jedi lightsaber, Kenobi's gift.
Grant him, I beg, if any craft remain
Without a pilot, some fair chance to prove
His mettle in an X-wing: time is short
And battle beckons: very much I fear
That Vader tracked the *Falcon* as we fled."
So saying, Leia followed Mothma back
To plan the fresh renewal of the war;
Chewie and Han assemble their reward;
310   Threepio trots to R2, who soon yields

DODONNA
TAKES R2-D2
The precious readouts, which Dodonna feeds
Into the mainframe's swift analysis,
Recalling Erso's very words: the flaw
Was hidden but destructive: just a touch
To the reactor module would provoke
A chain reaction and the Death Star's death.
Pondering all this, he turns to his research;
To him Mon Mothma soon entrusts command,
Departing, lest they perish one and all.

320   Skywalker, meanwhile, strolls in perfect bliss
Among the starfighters: the Y-wings stretch
Their long twin engines, like the blades of shears,

LUKE IN
THE HANGAR
The cockpit thrust ahead, and marked in gold,
For here Gold Squadron rested, what remained,
Mon Mothma's escort; crewmen scrub the crud

Of Scarif, painting every kill afresh.
After them wait, deep in the temple hall,
Red Squadron's X-wings, nimble as those cats
That ply the desert meadows, swift to strike,
330   Quadruple foils compact, four cannons mute
Which soon would dim the starlight with their fire;
The crews are busy fueling, hoisting up
The last proton torpedoes left in store.
Luke wonders, Was it thus his father fought,
As through the galaxy his glory spread,
Or in Z-95s? But as he gawks
He sees a pilot sink into his craft
With helmet checked in black and gold; nearby
Another's climbed the ladder, whose wise words
340   Instruct the rookie: here's the stick, the comms,
The target scope, the trigger, the eject.
Soon both note Skywalker: the rookie shouts,
Waving him over, swinging down at once,
BIGGS   His helmet doffed; and it was Biggs's face,
Old Biggs, than whom no finer pilot flew
The dunes of Tatooine, good Biggs who'd left
To practice at that pilot school. With joy
He shakes Luke's hand, presents him to his boss:
    "Here, Garven, meet my buddy: this is Luke,
350   The best bush pilot of the Outer Rim
(Though he'd say so of me) – on Yavin, Luke?
Among the rebels? Why, you said you'd farm
At least another season. Well, we're here,
And, like two shooting stars, we can't we stopped!
Now soon, as Garven says, we'll have our chance."
    So Dreis, forewarned by Mothma of a lad
From distant Tatooine, will not refuse
A new Red Five, replacing Gaul: the ace
Efficiently instructs the volunteers.

360   Yet even as they learned the X-wing's tricks
There came a klaxon through the busy base,
Summoning the rebel pilots: at their screens
THE DEATH   Technicians had discerned the Death Star's shape;
STAR COMES   Aye, as it streaked from lightspeed, who could miss

That mighty signature? Surprise was moot.
Beyond the edge of Yavin's crimson arc
The deadly sphere descended, swinging 'round
In orbit: thus a single hour's delay
Preserves the rebel base upon the moon.
370　There on that battle station Tarkin waits,
Lord Vader tall and silent at his side;
Both patiently attend the pull of time.

On Yavin IV the pilots sit intent
Upon Dodonna's careful briefing; mute,
But apt to turn, forgetful of the past,
To catch another's eye, and find him gone.
Dear guardian, count those unforgotten names:
CATALOGUE　Red Leader's first, the steady Garven Dreis,
OF PILOTS　The lance of Virujansi's cavalry;
380　And next Red Two, unerring in his aim,
Young Wedge Antilles, destined for renown;
Red Three in turn, Biggs Darklighter, was there,
Untested but undaunted, from the sands;
Red Four was Branon, rigorous and shrewd;
Red Five was Skywalker, in Pedrin's place,
So fresh he wore no flight suit, just a cloak,
Who'd come with Leia and the bootlegger;
Red Six was great Jek Porkins, brash and bold;
Red Seven was Harb Binli, Pedrin's peer,
390　Who flew that Eriadu might be free;
Red Eight was Dinnes, whose bright helmet bore
Six chevrons, tokens each of twenty kills
With Tierfon's Yellow Aces, tall and fair;
The grim lieutenant after her, Red Nine,
Nozzo Naytaan, Corellian to the core;
Red Ten was Garven's wingmate, Theron Nett,
With Red Eleven, Ralo Surrel too;
And last of all Puck Naeco, double ace,
The A-wing veteran, lately dubbed Red Twelve.
400　Such was Red Squadron; with them sat the Greens,
Ten X-wings more, and yielding place to none;
Gold Squadron last, whose battered Y-wings wait
For their brave pilots, Vander, Dex Tiree,

Evaan Verlaine, Lepira, Woolcob, Krail,
The seven heroes of Dodonna's plan.
There were the astromechs as well, staunch droids
Who flew behind the pilots, fixing faults;
And, at the back, tall Han and Chewie stood.
    General Dodonna now sets forth the facts:

410   The Death Star is the mystery weapon's name

DODONNA'S BRIEFING   Which pummeled Scarif, shattered Alderaan;
It dreads no grand assault: the rebel fleet
Would melt before its massive armament
Of turbolasers. Time is short: their base
Will soon be targeted, the moon destroyed;
But Princess Leia's readouts point the way,
Revealing secret weakness: just a touch
To the reactor module will provoke
A chain reaction and the Death Star's death:

420   A thermal port will trip it, one that leads
Straight to the system (so he demonstrates):
A thermal port, two meters wide at most,
Which snubfighters, not frigates, may attack,
Skimming the surface, lancing down a trench,
Aiming torpedoes only, since the shaft
Is ray shielded. At this a skeptic voice,
Perhaps young Wedge's, says it can't be done;
To which Luke Skywalker at once retorts:
    "If I could bull's-eye womp rats, slippery beasts,

430   By Beggar's Canyon in my T-16
Back home, and they're no wider than that shaft,

LUKE IS CONFIDENT   A slick computer surely cannot miss.
I fear the TIEs, for though so many kills
Adorn your helmets, I have faced their skill
Just once, in Solo's ship, and felt their teeth!"
    At this the veterans reassure the boy
With many a pointed anecdote: he'll live,
But when they sweep behind, a spiral twist
Can shake them, or a rolling scissor spin;

440   But, most of all, they must coöperate.
Luke thanks them, learns their callsigns, and is sent

To seek a flight suit. As he leaves his seat,
He notes Han Solo lingering at the back,
Absorbed in thought; the Wookiee too seems drawn
To old Dodonna's schemes and diagrams.
The smuggler stirs, catching Skywalker's ear:
        "Come with us, won't you, Luke? It seems a shame
A plucky fellow like yourself should cast

HAN AND LUKE His life away – we'd use you, share the cash.
450 But no rewards await the dead. These men
Have never seen that station: you and I,
We've been there, know they go to suicide."
        Thus Han; and yet the farmer lad responds:
        "There is a choice in suicide, but these
Have none: duty, not death, now draws them on,
Summoned ahead by those who went before;
I hear my aunt and uncle: even now
The sand entombs them; as my father fought
With Ben, without him I will fight in turn
460 For this reward: the name of Skywalker
Shall someday raise another in my place."
        So spoke the youth, and gave a curt salute,
Turning; but Han, without a grin or jibe,
Breathed a soft supplication to the Force
To guide the boy, with lips unused to prayer,
Then went to stack the boxes of his cash
Inside the *Falcon*; but Chewbacca moaned.

        Now through the temple's shady naves and aisles,
The tireless crews complete their tasks: they check
470 And recheck laser cannons, gyro coils,

THE REBELS Power couplings, stabilizers, shields, exhaust,
PREPARE Turrets atop the Y-wings' canopies;
Refill the fuel, insert the astromechs;
And hand those nervous pilots, as they sit,
Their helmets, blazoned bright. Luke dons his own,
As R2-D2 drops into his niche,
Battered but cheerful, blessed by Threepio.
Then thirty fighters rise and subtly slip

Into the freer air. Again Luke hears,
480 As clear as life, the gentle voice of Ben:
"Fear not: the Force stands ever at your side."
        Along the rosy, incandescent disc
Of Yavin they accelerate to space,
Like shooting stars which, being named, expire.
Then Leia joins the captains of the cause
Beside a glowing bowl, tight-lipped, intent:
Their ships appear on course; technicians gaze
At luminous screens and verify the comms.
        Upon the Death Star, Grand Moff Tarkin too
490 Stands watching their progression, unperturbed:

**TARKIN'S
ARROGANCE**

The latest gesture of a useless cause
He deems it, little thinking that huge mass,
His enviable weapon, could succumb;
He scorns to scramble fighter escorts, since
The turbolaser gunners need some sport.
        And soon indeed those cannons open fire,
As round the great gas giant X-wings swing:
Red Leader's orders crackle on the comms,
Bidding his men not chatter (though ahead
500 The wondrous target looms) but lock their foils
Into attack position. Switching on

**THE REBELS
APPROACH**

Deflector shields to double-front, they pass
Bumpily through the thick magnetic field,
Red Leader (that was Dreis), Red Twelve, Red Two,
Red Ten, Red Six, Red Seven, and Red Three,
Red Eight, Red Nine, and Red Eleven too,
Red Five – so Luke reported – and Red Four,
The other squadrons too, the Greens, the Golds,
Increasing to attack speed: close ahead
510 The Death Star fills, with every passing breath,
Vaster horizons, lit with pricks of light,
Bright frenzied bursts of turbolaser fire,
Some on the surface, some upon the towers,
Like distant sunrise dancing on the sea.
        Gold Leader then got set to make his run
Toward the target shaft; Red Leader bids
His squadron, flying low, distract the guns.
Wedge nips about the surface, Porkins tests

The turrets' patience, Dinnes barrel-rolls
520 Between two towers; but Skywalker elects

LUKE
ATTACKS
To turn his cannons on the fiercest patch,
His fingers hopping as the triggers snap,
His X-wing hurling orange bolts of fire.
As when, upon Lothal, where prairies stretched
About the stubs of broken cities, grass
Would suddenly ignite, kindled and fed
By passing gusts of chemicals and trash,
And rolling flame would churn the very wind,
Incinerating landscapes, razing towns,
530 Just so the waves of turbolaser blasts
From twenty turrets rolled about Luke's ship,
Blocking his bold attack, and off he spins
A little cooked, but undefeated yet.

Such was young Skywalker's first combat; soon
Together Biggs and Porkins follow suit,
Picking a tall deflection tower; Biggs shoots,
Pinpoints the fusion circuits, blows the whole,
Exposing those huge lasers to assault.
Yet brave Jek Porkins, covering Biggs's strike,
540 Preserved his wingmate, not himself, enmeshed
In turbolaser crossfire: ah, brave soul,

DEATH OF
PORKINS
Though Biggs in anguish begged that you pull up,
You would not disengage; the turrets barked;
Your wingmate heard you perish in the flame.

Tarkin, meanwhile, looks only to the base,
Whose moon will last just seven minutes more.
But Vader senses something in the Force,
Some fresh displacement, feeble, imprecise,
Whenever those snubfighters make a run.
550 He orders most TIE pilots to their ships,

TIES ENTER
THE BATTLE
Commanding them to crush the rebel scum,
Though he himself, lest this invasion prove
A mere diversion, waits upon events.
As when black birds of omen swarm the skies
Like swirling smoke afar, but from below
A sable choir in mourning for the year,
And farmers shiver safe inside their huts,

So from their bays the TIE fighters took flight
In tight formations, screeching into space,
560   Swift Victor Squadron's aces, tasked to save
The laser towers: some peel toward the south
To check Green Squadron's X-wings; some attack
The valiant Reds; Gold Squadron slips away.
As when the archers in a puissant host,
Ensconced behind the spears, would hear the word
To loose a volley, and the arrows dropped
In clouds across the shuddering regiments,
Just so the TIEs attacked the Reds and Greens.
Then second of Red Squadron to be slain
570   Was John D. Branon, rigorous Red Four:
Upon his tail the pitiless TIE attached,
Nailing his starboard engines, then the shields;
The X-wing buckles, burns. Another jumps
Behind poor Biggs, too tight to shake: like froth
Blown from the shaggy muzzle of a wolf
That hunts, but cannot reach, its frantic prey,
Just so the emerald lasers interwove

LUKE SAVES BIGGS
The X-wing's foils; Skywalker saves his friend,
Locking his target, earning their first kill;
580   And in his ears again Luke hears Ben's voice:
"Your soul must stretch beyond the passing hour";
So now he rakes the surface: frail it seems
And frail it proves, as every laser bolt
Disables or destroys. But from behind
Another TIE, far nimbler than Luke's craft,
Shadows him: left he rolls, and right, and left,
In vain: the enemy has touched him, grazed
The upper port nacelle; though R2 spins
To fix it, unrelentingly the foe
590   Pursues: to Biggs young Skywalker appeals,

WEDGE SAVES LUKE
But even as the TIE had locked its guns
On Luke, Wedge was the one who, banking in
From twelve o'clock, brought every bolt to bear
Upon the hapless TIE, which detonates.

On Yavin IV, Dodonna strokes his beard,
Catching the Princess' eye: they watch the bowl

GOLD
SQUADRON

Impatiently: their squadrons live, perhaps,
But time is trickling. Now Gold Leader spoke,
Reporting they had reached the narrow trench
600   In which the target lay. Krail and Tiree
Follow Dutch Vander down into the shade,
Deflectors double-front: the guns are thick.
But Vader, on the Death Star, saw them come,
Perceiving some grim purpose in their course,
And straightaway he acts: more TIEs are sent
To finish off Green Squadron and the Reds;
But he himself, selecting his two best
As wingmates, casts his sable cloak aside,
Ascending to the cockpit of a TIE.
610   Best he had ever been of all who sat

VADER
ENTERS

Behind a starfighter's controls, unfazed
By tumult or distraction, quick to pick
The unpredictable, unerring, lithe;
Best he still was in all the galaxy,
And best of all TIE fighters was his own,
Its fuselage distended and its wings
Bent inward like a bomber's, shielded too,
The latest prototype, the TIE Advanced,
Equipped with missiles: like a greedy fish
620   Infesting jungle pools, as quick to flit
As any prey, but ruthless in its bite,
So Vader now flew forth into the war
Flanked by his wingmates, Victor Two and Three.
     Aloft they soar, the hangar far below,
Discerning from on high the battle's course,
X-wings careening (since the Greens now faced
Wave after wave of fighters), TIEs ablaze,
Red Squadron holding tight, but to the side
The Y-wings streaking down the central trench.
630   There Dutch and Krail and trusty Dex Tiree
Had switched to targeting computers, locked
Upon the goal, but suddenly the guns
Go mute, foreboding ill; they stabilize
Their rear deflectors, but the foe appears

VADER STOPS
THE GOLDS

To port, at eight o'clock: the sensors wail
As Vader swings behind them: Victor Three

Covers him as he takes the leader, squares
His target dead away: that was Tiree,
Who falls in flames; Dutch asks for room, but Krail
640 Insists they stay on target; once again
Lord Vader shoots, the great Dutch Vander dies.
Too late, reporting ruin, Krail evades,
His clumsy Y-wing helpless on the horns
Of Vader's nimble ship: a final squeeze
Upon the TIE's soft trigger and he's gone.
 Such was the fate of brave Gold Squadron's run.
But Tarkin now is briefed upon their plan:

TARKIN WILL Softly an officer explains: the goal
NOT FLEE Is perilous indeed; he dares suggest
650 Evacuation; but the Grand Moff thus:
 "What, at the hour of triumph should we flee
From our own victory? Here shall I remain
And so shall all: so when the question comes
Of where we stood when Mothma was destroyed,
We'll say we watched immovable and smiled."
 So Tarkin spoke, forgetting to rebuke
The prudent messenger, for now the screen
Showed but three minutes 'til his dish would bear.

 Red Leader now got set to make a run,
660 Brave Garven Dreis, whom old Dodonna bade
RED LEADER Attack with Nett and Naeco, saving Luke
ATTACKS To follow in his wake with Wedge and Biggs.
Down to the trench they roll: again the guns
Hurl first a blistering hail of fire; eyes wide
For sudden foes, the wingmates cover Dreis
Who switches to computer. Far above
Luke was the one who first discerned the shapes,
Vader and Vader's servants, flying close
Into the trench behind Red Ten and Twelve.
670 Then even as Red Leader reached the goal,
Launching his twin torpedoes, Vader smote
The wingmates: that was Nett and Naeco's fate;
But Dreis' twin torpedoes, guided straight
By his computer, reached the target shaft.
Then old Dodonna, Leia, and the rest

Who still fought on, and Dreis himself, supposed

VADER STOPS
RED LEADER

That glory lay at hand: but 'twas not so,
For those torpedoes wrecked but the façade,
Impacting on the surface, launched in vain.

680 Yet Vader still pursues, and Dreis survives
No longer than to learn his shot went wide;
At Vader's hands he dies, quitting despair,
A patch of flame upon the metal plain.

    Just sixty seconds now remain. Luke views
The death of Dreis, then summons both his friends:
    "O Wedge, o Biggs, follow me to the end,
Full throttle down the trench, to shake the TIEs;
We'll pull up at the finish: nothing worse
Than Beggar's Canyon, where we'd stake our lives

690 Back home. And you, Artoo, hang on back there:
Get ready, at my word, to crank the power."
    Thus Skywalker, who boldly led them down,
Rolling into the trench past churning towers,
Past turbolasers turning far too slow,
Like steeds that spot the finish; Wedge and Biggs

LUKE LEADS
THE ATTACK

Hang back to cover Luke; the good R2
Prepares repairs; and then the turrets cease.
Again the tight formation of the TIEs
Descends astern, and Victor Two scores hits

700 Upon young Wedge's ship; at Luke's command
Wedge pulls aloft, his astromech at work.
But Vader lets him go, his hatred bent
Upon the leader: now the TIE Advanced
Reveals its power and speed, as up to Biggs
He rushes: though young Biggs of Tatooine
Seeks ever to impede their swift assault,
Darth Vader merely swings in step: his burst
Of laser bolts obliterates the boy.
    So Luke alone remains. On Yavin IV

710 Dodonna, Threepio, and Leia clutch

LUKE IS ALONE

The glowing bowl; gaunt Tarkin barely blinks
Upon the Death Star: thirty seconds tick.
Soon Luke's in range: gladly he switches on
The targeting computer. Vader gains,

Disabling R2 with his first barrage.
But even as Luke stared into his screen
He heard again the subtle voice of Ben:
"Luke, trust the Force: let go: the path is spread";
And Vader, right behind him, as he fought
720 To trap the last red X-wing in his scope,
Was puzzled by the power he now perceived:
The Force, it seemed, was with it. Ben again:
"Now you yourself are stepping on its path."
Luke shuts the targeting computer, breathes,
And stretches out: he feels the dying touch

VADER WILL Upon a daughter's cheek, the countless hours
KILL HIM Of planning and defiance, hears her vow
To fight for every inch, the parting kiss
Beside the boiling edge of Scarif's sea;
730 And yet Darth Vader, matching will to will,
The X-wing pinned, triumphantly exclaims:
        "So die, my little foundling of the Force;
I have you now, and, with you, final power."
        With that he pressed the trigger; from above
Come laser cannon blasts: Victor Three burns
As Victor Two skids to the trench's wall,
For like a kingfisher, with sturdy beak,
Plummets to cut the glassy lake and lance
A hapless fish, his glory and delight,
740 Just so the swift *Millennium Falcon* dove

RETURN OF Down on the TIEs, and Victor Two's TIE rolls
THE *FALCON* And tumbles into Vader, whose sleek ship
Spins from the trench as Victor Two explodes,
Debilitated, useless; Han proclaims:
"You're clear now, kid: blow this thing and we're home":
For so it was that Han and Chewie came
To save a friend, to save the galaxy.
Skywalker did not hesitate: eyes shut,
Since oft the eyes deceive, he took his aim
750 And launched his twin torpedoes clean away.
        Now nothing lay between the Yavin moon
And that vast Death Star's devastating dish:
Then Tarkin, with a chuckle, gave the word
To fire when ready: so the work began

Of using that great weapon: target lock,

DEATH STAR The final pause, the final safety check,
WILL FIRE Ignition of the kyber cores, which yield
Eight hypermatter beams, a livid green
As lucid as a pulsar; yet before
760 They meld in one apocalyptic ray
Luke's twin torpedoes reach the target shaft
And, penetrating deep, explode and scratch
The fierce reactor modules; these provoke
A chain reaction, melting one by one,

THE CHAIN Collapsing those deep reservoirs of power,
REACTION The hypermatter beams, which smite instead
The battle station's fundament. Han flees
Into the starlight, Luke and Wedge in tow,
While Vader barely bolts to hyperspace,
770 When, with titanic force, the kyber core
Blew up, the crystals' holy power again
Unchained at last; and instantaneously
Those turrets, trenches, towers, and massy plates,
The hangars and the barracks and the stores,
The garrison, the countless fighter swarms,
The dish that made the constellations quail

END OF THE Shattered for ever. So the Death Star died.
DEATH STAR As when the gradual dusk, lit by the wisps
Of silent insects, messengers of night,
780 Seems to rotate, and from the porch the eyes
Of weary children glitter with the sparks,
Just so the pieces of the Empire's pride
Hung glowing in the crimson planet's path;
Luke hears, a final time, Kenobi's voice:
"The Force, young Luke, stands ever at your side."

The *Falcon* and Red Five, Red Two, Gold Three:
No more remain, for twenty-seven fell
Of those three squadrons sent to save the moon;
Yet by their sacrifice the moon endures:
790 Across its sky the four survivors glide,

RETURN TO Each to a landing pad, where now the crowds
YAVIN IV Of rebels, cheering, weeping, greet their ships,
Technicians, crew, and generals, Threepio

And old Dodonna, gasping with the rest.
Luke first appears, his golden locks askew,
Hearing a single call amid the roar,

LEIA, HAN,
AND LUKE

Leia's, as through the throng she dashes, first
To grab him, twirl him; laughing, she declares:
    "Is this the farm boy or the stormtrooper?

800   Or Obi-Wan's apprentice? No, it's Luke,
Miracle-maker, prince of rebels, Luke!"
    To which Han Solo, rushing forward, adds:
    "The boy in the cantina! Did you think
I'd leave the glory, take the rich reward?
I'll have them both – and, what is more, a friend."
    And Leia, looking in the scoundrel's eyes:
    "It seems there's more than money in your soul,
For such a soul has room for many things;
Together we'll bring freedom to the stars."

810   Then arm in arm they seek the open air,
Pausing to hand poor R2 to the crews
Who'll soon repair him; Threepio will help,
Donating circuits, gears, and good ideas.
    Evening was settling on the leafy hills:
Among the mighty trees the temples peeked,
The crimson disc of Yavin filled the sky.
Behind them Chewie thinks of lost Kashyyyk.
Skywalker's thoughts are not of Tatooine:

820   He sees at last the path that lies ahead;
He seems to live the life of twenty men.

    Cease there, protectress; others may depict
That ceremony where, in brave parade,
All ranks of joyful rebels, frigate crews,
Commandos, pilots, officers, marines,
Filled the bright hall of thrones, and Leia watched
Skywalker, Solo, Chewie strut the aisle

MEDAL
CEREMONY

To where she stood, as silent as the sun,
Granting to each a medal made of gold

830   Amid the trumpets, and received their vows,
Sworn unto that indwelling power that binds
All living things and balances our fate,
To win the savage war among the stars.

BOOK IV

HOTH

One master, one apprentice: 'twas their Rule
And their undoing; of that Rule I sing,
A song of evil. Now I journey deep,
And every footfall echoes in the dark.
O muse of anger, whom the ruthless Sith
Alone have ever mastered or compelled,
Twin sister of my angel, let me pass
Uncursed into this blackness, let me tell
How hard th' imperial pride of Palpatine
10   Struck back against th' Alliance, though his will
Was bent indeed on riddling prophecy:
In wrath he bade his pupil hunt the foe,

That pupil whose black sorcery was surpassed
By his alone, Lord Vader, whom dark arts
Had snatched in secret from the clutch of death,
Who now before his master's hologram,
As though before an awful idol, knelt,
Upon his starship, worshipping afar;
And, breathing deep, the sable pupil spoke:

20   "What is thy bidding, master? Since by luck
The rebels broke rash Tarkin and his hope,
I've scoured the systems of the Outer Rim
With this armada and this giant ship,
O'er which thy mercy placed me in command.
At first no whisper of the rebel fleet
Was heard by spy or scanner; Yavin IV
Lay desolate. My ships dispersed. Three years
We sifted space: each habitable sphere,
Planet and moon, received its probes. Yet soon,

30   Though neither Ackbar's fleet nor Rieekan's troops
Were found, the rumor of another name
Was spreading: chief in arrogance and crime,
He led their bold commandos – young, they said,
But armed most strangely, with an ancient blade.
It seems this reckless rebel bears a name
Known once to me, and not unknown to thee,

REPORTS
OF LUKE
The name of Skywalker. A cunning fraud,
The work, I guess, of Obi-Wan, concealed
The seed of Anakin; by such a boy,

40   By him alone the Death Star was destroyed."

        So Vader, kneeling, spoke, his rasping breath
Reverent and slow. At this the Emperor paused,
The emperor Palpatine, whose patient schemes
Had wrecked the old Republic, twisting love
And loyalty to ceaseless civil war,
'Til senators and Separatists and droids,
Merchants and clones and Jedi all were burned

SIDIOUS'
HISTORY
In his ambitious flame; yet few perceived
The dreadful secret: ere his steps had trod

50   The path of politics, he'd long been dubbed
Darth Sidious, apprentice to the Sith,
And soon himself the master, steeped in spite,

In every arcane artifice of hate,
Apostle of the dark side of the Force,
Who wielded lightning, choked the souls of men.
With crimson eyes 'neath flesh as pale as death,
His voice malevolence itself, he spoke:
    "The Force is turbulent. All things, I feel,
Draw slowly to a reckoning. Thou alone
60   Wert spared from my great battle station's wreck:
Therein some greater purpose lies concealed,
Which we may dominate or thwart at will.
Recall the secrets of a vanished world:
Deep in the well of time, before Darth Bane
Arose from lonely ashes to restore
Our Order, instituting this stark Rule,
Which since that day, a thousand years, hath held,

THE JEDI   The Jedi once received their prophecy,
PROPHECY   To which unto the bitter end they clung:
70   In riddles it foretold a Chosen One
Fated to bring a balance to the Force
And overthrow the Sith forever. Thee,
Lord Vader, in their folly, they declared
The one elect; and thou, to my delight,
Didst prove the instrument of their demise.
But now this boy, the son of Anakin,
Is come, and now the Force is turbulent."
    So spoke Darth Sidious, and held his peace;
Yet his apprentice, answering, guessed his mind:
80   "Thou fear'st, my master, lest this eager boy
Should prove the creature of the oracles?

VADER'S   He cannot overthrow us: let him turn
PLAN   Toward the dark, an asset to our cause:
The Force is strong with him. If he refuse
Then I myself shall see to his demise."
    So spoke Darth Vader; and his master thus:
    "Again thy thoughts, my pupil, point the way.
Yet have a care: another pupil once
Fell to a Skywalker's bright blade. Look well,
90   Depending on the Force to guide thy search.

A SECOND   My task is different: what the rebels razed
DEATH STAR   I shall restore: a second Death Star, vast,

Impregnable, to shake the very stars.
To it bring this young Skywalker, to me:
Then thou and I shall judge this prophecy."
        So spoke the Emperor; Vader, kneeling, bowed,
His reverence like a wave, and made his way
Through the gargantuan *Executor*,
His flagship, fifteen times the size and length
100   Of any Star Destroyer. At the bridge
His officers await: Vader commands
A fresh dissemination of the probes
Even to systems void of life or air.
And straightaway the fleet obeyed his word,
Dispersing down the avenues of space,
The probe droids in their millions scattering far.
As when the soil relaxes and the clan
Combines, with many a song, amid the clods,
To walk the thirsty furrows, sprinkling seed,
110   Just so the cruisers and the carriers roamed

SEARCH FOR
THE REBELS

With Star Destroyers, littering Cophrigin
And Sha Qarot and Dresscol and Jinet,
Tibalt and Bovo Yagen and De'nel,
Zandrax and Intran, Kemix and Udine,
And thousands more, the nameless and the named,
Some undiscovered and uncharted. Months
Elapse, the captains nervously report
No progress, neither rebel fleet nor base.

        Late in the third long year since Yavin IV
120   Beheld the rebel triumph, on a day
Of drudgery, as another waft of probes
Diffused across another system, Jhas,
Its siblings, and its icy neighbor, Hoth,
The dividend of diligence was paid.
Down through Hoth's jostling atmosphere they fell,

PROBES
ON HOTH

The probes, their cargo shielded from the flame,
Scooping soft craters in the endless snow.
From crystal pits arise, like jellyfish,
Black horrid probe droids, Vader's nimble scouts,
130   Bulbous above, with spindly limbs beneath,
Floating along the freezing wind, to see

A haze of ice locked shimmering in the air,
A pale sun indistinct, mountains beyond,
Infinite whiteness blending land and sky.
They start to chart the emptiness of Hoth.
    Meanwhile, not far away, two pairs of eyes

HAN AND LUKE Note through their scopes the meteors' sudden strike;
Two riders, miles apart, wrapped thick in wool,
Atop sure-footed tauntauns, riding up

140   Along the ridges: one is Han himself;
The voice of Luke comes crackling on the comm:
    "Ah, Han, old buddy, there you are; I'm off
Across the valley. Nothing to report,
Just those fresh craters; I'll inspect one here.
A blizzard's on its way, we should get back."
    To this idea Han speedily consents,
Turning his tauntaun back to Echo Base.
Across the ice flats' painful glare he rides,
Between the DF.9s that guard the gate,

150   Dismounting in the bustling hangar bay.
There were the X-wings, tended by their droids,
The snowspeeders, T-47s, too,
The little arsenal that still defied
The Emperor's fleets, good Rieekan in command.
There was the *Falcon*, much the worse for wear,
On which Chewbacca labors with a torch.
    At once Han seeks the center of command,
Where Rieekan, Farr, and Leia chew their lips
In staring at the screens; they strategize.

160   Han offers General Rieekan his report:
    "We've placed the sensors, General; Luke's still out
Checking some meteors; aye, they're falling thick.
But, General, there is this: I cannot stay.
The bounty hunters, whom I'd hoped to shake,
Have not forgotten – well, who has? – my name;
The Hutt's black death mark stalks me; Ord Mantell,
Where lately we ran into one, was proof.
I've got to pay back Jabba or I'm dead."
    Thus Captain Solo, whom the general thanks,

170   Though Leia barely bids the man farewell;
Yet once the smuggler's left them, she makes haste

To stop him in the icy corridor:
A passion rising in her eye, she speaks:
  "So you'll depart? I thought you said you'd stay.
Come, Han, we need you: every rebel looks
To you and Luke to lead when battle roars.
You've wanted riches: settle for such fame,

LEIA AND HAN

And let the name of Solo help the cause,
A name we need, that this Rebellion needs!"

180   So spoke the Princess, hand upon her hip;
To her the cocky captain made reply:
  "Aye, this Rebellion, which th' Imperial fleet
Will soon be blasting off this icicle,
Who knows what it may need? But, Princess, you,
What do you need? Not me? Ah, surely not!
As for myself, I need my life: the Hutt
Needs me or money; no, it's you they need,
This merry band of rebels. I must go!"
  So spoke the smuggler, hastening to his ship

190   To labor with the Wookiee on repairs,
The lifters and the hyperdrive, for hours.

  But what is this? Across the icy floor
Luke's droids, interpreter and astromech,
Arrive to interrupt: a grim report
From Princess Leia: deadly dark descends,
The night of Hoth, in which no creature lives,
But Luke has not checked into Echo Base.

LUKE IS
MISSING

One second Solo stares, then yells for word
Of who's still out there, but reports confirm

200   That Luke has not checked in at either gate.
Then brave Han Solo did not hesitate:
The speeders were too brittle for the cold,
So straightaway he climbs a tauntaun's back;
Deck officers protest, but Han replies:
  "Of course I know the temperature! Why else
Would I dare venture out to get my friend?
Oh, if I freeze, I'll see you all in hell!"
  So out he rode, past other tauntaun scouts
Who now were riding back into the base,

210 The toughest rebel troops: they brush the ice
From harnesses and whiskers; 'round their necks
They wrap thick thermal sheets; numb lips accept
The hot concoctions of less hostile worlds.
Thick doors debar the dropping temperatures,
Lest snowspeeders and X-wings, droids and ships
Congeal together. At that gate she waits,
Leia Organa, uniformed in white,
Before it shuts; nor Luke nor Han appears
Among the last to struggle in, cheeks blue,
220 Tauntauns half-dead. Beside her Chewie mopes,
Behind him R2 and C-3PO,
Fretting and waiting, reckoning up the odds
That flesh could ever last the night of Hoth.
They're turned away, it's over. Chewie moans
To mark the gate's inexorable descent.
As when a pet, agèd and sick, its breath
A beat of ceaseless suffering, lies confused
Upon the table, little guessing death
Approaches in the doctor's gentle touch,
230 And then its master cannot bear to look
LEIA'S Nor look away, so Leia strove to shut
DESPAIR Her eyes, the horror swelling in her heart.
She stumbles off, roaming the frigid gloom
Of bustling tunnels; all seems pale and slow,
All effort tending only to defeat;
She cannot sit, nor stand, nor rest, nor weep;
Always the vision of dead eyes, dead lips
Recurs; she'd rather stay and perish too.

Meanwhile into the blizzard's midnight maw
240 Han turned the tauntaun's horns. Oh, loyal beast,
That did not shirk that crystal wind, that swirl
HAN IN THE In which all forms dissolved, where up was down,
BLIZZARD Your toes and tail like iron! On they push,
Though scanners show no life, and ever on,
Though time seems stopped. Twice Solo must descend
To wrest the creature's leg from a crevasse,
And twice remount, though up into his brain

The cold is creeping; heart supplies the will
To disregard the lullaby of ice.
250   At last the mewling storm subsides, the crests
Of distant hills delineate the world;
And there, ahead, gray on the downs of white,
Lit just by softest starlight, stretched a man,
His temple bloody and his frozen glove
Curled tight about a saber's silver hilt.
Solo dismounts and staggers up, but Luke
Lies senseless in his arms; the smuggler's pleas

HAN FINDS
LUKE
Are punctured by the tauntaun's lethal groan.
As when an AT-ST, pride and joy
260   Of bandits whom brave villagers defy,
Will lurch into a trap, a pit, to trip
And tumble in a heap of fiery steel,
Just so the reeling tauntaun, with a groan,
Seemed to float down in death, its loyal days
Exhausted. Yet just then Luke's icy lips
Stir with the faintest syllables: "Ah, Ben,
Ben, Ben, to Dagobah." No more. Han's heart
Surges, for Luke still lives, if but to die;
At once he plucks the lightsaber, his mitts
270   Fumbling to activate its cool blue flame,
And crawls to where the tauntaun carcass lies;
Braving the inner stench, he slices wide
Its spilling belly, shoves his rigid friend
Into the guts: heat lingers in the blood,
To warm him in the wasteland, while Han toils
To raise the shelter. Soon a feeble tent
Protects them both against the searing air.
    There in the little circle of the lamp,
Beneath a thermal blanket, Luke awakes,
280   And Solo, sponging off the blood, exclaims:
    "Hang on, kid, you can make it; you're alive!
Must have gone sliding down some deep crevasse.
What was it you were muttering? Dagobah?
Just rest now; at the morn, if we survive,
I'll flag a speeder, won't be long before

The Empire comes and kicks us off this rock,
And I can't hope three times to save your life."
    Thus Solo; Luke produced a slender smile;
With sparkling eyes he answered Solo thus:
290   "I won't forget it, Han, and I foresee
I'll have a chance to settle up the score.
Yes, rest; but not before I tell my tale.
Han, I have seen him – oh, but first the brute.
I rode, once we had spoken on the comm,

LUKE'S TALE   Toward the crater I would never reach.
The snow was up already from the north,
Dusting the upper air; a rock dislodged;
My tauntaun snorted, gargled in her fear;
But, even as I soothed her, from behind
300   A mammoth paw smashed down upon my head,
Knocking me from the saddle. When I woke
I found I dangled like a butcher's treat
In some front window, which the crowds admire,
Downward, my feet stuck frozen in the roof
Of that mad monster's lair, a cave of ice,
Blue as the sea that washes tropic isles
But cold as Hoth itself, disfigured, clawed
By furious hunger. Out of sight, but near,
Bones crunched beneath the snarls of appetite –
310   My tauntaun's fate, torn by the lonesome moans
Which often, from the warmth of Echo Base,
We used to shrink to hear, ere doors were shut:

THE WAMPA   Indeed it was a wampa, ten foot tall,
Black horns like daggers bent about its mouth,
White as the snowy world it ruled in blood.
Helpless I dangled, couldn't reach my feet,
Nor budge them. Far beneath my aching head

LUKE'S   I sensed – not with my eyes – the lightsaber,
SWORD   Ben's gift, with which, on all those risky raids,
320   I'd clumsily pursued the foe. To it
I spoke in desperation, fingers clenched:
'O blade of light, o heart of crystal, hear
The son of him whom once you served: attend

As dire a need as any Jedi Knight's:
Aid me against this slaughterer of men,
And for my part I'll somehow learn to wield
Your deadly beauty with the same sure skill
As when you flickered in my father's fist.'
Just so I spoke, and instantly the blade
330   Leapt upward to my grip, and none too soon,
For barely was I free before the beast
In frenzy turned the corner, soaked in gore,
Teeth chewing on the frosty air, its eyes
Like hell; I leapt aside, but as I leapt
The searing saber seemed to turn itself,
Striking a shoulder, slicing off the limb.
The monster, screaming like a child, collapsed
In raging agony; I did not stop,
But through the jagged passages I fled
340   Up to the swirling surface; even there
In blind defiance of the blizzard's roar
I ran, I crawled in terror, 'til I dropped:
My frozen face fell hard upon the snow,
And death by numbness seemed to shut my sight.
But then – oh, Han, this is the strangest part –
I glimpsed, amid the white, a human shape,
LUKE'S VISION   The form of man, but insubstantial, pale,
Standing far off, in sandy robes, concealed
Beneath a drooping hood: I tried to call,
350   The sound was snatched away upon the wind.
Yet then that figure, casting back the hood,
With quiet mirth addressed me, and I heard:
'O son of Skywalker, is Hoth so cold
You do not know Kenobi? Now take heed.
Far distant lies the sphere of Dagobah:
KENOBI'S   Few know it, fewer reach it; there you'll go;
INJUNCTION   There dwells a hermit, Master Yoda, he
Who showed me first th' indwelling power that binds
All living things and balances our fate;
360   On Dagobah your own, with Yoda, waits.'
Just so Ben spoke – for it was Ben – Ben, Han!
Haven't I often told you how Ben's voice

Whispered within me as the Death Star fell?
Now dreams are real again, and duty calls,
Aye, duty, there, with Yoda . . . Dagobah . . ."
    So spoke Luke Skywalker, and shut his eyes
In heavy slumber; Han with tender touch
Tucked up the thermal blanket and remarked:
    "Alas, now here's delirium indeed,
370   That monster's last revenge! Poor kid, just sleep,
And wipe these crazy visions from your brain."
    With that his vigil through the night commenced.
As when a boat, too slender for the storm,
Bobs on the crests, shooting into the troughs
In some fierce hurricane, yet still escapes,
Just so that shelter in the snow survived,
Buried but breathing, 'til the flare of dawn
Restored the peaceful contour of the sky.

    Now in the Juris sector, at Qeimet,
380   Lay the *Executor*, Lord Vader's ship,
That Super Star Destroyer, with her fleet,
Death Squadron, tasked to crush the rebel base,
Th' *Avenger*, *Conquest*, *Stalker*, *Tyrant* too,
And fearsome *Devastator*. Countless probes
Were now reporting; Admiral Ozzel stalks
The flagship's bridge, Flag Captain Piett stares
HOTH   Into the screen where first reports from Hoth
IDENTIFIED   Show artificial structures. Piett frowns,
Recalling Hoth as void of human forms;
390   But Kendal Ozzel was a jealous man:
Scoffing, he answers Piett with contempt,
Suggesting rather squatters, smugglers. Him
The sudden voice of Vader overruled:
    "That's it. Those are the rebels. Set your course
For Hoth alone. And there is Skywalker."
    So spoke Lord Vader. Like a woeful gang
That hears the lash and suffers to transport
The dreary spice of Kessel's precious mine,
So those proud captains, facing Vader's mask,
400   Snap to their work at once: th' armada points

Its prows to Hoth, and at the admiral's sign
Its ships leap one by one to hyperspace,
Hurtling along that velvet whirlwind.
      Now, as they speed, Lord Vader summons Veers,
His loyal general, schooled in bitter war;
And thus Lord Vader speaks his strategy:
      "Prepare your walkers, Veers, and load the troops.
From orbit our destroyers shall dispatch
TIE Interceptors, sleek and slippery, quick,

410 Who'll strike the generator, lest a shield
Impede your march upon the rebel base.

VADER'S
STRATEGY
Beware their speeders. Bring the prisoners here.
When all is done I'll come to claim the prize."
      Just so Lord Vader fixed the hour of doom
Upon the enemy; and Veers obeyed.
But the assault went otherwise: that fool,
As crude as stupid, clumsy as inept,
Ozzel, thought fit to take them by surprise,
Exiting lightspeed close to Hoth's cold star:

420 His starships' signatures alert the foe,
And straightaway the rebels boost their shield,
Deflecting all bombardment. Thus the fleet
Can do no more than settle a blockade:
So Ozzel, with young Piett, soon reports.
As when a bantha, in the desert waste,
Will pause, and sniff, and nibble some sweet shrub
Beneath a ridge where lurks the mighty krayt,

DEATH OF
OZZEL
Just so the admiral shuffled to report
His final failure: Vader's iron hand

430 Unseen constricts the flesh of Ozzel's throat;
He staggers, strangling; to his vacant place
Vader promotes young Piett. Now his plan
Is changed: the generator shall be first
To fall to Veers, then Vader from the east
Shall lead the legionaries of the 1st.
      So Vader spoke, and eager Veers obeyed:

HOTH
INVADED
At once six AT-AT walkers are dispatched,
Cradled by carriers to the snowy ground:
Therein his hardy snowtroopers lie hid

440   By hundreds, ready for the frozen war.

Meanwhile Luke Skywalker, whom Han had saved
From death, attended by the med droids, floats
In bacta tanks, 'til soon the shaking stops.
Recovering, Luke awakens with his friends
Gathered beside his bed; Han Solo speaks:
    "Well, there's the hero, looking not half bad,
Aye, fit to pull a gundark's ears clean off!

LUKE IN THE That's two you owe me, junior: don't forget.
MED BAY And you, Your Worship," (this to Leia) "seems

450   Your scheme to keep me here is paying off:
Something about the shield of Echo Base,
A gorgeous guy, true feelings we conceal . . ."
    Thus Solo, whom the Princess, as she rose
To seek her duty, answered with a sigh:
    "If only bacta tanks and droids could treat
Such vast delusions. One thing still escapes
The laser of a smuggler's intellect:
The slightest notion about women. Look!"
    So Leia spoke, and, stepping briskly, strode

460   To plant a kiss on Luke; then she departs
To Chewie's mirth, Luke's cheer, and Han's chagrin.
    But soon another mission summons Han,
For Rieekan's sensors have detected this:
Some bulbous form, with spindly limbs beneath,
Floating along the freezing wind: at once
The smuggler and the Wookiee sneak outside
Across the snowfields, blaster pistols drawn
In clever ambuscade. Behind the drifts
Han glimpses metal – no, antennae; hears

470   The evil burble of a subspace code.
Then Solo thinks no more of cold and frost,
The *Falcon*'s foibles, Leia's jibes, his debts:
Chewbacca's roar distracts it; Han, behind,

HAN KILLS Pops up to shoot, dodging the answering bolt,
A PROBE Nailing its weapon system; it explodes,
Knocking the Wookiee and the smuggler down.
His vision cleared, Han fumbles for the comm

To offer General Rieekan his report:
"Some kind of probe droid, General: no, not hard,
480   It must have had a self-destruct. Good bet
The Empire knows we're here. Evacuate?
I think that might be just the right idea."
     So Solo spoke; with Chewie he rejoins
The bustling rebels in the base: long months
Of discipline in desperation guide
The steps of silent troopers to their posts.
Droids roll or totter down the icy halls
To where the last equipment's being stowed
In thirty GR transports; captains check
490   Abandoned offices, wiping the drives,
As pilots rev the engines of their ships.
The rebel leaders congregate, agree
To split the duties: steady Toryn Farr
Shall ope and close the shield, coördinate
The mighty ion cannon; Derlin dons
His warmest uniform and vows to save

REBEL
PLANS

The generator; Rieekan goes to load
The transports; so to Princess Leia falls
The task of pairing every transport's flight
500   With escorts of the X-wings that remain.
She hastens to the hangar's din, intent
On duty. There the pilots gather round
To hear the Princess' orders: to the north
The snowspeeders must wait for Derlin's word,
While transports, with their X-wings, one by one
Slip through the tight blockade: the ion gun

LEIA'S
BRIEFING

Shall clear their flightpaths up to open space.
They cheer; she seeks the center of command,
The pilots jogging to their stations, keen,
510   Prepared for war. A latecomer limps in,
Luke Skywalker, well thawed, who'd lately slain
A wampa in the waste; his gunner, Dak,
Is waiting at their speeder. Back to back,
Helmets of Rogue Group strapped upon their heads,
They take their places in the nimble craft.
Another cheer: behind the ion blasts
The leading GR-75 had burst

DAK   The Star Destroyers' ring: the *Tyrant* rolled
        Disabled by the aim of Toryn Farr.
520   Then to Commander Skywalker Dak cried:
          "Ah, sir, the Force is with us! Just as you
        Took down the Death Star, so today my heart
        Could crush the mighty Empire by itself!"
          Luke, grinning, bade him look to his controls,
        The cable and harpoon, the turret gun,
        As, lifting off, they joined the other Rogues
        That streaked, at Derlin's order, for the front.

          There to the north, where just behind the ridge
        The shield's great generator lay concealed,
530   A trench, well fortified with laser towers
        And DF.9s, was dug, wherein the troops
        Keep steady silence; Sergeant Callum views
        The blowing snow before him: five black shapes
        Seem distant rocks, but his binoculars
        Reveal five AT-AT walkers, huge as beasts
        Of armored steel, some twenty meters tall,

THE AT-AT   Pacing the wintry plain on four long legs,
WALKERS   Cannons for tusks, transporting countless troops
        Prepared to storm and pillage Echo Base.
540   As when a comet, sliding 'round its star,
        Is calculated finally to impact
        A helpless moon, obliterating all,
        Just so that veteran eye assessed the path
        Of Veers's strike force: quickly Callum calls
        For air support, and Derlin sends the Rogues,
        For though his laser turrets take their aim,
        The walkers' armor blocks those bolts; the foe
        Replies with AT-AT cannons, striking hard.
          Across th' embattled trench the speeders streak,
550   Skimming the flats, dodging the cannon fire,
        A dozen dauntless pilots holding tight.

ROGUE GROUP   Then Skywalker commands the squad to switch
        To Pattern Delta: splitting up, they peel
        To left and right, then bank and interweave
        The AT-AT legs. Alas, against the steel
        Of AT-AT armor, what can blasters do?

As often as Dak nails a joint, the glow
Rapidly dims; the heads deflect all shots.
Now incidents of battle take their toll:

560   Speeders are hit, unspooling threads of smoke.
Luke bids his squadron switch to their harpoons
And snare the walkers' ankles; on his wings
Hobbie and Wedge, Rogues Four and Three, protect

HARPOONS
AND CABLES   Luke's daring vector; yet the target shoots,
Striking his speeder, frying circuits; Dak
Slumps lifeless in the seat: but Wedge instead
Will let his gunner, Janson, take his aim,
Pointing the stiff harpoon. A hit! Wedge threads
The cable once and twice and thrice about

570   The AT-AT's gait; it falters, topples, breaks
Its armored neck, and Hobbie, swooping swift,
Blows it to pieces. From the trench a cheer
Shows the defense still holds, though even so
The walkers and those chicken-leggèd scouts,
The AT-STs, devastate the line,
Shattering the towers and DF.9s, huge holes
Blown in the snow, from which a ragged hedge
Of laser-rifle barrels still resists.
      Again Luke grimly looks to the attack,

580   Enlisting Zev, Rogue Two, the very man
Who'd rescued him and Solo in the snow;
Ah, but that seemed another age, as now,
With Zev and Hobbie in position three,
Quite tight, quite low, amid the tufts of flak,
They ready their harpoons; but Zev was caught:
Flaming, he burst, and Hobbie just escaped,

LUKE
CRASHES   But Luke was hit again; computers fried,
Smoke seethes about him; furiously he seeks
An angle for th' inevitable crash.

590   As when a smooth, flat stone, which patient eyes
Have sought for minutes on the beach, is skimmed
Across the rippling surface, scudding quick,
To sink at last, a record-breaking throw,
Just so Luke's speeder plowed the plain, to stop
Right in the rearmost AT-AT walker's path.

The tremor of its footfalls wakes the brain:
He pushes up the canopy, retrieves
His sword and some explosive just in time
Before the mammoth, with gigantic weight,
600   Crushes the cockpit 'neath a steely foot.
Then Luke addressed the remnants of his friend:
     "Ah, shall this broken coffin, Dak, encase
Your icy flesh, no epitaph attest
The heart that fought the Empire to the end?
Take this instead, a hero's funeral pyre."
     Thus Luke, and from his flight suit belt he shoots
A cable, latching to the beast's steel hide,
Winching aloft to dangle there beneath
The undercarriage: there his saber flares,
610   Cutting a sudden fissure, where he stuffs
A brace of thermal detonators; down

LUKE DOWNS
AN AT-AT

He drops into the snow. The walker's chest
Muffles the tearing detonations, down
The AT-AT monster crashes; Luke avoids
The burning of its screaming denizens
Above Dak Ralter's body on the plain.

     Now, as the battle boiled, there came a calm
For Luke: the AT-STs spring ahead,
Their double cannons clearing out the trench,
620   Struck by rifles' futile flash; none note
A single flight suit at the heart of war.
Over the snow he stumbles, up the ridge
That hides the transports, watching from on high
The three last AT-AT walkers reach their goal.
As when a squishy plank, in which the bugs
Have feasted on the damp and the decay,
Is lifted and they scurry from the light,
Just so the rebel troops were scattering, shot
By idle gunners. Veers directs his scope
630   Toward the generator, cranks the power:
Two livid bolts divide the bitter air;

VEERS
VICTORIOUS

It buckles with a cataclysmic crack.
The shield has crumbled. Ships from orbit launch

A ruinous barrage upon the base,
And straightaway the grim 1st Legion drops
Toward the east. Young Skywalker makes haste
To where good R2, in the X-wing, waits.
Calling farewell to Wedge – for Hobbie too,
Like Dak, like Zev, lies dead upon the field –
640 Luke climbs the ladder, sinks into his seat,
Rising away from that disaster, tight
Behind the final transport's swift escape;
The ion cannon, firing still, protects
Their breakout to the liberty of space.

Meanwhile the turbolasers of the fleet
Pummel the surface; Echo Base beneath
Shudders, the ceilings fracture, chunks of ice
Smite the *Millennium Falcon* in its bay.
There Han and Chewie work as if possessed,
650 With solder, spanner, imprecation, prayer,
HAN AND Upon the hyperdrive; technicians flee,
CHEWIE Each to a transport; even droids depart;
And still the duo labors, 'til the voice
Of Princess Leia echoes through the halls:
"Get to your transports! Snowtroopers approach
Our headquarters; get to your transports now!"
Then Solo, leaving Chewie to repairs,
Sprints through the glacial labyrinth: it's from there
At headquarters that Princess Leia speaks.
660 The corridors are broken: cords and vents
Litter the ground, the sparking tips of wires
Illuminate the wreckage; few remain,
And those are hustling for the southward gate.
HAN SEEKS Han finds his destination: that close room
LEIA In which Mon Mothma and old Ackbar planned
The raids and picked the targets; it's been smashed,
But still inside are Farr, that droid of Luke's,
And Leia, fiercest at the final hour.
To him the startled Princess turns to speak:
670 "Han? Why are you still here? The *Falcon's* cleared
For takeoff since this morning. Chase the blast,

We've hardly lost a dozen transports. Go!
There's still some time before they storm the base."
    Thus Leia; Solo, breathless, made reply:
    "A smuggler I may be, Your Worship, but
Rebel enough to care about the fact
It's clear this mad Rebellion cannot last
Without you, so I'll get you to your ship
And clear your own departure from this rock!"

680   So Han declared, and Leia acquiesced;
Farr too concedes, departs; the Princess calls
A last evacuation on the comm.
Then even as word came the mighty 1st,
Cream of the Empire's legions, Vader's fist,
Had blasted through the eastern battlement
They fled, two human beings and the droid,

ESCAPE OF   Through the last scenes of Echo Base, their home,
HAN AND LEIA Whose structures are disintegrating: walls
Shake off their icy ceilings; tunnels choke,

690   Collapsing, one near kills them; with a cough
Han signals Leia's transport to depart.
Instead, his steady strength about her waist,
He lifts her over every obstacle
Toward the proud *Millennium Falcon*'s bay.
C-3PO can barely keep the pace;
Dread only of desertion, being left
A brass maroon upon a sea of foes,
Encourages his tottering metal steps.
The guns of snowtroopers seem right behind.

700   At last a Wookiee howl, its echo stark
Around the empty hangar, marks the end:
They rush the gangplank as the engines bawl,
And none too soon: behind them blasters bark,
Though Chewie's cannon buys them time to lift
And point the double prow toward the light.
    Watching the *Falcon* fly, a shadow stands
Amid the ruin of the secret base.
As when a cairn, which pilgrims worked to raise
Deep in the wastes of waterless Jakku,

710   Stands guard, an awful warning to be read

By those with eyes to read, a dusty shape,
Just so Darth Vader watched the rebels go,
But in his heart, half god and half machine,
He laughed, for though young Skywalker had fled,
He knew not yet the power of the Force.

BOOK V

DAGOBAH

INVOCATION

Harsh spirit, now I'll shirk your evil eye;
    Nameless I'll go, concealed I'll slip away
    Far from the envy, frenzy, and regret
Of your insidious domain; the brave
May balk at exile, but the wise accept,
Knowing they cannot change, their weary lot,
'Til patience may receive its due reward.

    Up through that clear, cold air Skywalker soared,
Along with R2-D2, trusty droid,
To space, the chaos of the cracked blockade
Far back behind; the other ships perform
Their separate jumps to different rendezvous.

But Luke himself selects another course,
Much to R2's alarm, who beeps and twirls,
Asking what's wrong; but Luke, his blue eyes bright:
   "All's well, good fellow; aye, 'tis for the best.
We won't regroup or seek new hangars yet.

LUKE SEEKS
DAGOBAH

Our destination is a distant dream:
We jump to Dagobah, for somewhere there

20

A hero dwells, preëminent in war,
Yoda, the Jedi Master. Clear I heard
The word of Ben Kenobi in the snow."
   At this, on manual control, he guides
The X-wing to the nav computer's path,
And R2, not without misgiving, jolts
The hyperdrive to lightspeed; off they leap
Past Ione (although they knew it not,
Deep in the unreal lane of hyperspace),
Past Burnin Konn and Polmanar, beyond

30

Seswanna's settlements, past Shumavar,
'Til they broke back at last at Dagobah.
   Far from the hyperlanes it lay, lone sphere
Hugging its dim white star; no city, mine,

DAGOBAH

Colony, port, or prison marked its place
Upon the stellar map; 'twas just a name.
Luke nonetheless (though R2 counseled care)
Pointed the fighter's nose into its airs.
No villages appear upon the scan,
Nor any tech, but massive signs of life,

40

Life surging from the marshy continents
That weigh upon the surface, hid by cloud.
Oh, how that atmosphere was thick! The droid,
Exposed behind the cockpit, felt it streak
In soupy vapor down the fuselage,
Yellow and white, an oily, cloying fog;
The X-wing starts to shake, the scopes are dead;
Luke starts the landing cycle on a hunch
And none too soon: they hurtle through a tree,
A wood, whose brittle branches seem to bend

50

In welcome to the wastes of Dagobah.

   Into a pool amid th' eternal swamp
The fighter shuddered, fastened in the mire;

Skywalker lifts the canopy and stares.
About the pillars of an ancient glade
The murky water stretches; twilight looms
Far back into the endless trees; gnarled roots

THE SWAMP Of human height invade the liquid earth,
Their unkempt tendrils motionless; the air,
Rich with the taste of growth, hangs heavy; smells
60 Of spongy moss and shiny algae waft.
Only the mist seems wakeful, curling thick,
Concealing and revealing every shape;
But over all a patient stillness reigns,
Made louder by the distant flap of wings.
As when the apprehension of the truth
Torments a sleeper, dodging his pursuit
Through gilded rooms and polished corridors,
Until at last he startles, wet with sweat,
Just so Luke's gaze went flitting through the mist
70 From trunk to massy trunk, from pool to roots.
He hops from fuselage to shore; R2,
Hoist from his niche, falls off the shifting ship,
Bobbled and soon submerged beneath the swamp.
Then Luke, relieved to spot his periscope,
Directs him to the shore. Yet Dagobah
Was filled with risk, as now a muscled spine,
Some nameless monster's, arching through the ooze,
Plunges for R2's periscope, his chirps
Sucked down. In vain Luke points his pistol, yells:
80 Only the bubbles of the droid remain.

R2-D2 NEARLY Luke challenges the rippling ooze itself,
DEVOURED Blaring his rage; but ere he'd lost ten words
The droid, ejected from the carnivore
Like bolt from bowcaster, shatters the sheen
Of algae, launched across the heavy air
To land among the roots; he's hauled upright
By Luke's firm grip, regurgitating bog,
To hear the comfort of his master's voice:
        "So droids, at least, are little to its taste!
90 And yet I dread the omen. Oh, Artoo,
What folly to dismiss your wise advice!
Alas, this ship can never rise again
From such a watery pit; forever stuck

Among the horrors of this swamp, we'll wait
To starve or be devoured. Have I gone mad,
Willing myself a nobler destiny,

**LUKE SENSES
A PRESENCE**

My visions mere delusions? All the same,
If I was crazy, crazy I remain,
For something on this planet, in the mist,

100

Some whisper in the silence strikes my thought
As quite familiar. When I used to stare
Toward the setting suns of home, I guessed
Adventure lay in store; the Force itself
Ordained it, Artoo, and this creepy place
Exudes its power. So come, we'll pitch a camp,
Get you some voltage and get me some food,
Then ponder how to reach this Yoda's seat,
If he exists – if any here exist."

    Thus Skywalker. The astromech and youth

110

Settle their simple kit on scarce hard ground
Some distance from the crash; long serpents slide

**THEY MAKE
CAMP**

Across it, 'round the space chests; Luke unpacks
A scanner, comlink, rations, and a lamp,
A portable reactor for the droid.
And yet his first uneasiness persists.
Blaster in hand, he checks the forest, watched
(He senses) by a mind unseen. He shouts;
No answer echoes from the bog but this:
    "Why shout? Here do I linger, not far off;

120

Put down your weapon: look, I mean no harm."
    Luke whirls, but drops the blaster; no dread beast
Confronts him from a cradle of the roots:
Rather a two-foot humanoid, green skinned,

**A LITTLE
CREATURE**

Wrapped in a rag, supported by a stick,
With pointed ears curled outward to the side,
Was resting wry and perspicacious eyes
In his. The creaky voice is laced with mirth,
Asking why Luke has come; the youth replies:
    "Why, little fellow, would you like to help?

130

I wish you could! But no, a fated quest
Unfolds: I seek a mighty man of war.
Yet now this slimy mudhole grips my ship,
And toil awaits; you should be on your way."

Meanwhile the creature, hobbling on his staff,
Had climbed one chest, was rifling through the next:
Tossing its contents messily, he spoke:
   "But why depart, if I can stay and help?
This slimy mudhole, which I call my home,
I much regret that it has claimed your ship.
140   You see, morasses, not great men of war,
I count among my neighbors; is it war
That makes a hero? Ah, but what is this?"
   Chattering like that, he fishes from the box
One item, clutching in his three-clawed fist
A little flashlight, fighting off R2.
As when a tiny child unwraps a toy
Of no great worth to others, but to her
As prized as kyber, fabulous indeed
As Zenda's scarlet jewel, and cries of joy
150   Track her about the playground of her home,
Just so the agèd creature laughed to shake
The flashlight; to Luke's protest he replied:
   "Let it be mine, or I shall help you not!
Ho, you agree? Well chosen! Such a price
Is heavy, yes, but not too heavy, no.
Whom do you seek, then? Jedi Master? Ah!
Yoda you seek, and Yoda shall you find:
For I shall take you to him. Nonetheless,
All things in order: first it's time to eat,
160   The table calls the Jedi also, no?"

   With many a chuckle thus the creature led
The wary youth through steaming bog and fen
Beneath the twisted roots, for much Luke wished
AT THE HUT   To meet the sage, even with such a guide.
And soon the travelers reach a tiny hut
Of rounded walls, tucked in beneath a tree.
The heavy rain beat hard, but dry inside
The bustling creature and cross-leggèd youth
Discuss Luke's goal; a tiny pot of stew
170   Cooks on the miniature hearth, its taste
Abominable to Skywalker's soft tongue.
Bidding him eat, the little host inquires

Why Luke should wish to learn the Jedi's ways;
To which the eager answer came at once:
    "The path I follow was my father's too:
For he was once a Jedi, such a Knight
As fought for peace and truth, before the dark
Eclipsed the proud Republic. Long indeed
Was Leia's tale: I'll recollect the gist.

180   In brief, the Separatists, in freedom's name,
Backed by a host of heartless battle droids,
Led by the cruel Count Dooku, would secede;

THE CLONE
WARSThree years they fought the Jedi and their troops,
Those millions of devoted clones; that war
Was bitter and its battles even now
Bring tears when named, and reverential awe:
Ryloth, Felucia, Teth, and Utapau,
And Geonosis, where like some vast wave
The battle droids descended, Jedi fought

190   Against an army; and in all those deeds
My father had his place: himself he slew
The cruel Count Dooku, with this blade I bear,
Anakin Skywalker, whose name resounds.
But now the Jedi are well nigh extinct,
For Obi-Wan Kenobi, whom I knew,
Has perished: only Yoda now remains,

REPORTS
OF YODAKenobi's teacher. He it was, they say,
Who steered the Jedi Council, and his sword
Saw many a siege and battlefield before

200   The clones' betrayal and Darth Vader's hour,
Yoda, the last of Jedi, and the best.
But why must we delay? The hour is late,
The frail Rebellion flees into the stars,
And here we sit beside a crackling fire!"
    So spoke young Skywalker, and moved to rise,
Bumping against the ceiling where he sat.
At first the little host made no reply,
Stirring the pot, his eyes half shut, intent
On memory; then at last he sadly spoke:

210   "Indeed, your father did not lack for power:
He was the best, not Yoda: best with sword,
With every mindful art, and most of all

The Force flowed through him as through channels carved

By ancient waters; well I recollect
The day he saved the chancellor: how upright,
How handsome in his piety he stood
Before the grateful Council. Aye, but fate
Claimed him and everyone; and so it must.
And now at length his offspring comes to learn.

220 Alas, is this a Jedi Padawan,
So quick to anger, quick to look away?
Another was the same. Shall he be trained?
Long have I watched him from afar, his mind
Fixed always on adventure, not on life;
Are Jedi so preoccupied? Too old,

SHALL LUKE
BE TRAINED?
I think, is he, too used to recklessness.
Eight hundred years I've taught them: well I know
A Padawan is wholly serious,
Wholly committed, body, mind, and soul –

230 Perilous else, for, hastily enrolled,
The hasty pupil soon forsakes the way."
　　　So Yoda spoke; amazement filled the youth,
For now the gentle creature seemed transformed.
As when a child, on steady study bent,
Puzzles around a problem, sketching facts
In bafflement, 'til suddenly the pen
Perceives and proves the answer of itself,
So Luke abruptly felt the master's power.
With awe he bends, yet desperately protests:

240 　　　"I am my father's son – that is the truth –
Though not his equal; little I deserve
This life, for I was raised to harvest dew;
I claim no more than fighter pilot's skill;

LUKE'S
PLEDGE
This saber is a cudgel in my hand.
Yet also this is true: when I gaze off
I look not to myself but to the Force,
In which all things arise and fall away.
My life is little, but in your firm care
I place it now forever, unafraid."

250 　　　So spoke the pupil, and the master's mood
Softened, for even then old Obi-Wan
Was present in his thought, a voice unheard

That counseled patience for impatience, trust
In such sincerity. So in a breath
Yoda consents, although his tone is grave:
        "Be then my student, aye, like Obi-Wan
Once was, the final Padawan I teach.

YODA CONSENTS

Your life I take, another life I give;
But fear you must accept, for life is fear,

260 The breath of that indwelling power that binds
All living things and balances our fate.
A fool approaches wisdom unafraid."
        At that the pair in silence ate their meal,
Then slept in silence, and at dawn arose
To start the quest for knowledge in the dew.

        Skywalker firstly, ere the thin gray morn
Had reached the arching roots, sprinted and stretched
Amid the skeptic whistles of R2.
Chuckling, the master, who, well fed, emerged

270 Some minutes after, bade him listen, sit.
No spoken lesson follows: Luke perceives
His own impatience with his patience knit,
The one, the other triumphing; at length
The master, sitting, bids him stand and step

LUKE WALKS AND RUNS

Among the misty sinkholes and the stones.
Fearful, the youth moves gingerly; he trips
But rights himself each time before a fall.
The master bids him run: about the tree
That topped the hut he courses, leaping clear

280 Of gnarly obstacles, 'til strength is spent.
At this the philosophic tutor spoke:
        "Now you may listen, while your muscles ache.
To listen is the first of Jedi ways,
Not to my voice, but to the world about.
Will you ignore what would converse with you?
Each object bears a name, unspeakable

LANGUAGES OF NATURE

By us perhaps, as it speaks not our own;
There is a language of the rocks, of air,
Another of the grass, which makes its words

290 In whispers; proudly talk the towering trees,
Fiercely the flames, deeply the shifting earth.

Listen and learn their languages, their names,
And teach them who this Skywalker may be."
  Luke, marveling, must obey; a single rock,
Belched at the outset from the planet's core,
The glaciers' toy, chiseled and split, its edge

LUKE LISTENS Speckled beneath the tendrils, greets his thought;
The gurgle of the swamp explains its sloth;
Even the mist communicates itself.

300 He feels the birds' unwearied wariness,
The malice of the monster in the mire;
He senses R2-D2's loyalty
And hidden depth of memory; he discerns
The ancient power of Yoda like a tomb
Of golden stone upon the lonely sand.
Unsummoned he arises: now his steps
Are planted with the favor of the trees,
The fen directs him to the firmer ground;
The air seems happy to uphold his leap.

310 Unconscious of the passing day, intent
On his connection to these paltry things,
He hops for hours, studied by Yoda's eye;
But when the dimness of the sun's ascent
Reached noon, they ate, and Yoda took his place
On Skywalker's strong back, bidding him sprint
By paths untrodden yet on Dagobah.
As when a salmon, ere it quits this life,
Filled with the ache of duty, leaps ahead
Against the ceaseless pressure of the brook,

320 Persisting 'til it reach its natal pool,
Just so Luke pushed across the reeking fen:
No more the notes of every separate thing
Sound singly in his ears: a melody
Unites them, layers them; so from tune to tune
It makes a way, now jubilant, now grim,
As Luke, a silent singer, picks it up.
  Attached upon his leaping pupil's back,

YODA'S Yoda conceals his joy and his alarm:
CONCERN His joy, because no Padawan before

330 Had made such easy progress; his alarm
Because such power, untamed and raw, might yet

Be turned to ill and evil agency.
So even as Luke leaps from rock to rock,
His gentle teacher counsels vigilance:
 "Each thing, o son of Skywalker, all life
Is turned toward the light; thereby the dark
Has being in the light's eternal shade:
Thus light and darkness meet in every thing.
Yet you would be a Jedi, not a Sith:

340 Beware, therefore, the dark side of the Force,
The way of fear unmastered, rancor, rage.

THE
DARK SIDE
The dark side must consume them, those who start
Down its relentless path, while those who seek
To dominate and make a slave of fate
Make only their own slavery: so it was
With Obi-Wan's apprentice, Vader, him
Whom you have seen, and terror hedged him 'round,
Who at our first encounter was a child.

 "Long is the tale, and long the sorrow too.

350 There was a tax dispute, a minor fuss:
The sly Trade Federation and its droids
Had blocked Naboo; our worthy Qui-Gon Jinn
Was dispatched by the Council to restart
Negotiations, or to save the queen;
And with him went Kenobi, still a youth;

NABOO
INVADED
But all in vain: an unprovoked attack
Crushed all resistance on Naboo; our Knights
Could barely save Queen Amidala, her
Who far surpassed all rivals: grace and wit

360 Sat on her lips, and beauty in her eye.
Up through th' encompassing blockade they fled,
But not unscathed: her shapely silver ship
Sought Tatooine, your planet, for repairs.
At Espa there the Jedi met two waifs
Amid the dust, a mother and a son

THE BOY
Conceived in mystery, whom no father sired,
A boy of nine, but mighty in the Force.
Then Jinn, a Knight so studious in lore,
Believed that ancient prophecy fulfilled

370 Whose riddles had foretold a Chosen One
Fated to bring a balance to the Force.

To Coruscant the queen and Jedi came;
Before the Council Qui-Gon brought the boy,
The Twelve: and there were Windu and Piell,
Billaba and Rancisis and Eeth Koth,
And Tiin, who fell to Sidious' red sword,
Ki-Adi-Mundi, Gallia, Yaddle too,
Dear Yarael, Plo Koon the undismayed,
And I, grand master, who performed the tests.
380   Indeed the boy was mighty, though untrained,
But suffering and the dread of loss had marred
A rising mind; within his soul I saw
A clouded future. So the Council spoke,
Forbidding any training, urging Jinn
To leave it be; but fate willed otherwise.

AMIDALA'S RETURN   For Amidala watched the Senate balk,
Abandoning her planet and the law,
Addicted to procedure: though her maids
Begged her to stay on Coruscant, she vowed
390   To liberate or perish with Naboo.
And so with Jinn, Kenobi, and the boy
BATTLE OF NABOO   She faced the Federation and its droids.
A dreadful battle then engulfed that world:
Even the Gungans, allies at the last,
Were not enough for victory, though the queen,
Scaling the fortress with her palace guards,
Herself dethroned the viceroys: there was Maul,
A hellish warrior schooled on Malachor,
The Sith or Sith's apprentice – always two
400   Perpetuate that endless chain of hate –
Darth Maul of Dathomir, whose dual blade
Met both the Jedi's sabers. Qui-Gon fell
Not unavenged, for Obi-Wan dispatched
His master's killer, heard his master's breath
Expiring with a sacred last request:
The boy, the Chosen One, was to be trained
QUI-GON'S REQUEST   As Obi-Wan's apprentice. Such a plea,
The very voice of Qui-Gon's blazing pyre,
The Council did not dare to overlook.
410   Yet, as the boy grew up, Kenobi's word
Was seldom much respected: recklessly

He made the Force itself his guide; the path
Toward the dark side opened to his feet.
He missed his mother, broke the Jedi's rule
Against the love of one: his heart was turned

VADER   To one wise maiden, and her own to him;
But even as they pledged them, visions showed
His mother murdered, and he took revenge
Most savagely, thus yielding to the fate

420   That made him Vader, not the Chosen One –
The tool of Sidious, the Jedi's bane."
        So Yoda spoke; in Skywalker's mind's eye
The tale unfolds as if upon a loom
Embroidered: swift invasion of Naboo,
The speeches to a thousand senators,
The battle of the Gungans and the droids,
The pyre of Jinn, the Council giving way:
The more he looks behind, the more he sees
Ahead, but tending only to defeat;

430   Yet Yoda guides him back from his despair,
Bidding him shun seduction by the dark,
Forever mindful of the living Force.

        So stage by stage, combining feats of strength
LUKE'S   With feats of intellect and tales of old,
PROGRESS   Behind his master Skywalker progressed;
His words grew fewer and his motions brief;
No more he struggles with necessity,
No more desire impinges on the right;
Unfazed the creatures of the earth and air

440   Await his coming. To the solid stones
The patient teacher points the pupil's thought:
The light of life is missing from them, yet
The light of being fills them just the same;
And, being known and named, they may obey
MOVING   A firm direction. Soon Luke learns to will
ROCKS   Pebbles and sticks together, next to lift
A weighty rock aloft. Then Yoda sets
A grander challenge: Skywalker shall stand
Upon his head (an easy pose for him)

450 With Yoda perched upright upon his boot;
And then the Force, not Skywalker, shall stack
Five stones as Skywalker elects. Luke gulps,
Sensing a test and doubting he'll succeed,
But tries: the first stone inches to its spot;
The second rises, sinks atop the first;
The third, a flinty fragment, wrapped in moss,
Cuts elegantly up, then down again
In place; the fourth – but now R2's alarm
Invades the stillness: frantic tocsins, whirls,
460 And peals of panic knock both stones and youth
To earth, as Yoda leaps to safety; Luke
Dashes toward the astromech, beholds
The X-wing sinking quickly in the swamp.
Luke, wading some way in himself, exclaims:
    "This is the end; I'll never get it up!
What hope in even trying? Here I'll stay
THE X-WING   And train forever, while the others' deeds
HAS SUNK   Fill annals. Now where are my loyal friends,
The rocks, whom I preferred to starfighters?"
470   Thus Luke, who cast himself upon the ground;
To which his little teacher made reply:
    "Alas, you are so certain of all things.
The certainty of youth is like a storm
That rips the sky and terrifies the birds
And next day is forgotten. Do I speak
To clouds or mutter precepts to the trees?
What can be done eclipses what cannot.
The student must unlearn what he had learned.
Your friends, the stones, are small, but Dagobah
480 Is naught but stones and water. Look at me:
YODA ON   Is size my measure? No? Indeed it's not:
THE FORCE   An ally stands behind me and within,
Perceived by few, yet felt by everything,
The note of life itself, the energy
And music of the galaxy, the Force.
Its instrument am I, and so are you:
This starship brought you hither, but to me,
To this one spot upon the globe, you came

Unguided? Nay, as much as any rock,
490 Your starship stands in union with the shore.
I do not try: I do, or I do not."
      At that the master raised his tiny palm,
His eyes half closed; Luke sits upright to watch.
At first no gurgle stirred the depths. The slime
Trembled perhaps; perhaps it was the fog;
Yet then the bubbles, clustering thick, break forth,
Sketching the sunken treasure: first the tip
Of one long cannon, hung with weeds, appears:
Next is the sensor window of the nose,
500 The nose like some huge fossil, shedding mud;
Then R2's perch, the cockpit, and a wing

THE X-WING
RISES
Still proudly bearing Rogue Group's famous mark,
'Til over the morass the X-wing hangs,
Flowing with water, draped in filth, but free.
Confounded, Luke regards its stately course
Toward the silent shore, where Yoda waits,
Who drops his hand and leans upon his stick.
Touching the solid fuselage, Luke speaks:
      "Impossible, yet real; unreal, but fact!
510 What dream is this, from which I won't awake?
Is everything in nature overthrown?
Is this a legend or the solid world?"
      To which the Jedi Master made reply:
      "Such questions you will answer – yes, and soon;
And on your answer all depends. Some choose
The paths of certainty, and live content;
Some choose the same, but soon regret their choice;
Few take the road of mystery: fearsome things
Await in mysteries: fateful prophecy,
520 Terror beyond all limit, lofty bliss,
The present and the future and the past
Perceived together, inescapable;
And so all things may soon seem strange indeed.
Aye, death, that constant measure of the world,

THE FORCE
AND DEATH
Shall prove a hidden kingdom of the Force,
Wherein, perhaps, the selfless may persist,
Forsaking love and hate, aligning thus
With only nature; Qui-Gon taught the way.

Alas, another method, born of hate,
530　　Of rash defiance, not of harmony,
Seeks to break death itself: such were the arts
Of old Darth Plagueis, whom they called the Wise.
Deepest into the dark side had he delved,
Deepest of all the Sith, 'til life itself

DARTH
PLAGUEIS
Was clay to mold, to fashion, or to crush
Between his fingers, even to revive
The dead. And yet that master, by their Rule,
Took an apprentice, passing on his lore.
There was a youth, a scion of Naboo,
540　　Last of an ancient line, Sheev Palpatine,
Learned in the law, soon steeped in evil: soon
The pupil sought the teacher; Plagueis taught

PLAGUEIS'
PUPIL
The art of whispers and the art of lies,
The skill of killing with the fingertips,
Dominion too (he reckoned) over death;
And thus was born Darth Sidious the Cruel.
Yet soon old Plagueis perished in his sleep,
For evil knows no gratitude: the youth
Murdered his master, cackling at the blow
550　　That took the wary prophet unawares.
And so the secrets of Darth Plagueis passed
To him alone. The malice of the Sith
Possessed him all the more, and subtle plots
Were hatched against the Jedi: few perceived
The Sith's return, until he chose at last
A new apprentice. So young Vader fell,
Whom hope seduced, a hope that his beloved,
Betrothed in secret, might escape her fate,
Though visions showed her perishing in pain;
560　　And in that hope he turned toward the dark.
Such were the lies of Sidious, long planned,
Whereby the Jedi Order was destroyed;
But fate is not so easily defied,
And Plagueis's arts were treacherous: no, not she
But Vader was preserved, a living death,
While she preferred to perish than to turn,
Forsaken, aye, but not forsaking love,
Foretelling, even as death's fingers clutched

Her heart, that he might someday be restored –
570 An empty hope, alas! But 'tis no dream,
Impossible, yet real; for I was there."
So speaking, Yoda, weary from his feat
And from such recollections, leads them back
Toward a supper and the balm of sleep.

Yet sleep had little purchase over Luke,
Who dreamed of agony, of clenching jaws,
LUKE'S DREAMS Childbirth's devotion, courage unto death,
Tears of a young Kenobi, infants' wail,
A young girl gazing from a lofty town
580 Across a lake, 'neath snowy mountains sheer:
Her mother's and her father's hands had met
Upon her shoulders, and her robe was white,
Her face unseen. The restless Padawan
Escapes these portents with the breath of morn;
Solitude calls, among the snakes and fog,
With meditation. Now, in passive pose,
LUKE He weighs a dictum of his master's, thus:
MEDITATES *There is no why.* The answer must be this,
That only mortals ask, for life itself
590 Is incompleteness, and the why is what
Is not, or is not yet. That is control,
The knowledge of what lies beyond control.
Yet, as he pondered, distantly he felt
A wind of ill that left the air unswayed,
An icy turbulence. He shuts his eyes,
The better to pinpoint the source; yet soon
His master interrupts, for Yoda too
Has joined him and discerns the reverie:
"You feel the cave. It summons you to look.
600 Be wary: in that place the dark side waits,
A nest of evil. Yet naught lies within
But what the visitor himself has brought.
You will not need your weapons, Skywalker."
Thus Yoda; but Luke brought his father's sword,
The blaster too, and warily approached
The misty gate beneath a mammoth trunk.

Its slimy threshold sinks beneath his step

THE CAVE   And lizards scurry for the blackness: Luke

Descends unseeing. Soon a distant glow

610   Intensifies, as though discerned afar,

A fleeting vision of a vanished age:

There, 'neath a darkened heaven, glowing bright,

A sprawling city, infinite, enclosed

A temple topped with five ascendant towers,

Four guarding one; but to the lofty gate

A perfect army marched, its armor white,

Rank upon rank, battalions locked in step,

Grim weapons in their hands: and at their head

A single figure, cloaked in black, strode on

620   Across the threshold, past tall pillars crowned

By carven figures, Sages, Knights of old,

LUKE'S VISION   And in his hand there blazed a sapphire blade,

His tool of evil, murder, slaughter loosed

On any, all who dared maintain the right;

But even as those troopers opened fire,

The figure turned and, horrible to say,

Perceived Luke's gaze: that figure Luke knew well,

For it was Vader, like a storm of night,

Armored and gloved and helmeted and masked:

630   The distant vision fades but, breathing cold,

Vader advances, saber turned to red,

Lighting the cave; Luke's own, a feeble blue,

Is lit: then Vader's double-handed blow

Is met and parried, met and met again,

'Til Luke, as though time trickled, saw his chance

VADER IN   And slashed the spectre's neck: the helmet rolls
THE CAVE   To earth, sparks scattering from a headless trunk.

The mask stares up at Luke, its glossy eyes

Still evil, then it vanishes in smoke,

640   Showing the human face beneath: the boy

In horror sees that visage is his own,

Blue eyes unblinking, stuck in sudden death.

The awful omen holds him, boding ill,

Until at length all fades, and from the cave

He climbs distressed, to hear his master's word.

Yet nothing further Yoda will provide,
Nor even hear the vision's elements.
He bids Luke meditate again upon
There is no why; and thus the dusk descends.

650   Yet worse and worse the pupil's visions grow
Amidst his training: suffering of his friends,

DREAMS OF Of Leia, Han, and Chewie now appears
HIS FRIENDS Within a city hanging in the clouds
Of subtle tincture, coral, cherry, rose,
Violet banks and piles of gilded fog;
Upon a pad the battered *Falcon* sits;
But there, inside the floating city, pain
Torments them: Chewie howling in a cage
Of piercing sirens; Han enduring heat
660 And, past endurance, electricity,
His shrieks unceasing; Leia sinking down
Beside his beaten body as she weeps.
No sooner does he sleep than visions come,
Yet waking only yields to sleep again.
He counts the beats to Dagobah's pale dawn,
Then seeks the misty woods; already there
Sits Yoda, mirthless, sorrow in his face;
He fidgets with his stick and mumbles this:
  "Such is the burden of the Force, to know
670 Where others only guess; to guess, where else
No inkling of the future or the past
Troubles the simple spirit. Luke, 'til now

YODA'S The past has opened to your insight; these,
CAUTION These dreadful visions of your friends' despair,
These are the future; Bespin is the place.
You wonder if your valiant friends must die?
The past is fixed, but what the future shows
Is ever shifting. Here temptation waits:
For if you end your Jedi training now,
680 Choosing the quick and easy path, before
An ally stands behind you and within,
How shall you conquer Vader? Luke, on you
And on your choice the galaxy depends.

Depart and you will save your friends, perhaps,
But all their love and labor shall be marred."
    Thus Master Yoda; Skywalker replied:
    "I cannot calculate or sacrifice
My friends for some advantage – never! Twice
Han Solo risked his life for mine, a debt
690   More sacred than the galaxy itself.
Vader awaits me – so my vision showed –
Vader, who killed old Ben: though incomplete
I'll face him: so my spirit shall be whole;
And maybe Han and Leia shall not die."
    So spoke young Skywalker, and called R2,
Donning his flight suit, packing up the camp.
Then to the X-wing's cockpit he ascends,
R2 in back; hastily waves farewell;
Promises to return. The engines growl,
700   The fighter lifts, and Dagobah below
Rolls like a misty dream, its glittering fog
Alive at dawn. To hyperspace he leaps.
    Long Yoda lingered, watching him depart,
Catching the last glint flickering in the sky;
Beside him, heard and witnessed with his mind,
A form of man, but insubstantial, pale,
Was standing, whom the Jedi Master named:
    "I was not wrong, Kenobi: now the son
Exceeds the father in his recklessness.
710   That boy, you say, is our last hope? But no,
There is another, though on Luke alone,
So unprepared, unready, soon must fall
The burden of the truth. Matters are worse
Than if he'd never come to Dagobah."

LUKE WILL DEPART

YODA AND OBI-WAN

BOOK VI

THE PURSUIT OF THE *Falcon*

I n evil there is much that we admire:
Precision, purpose, vehemence, and zeal –
Yet virtues bent to darken the delight
Of lofty reason soon are base, corrupt:
I will not make a rhapsody of hate,
Though you, dark angel, tempt me: those who mourn

The hollowness of power, the grief of greed,
On them descends the wreath of poesy;
No, tell how the *Millennium Falcon* fled
In fear of Vader and th' *Executor*,
Even as Luke arrived at Dagobah;
What steered Death Squadron into that thick stretch

10

Of asteroids filling the immense frontier
Between bleak Hoth and dim Anoat's star?
A single freighter, battered and forlorn.
　　　　With hesitating step, with fluttering heart,
Piett brought word to Vader in his cell.
In baleful meditation sat the Sith,
Communing with the Force, his helmet off,

VADER'S ARMOR 20 White scalp exposed, which searing lava scarred
With livid marks and deep. Around him flit
The delicate devices of the droids
Tasked to maintain his armor's circuitry,
The respirator and the durasteel
That knit the limbs, the muscles, and the joints,
Replacing organs of the lungs and blood,
Shielding the brittle flesh of that dark soul
More god than mortal, more machine than man.
Now he was pondering this enigma: why,

30 If Skywalker had fled the icy base
Upon that ship, why now among the rocks
Did Vader sense not him but that fell girl,
The Princess, Leia, Bail Organa's child?
Not for her sake the Emperor had dispatched
Th' *Executor*, yet vividly the Force
Moved near her. So Lord Vader meditates,
And so poor Piett found him, helm restored,
Who now makes his report before the mask:
　　　　"My lord, the latest update on the chase:

PIETT'S REPORT 40 The YT-1300, which escaped
With rebel spies, was tracked direct from Hoth,
A nimble vessel, though defective: twice
She prepped for lightspeed, we for swift pursuit,
Yet then she seemed to shiver, hanging there
Helpless in space; we aimed the tractor beam;
But then she swung aside, a kind of twirl,
And led us such a chase as ne'er I saw:
Avenger and the fighters drove her back
Against the *Tyrant* and the *Stalker* too,

50 Harried by TIEs. Among the three vast ships
The cunning freighter threaded, luring us

To near-collision and -disaster; yet
Four fearless TIEs stuck with her every step
Along her fickle course. Now here, my lord,
We reach a problem, since between the stars

AN ASTEROID
FIELD

Of Hoth and bare Anoat floats a field
Of asteroids, dense, impassable, the grave
Of any pilot who defies their odds,
Where boulders bound, where twirling mountains smash,

60   A thresher, churning, stretched across the sky.
Into that zone the dancing freighter flew,
Our anxious TIEs behind; I tasked my best
To guide them through the rubble, but in vain,
Since of those four the first was pulverised
By random rock, the second by a stone
That choked its ion engine; for the rest,
Their last report described a mad pursuit
Down canyons, over mesas; nothing more.
Aware, my lord, how much the freighter meant,

70   I blocked the foe's escape with half the fleet,
Bidding the rest plunge straight into the rocks,
Probing the boulders, blasting out a path;
TIE bombers too are scattering seismic shells
Along the biggest, to dislodge the foe
From any crack, while fighters cruise the field.
All this is done, yet nothing, not a hint
Has surfaced. Aye, they must have been destroyed,
Pummeled to bits, the same as ours. My lord,
Each passing minute brings fresh injury

80   To ships, to squadrons; should we not withdraw?"
       Thus Piett, but to that suggestion came
The harsh voice of Lord Vader in reply:
       "No, Admiral, they're alive. What do I care
For asteroids? Sweep the field until they're found;
Use every Star Destroyer, every TIE.
I want that freighter, not excuses. Go,

VADER'S
REBUKE

But steer th' *Executor* to open space:
My next transmission, Piett, must be clear."
       So Vader spoke, whom Piett fast obeyed,

90   Though Vader, in frustration, now prepared

To summon reinforcements to his search,
The bounty hunters, killers, villains, scum,
That galaxy's most ruthless renegades.

      Meanwhile the undetected *Falcon* rests
In one enormous asteroid, quiet-like,
For thither, down a cavern's winding course
Five times the freighter's breadth, for half a click
They'd flown into the blackness, 'til at last
Han Solo set her down. Then with a grin

100   To Leia, Chewie, and C-3PO

SOLO'S
OPTIMISM
He did his best to bolster their morale:
    "Come on, we've been in tougher scrapes before!
Where was it I first met you, Chewie? Right!
Chained in a pit, unfed, knee-deep in mud,
The sport of troopers; ah, but we pulled through,
Winning this ship, if nothing else – a beaut.
And you, Your Worshipfulness, recollect
The Death Star (than which I would like to see
A fortress more impregnable) had booked

110   Your execution; yet Han Solo came

And soon you saw it shatter in the sky.
You, Goldenrod, you'd still (except for me)
Be pitching package tours of Tatooine.
No more forebodings! Someday we'll look back
And chuckle that we thought our luck was out.
Meanwhile we take our time, power down the ship,
We eat, we fix the hyperdrive, we let
The Empire chase some asteroids. All is well!"
    So spoke Han Solo, lifting up their hearts

120   Somewhat. C-3PO is sent to learn

The ship's afflictions, couched in dialect;
Chewbacca shows the way, and Leia's left

HAN AT THE
CONTROLS
To watch the captain handle his controls.
Those consoles and the panels overhead
Were bright with timeworn knobs, which Solo touched
As lightly as an organist his keys;
Concern, relief, affection for his ship
Play out upon his lips, his chin; she thinks
Of Bail Organa, how he'd chew the text

130 Of some fair exhortation to the right,
Ere the Republic proved an empty name.
Han had no family; neither, now, did she.
The consoles dim, the engine hum subsides
As Solo sets the power to minimum;
Yet suddenly the battered *Falcon* bucks,
Tilting and groaning on her landing gear.
As when the water sloshes in a bath
In which the bather slips, catching himself
Against the lip, and bubbles flood the floor,

140 Just so the cabin lurched, and Leia tripped

A LURCH Into the arms of Solo where he stood.
They peer outside, alarmed, and listen close:
There's silence. Rapt by th' enigmatic dark,
Neither can speak, but suddenly both sense
Their hands, their limbs are touching; both recede,
Han with a grin and Leia with a frown,
Though strangely mixed with more than dignity.
Han hurries out to find C-3PO,
Whose shrewd suggestions he must hear, critique,

150 Dress as his own, and send Chewbacca's way;
Leia decides to overhaul the shields,
Welding the static dissipator, which

HAN ASSISTS
LEIA She struggles then to wrench back into place.
Han, from the hold, pities her, comes to help,
Stretching an arm around her, which at once
The rebel leader, with a glare, repels,
Returning to her work and groaning thus:
  "If I must be Your Worshipfulness, show
Some reverence, if a scoundrel's heard that word.

160 Now and again you seem, from time to time,
More than an irritation – nice, perhaps;

LEIA LIKES
NICE MEN I like nice men, not scoundrels. Come, do not
Caress my fingers; see, my hands are foul."
  Just so she spoke, for thus had Solo touched
Her palm where it was reddened by the steel;
To which the smuggler wryly made reply:
  "My hands are also foul, and do not shake,
But yours are trembling. What, am I not nice?
Better to be a scoundrel, Leia, since

170 I think your life lacks scoundrels. As to 'nice,'
  Is it so nice to push my help away?'
   At that their eyes, which ever closer drew,
  Were closed, and, quivering, lip with lip had met.
A KISS As when paired stars, which gravity has knit
  Into an ever tighter orbit, meld
  And fuse their elements in one vast fire,
  Such was the kiss of Leia with that man
  Whom she would lose, and whom she would restore.
  And yet C-3PO, whom human ways
180 Confused, burst in just then to advertise
  Some progress on the power flux coupling; Han
  And Leia part, each wondering at events,
  He to the hyperdrive, where Chewie sweats,
  She to the cockpit, where, in Chewie's seat,
  Her mind first spins, then slows; unbidden, dim
  Come faintest memories of a woman's face,
  Smiling, but sad, as though she must depart,
LEIA Her dark eyes rich with beauty. Was it she,
REMEMBERS The one who bore her, ere the regnant queen
190 Had fostered her on peaceful Alderaan?
  It seemed a vision of a vanished age.

   So Leia roamed in recollection, yet
  Outside the cockpit flapped a leathery wing;
  She starts from Chewie's seat to stare again
  Into the blackness: nothing – something – then
  A horrid squealing mouth, six inches wide,
  Round as a medal, planted on the glass
  And sucking uselessly, appears: she screams,
  Runs to the others: yes, they've heard the clangs
200 Of creatures in the cave outside: Han steps
CREATURES To grab his blaster, Chewie in pursuit,
IN THE CAVE And Leia next: they don the breathing masks,
  Advancing down the gangplank to the dark,
  While Threepio hangs back to guard the ship.
   Thick was the vapor, thicker still the stench
  In that weird hall; beneath their feet the floor
  Is slippery, springy, though invisible.

Beyond the *Falcon*'s floodlights, perfect night
Extends forever. 'Round the ship they prowl,
210   Chewbacca's bowcaster, Han's pistol poised
To face whatever evil lurks: Han wheels,
Blasting a drake-like shape of silicon
MYNOCKS   Which flops from fuselage to earth. He groans,
Announcing mynocks, pests that oft infest
The asteroids of the deep, eager to feed
On spaceships' cables: he and Chewie check
The hull, lest all their labor be for naught.
And so the deadly danger, unperceived,
Is now unfolding, as more mynocks flap
220   Before their eyes: Chewbacca takes his aim
Missing; into the blackness burns the shot,
At which that cavern heaves again, the crew
Staggering. Then Solo, with a frown of dread,
Lowers his pistol at the floor and fires.
As when upon Tremaal, where liquid rock,
Pent deep beneath the surface, swells and builds
And quakes the crust, foreshadowing a burst,
Just so the cavern shuddered at that shot,
The *Falcon* lurching, teetering to and fro.
230   On reeling feet they scramble to the ship,
A HASTY   Bouncing around its passageways; Han cries
DEPARTURE   To Chewie to take off, though Leia notes
Th' Imperial fleet's still out there; Solo drops
Into the pilot's seat and opens up
The throttle, speeding like a searing bolt
Along the tunnel. Far ahead they spot
The entrance of the cave collapsing fast,
Edged with stalactites; Leia, staring, grasps
What Han had first deduced: that was no cave.
240   Barely the *Falcon* fled the massive mouth,
THE   The behemoth's, the mighty exogorth's,
EXOGORTH   The space slug's, hugest of all forms of life,
Long burrowed in the asteroid, as a fruit
Will house a worm; and so their twirling ship
Had sat inside its mammoth gullet; up
It heaves its jaws toward the engine glow

In vain: the brave *Millennium Falcon* soars
Just past the tips of its titanic teeth.

Meanwhile aboard th' *Executor*, beyond
250   The churning rocks, Darth Vader stalked the bridge;
BOUNTY   Yet there no trembling officers attend
HUNTERS   But rather bounty hunters, whom his scheme
Had gathered, loyal to no cause but cash,
With dreadful tools and weapons. They were six,
Best of the worst and grimmest of the grim.
The foul Trandoshan first, heir of Cradossk,
Sadistic Bossk, the Wookiee-killer, he
BOSSK   Whose cold reptilian craftiness had stalked
Unnumbered fugitives, whom in his ship,
260   The dread *Hound's Tooth*, he stowed like specimens;
Now at the heart of the Imperial fleet
Bossk swaggered, growling down its officers.
4-LOM AND   Behind him 4-LOM waited, bug-eyed droid,
ZUCKUSS   Whose metal mind rejected subtlety,
Turning to banditry and blackmail, theft,
And murder for its protocol; his peer,
Zuckuss, the mystic findsman, to his left
Fondled a rifle, sucking through the tubes
That served the cold ammonia to his lungs,
270   Insectoid Gand: with 4-LOM he'd appeared,
For rumor held that Solo was the mark,
That blackguard whose deceit had once marooned
The hapless pair as prey of scorpion droids.
DENGAR   There too was Dengar, whom in livid tales
The crooners back at Chalmun's celebrate
For Clone War feats, unrivaled in conceit
Or bold ambition, henchman of the Hutts,
Curling his lip in scorn of life itself;
And he had claimed the Wookiee, whose vast clout
280   Had dropped him, with a detonator, down
Into the filthy streets of Nar Shaddaa.
Beside him stood the one I dread to name,
IG-88   The steel assassin, IG-88,
Which took its maker's life and roamed the stars,
Horrific robot, tall and slender, sleek,

With limbs of battered chrome, its head aglow
In scarlet sensors, mercilessly quick,
A heavy needle dart gun in its grip.
Such were the five, deferring to the sixth,
290 The shrewdest and the deadliest of all,
BOBA FETT That fateful mercenary, Boba Fett.
How do I dare do justice to your deeds,
Iconic warrior? At that catalogue
I shiver: from Kamino's sea you sprang,
The cousin of the clones, your father's twin
And his avenger, were the prayers of sons
Worth half their rage. What piety to vow
Reprisal on the Jedi! With a crew
Of killers you traversed the age of war,
300 Outliving mighty Windu and your oath,
Then took to hunting in that storied ship,
The sleek *Slave I*; all trembled who beheld
Your Mandalorian armor, beskar-faced,
Jetpack, twin pistols, rockets on the wrists,
And flamethrower, in service of a mind
Most cunning and a will of adamant.
Fett's grim research and industry had named
The boy by whom the Death Star was destroyed,
Reporting it to Vader. Here again
310 He faced the dreadful Sith, and heard this speech:
    "So, bounty hunters, learn your task, in which
A rich reward awaits the victor. Know
VADER'S The swift *Millennium Falcon* is the mark,
TASK Missed by my fleet amid this field of rocks;
Upon her, rebel operatives have fled:
A Wookiee and a smuggler and a girl
And some young boy, a lad of little worth —
Aye, Solo's vessel. Use what means you wish,
But bring them back alive: the one who dares
320 Disintegrate them shall endure my wrath."
        So spoke Lord Vader, and that greedy band,
Who owned no law and no allegiance, quaked,
Departing to their ships, intent on gold:
Bossk seeks the *Hound's Tooth*, Fett his Firespray,
The Gand the old *Mist Hunter* with his peer,

While Dengar boards the JumpMaster, the droid
His own *IG-2000*, hideous craft.

Yet, as they went aboard, word came at last:
Th' *Avenger* had them: right amid the fleet

330 The slippery ship had reappeared and shot

CAPTAIN
NEEDA Across the tip of Captain Needa's prow,
Who straightaway gave chase, and from the bridge
Addressed th' *Avenger*'s officers and crew:
"Now, Helm, look sharp! This is the fatal hour:
To us the glory of this victory falls.
Scanners, be wary; gunners, take your aim,
Crippling her shields. Prepare the tractor beam,
Prepare a signal to th' *Executor*
Announcing our success. Promotion waits,

340 Awarded by Lord Vader's open hand."
Just so you spoke, poor Needa, but alas!
No ordinary pilot was your prey:
For even as the speedy freighter's shields
Had bent and buckled – one more hit would leave
The *Falcon* hanging helpless – even then

THE *FALCON*
VANISHES That frisky ship performed a Segnor's Loop,
Skidding to face them, wheeling to attack,
Pointing at the *Avenger*'s bridge itself.
In consternation Captain Needa cries

350 For shields, the turbolaser batteries turn
Too gently: now like lightning 'cross their view
The freighter flashes – and then disappears.
Astonished signal officers report
Its absence from the scope: no trace remains,
Though frantically they double-, triple-check.
Then all the glory left the captain's face:
He stammers his amazement; soon the news
He bears to Vader in a shuttlecraft
Produces not promotion but his death:

360 Apologies mean little to the Sith

DEATH OF
NEEDA But proof of failure: so at Needa's throat
The flesh constricts as Vader's iron grip
Throttles him at a distance; on the floor
He learns at last the nature of his lord.

At once Darth Vader bade them calculate
All possible trajectories of the foe,
Though well the trembling Admiral Piett guessed
The *Falcon* might be anywhere at all.
The admiral puts all sectors on alert,
370 Then sends Death Squadron off to scour the stars.
     Little poor Piett and his captains knew
The frail *Millennium Falcon* was not far:
Its hyperdrive, as from the rock they'd raced,
Had fallen flat again, to Han's despair

**HAN'S
GAMBIT**
And Chewie's rage, since helpless 'neath the guns
They dangled; Leia'd watched in disbelief
As Solo spun the ship about, all power
To front deflectors, charging at the foe,
Though Threepio forewarned him of the odds;
380 But even as they'd overshot the bridge
Like lightning, even then Han Solo's hand
Had flicked th' inertial dampeners, stopping cold,
Attaching to the superstructure's heel.
     As when the coral trees of Atollon,
That world unpeopled and uncharted, shook
To show the Bendu, camouflaged in dust,
Just so th' *Avenger*'s dappled surface yields
The hidden freighter as the trash is dumped:
For ere the warship streaks to hyperspace
390 Chewbacca cranks the manual release
And off they softly tumble, whom no scan
Has yet suspected, 'mid the twirling junk –
As Leia notes, the other twirling junk;
Yet she bestows one kiss for Han's success,
Success indeed which neither can believe.
Th' *Avenger* leaps away, the fleet is gone;
Amidst the starlight and tranquility
The *Falcon* flares its engine, backup drive
Retrieved from storage, rusty, clunky, yet
400 Enough to nudge them past Anoat's star.
     There might the history of Darth Vader's chase
Have ended, thence the *Falcon*, soon restored,
Have reached the rebel rendezvous; but you,
Relentless Boba Fett, while others toiled

On distant leads, reflected thus afresh:

The target had not jumped before it wheeled
Against the Star Destroyer; why, therefore,
First face the cannons, afterward escape?
Only one answer fit, however odd:
410 The target had not jumped at all, and so
Must still be at th' *Avenger*: straightaway
He tucks the Firespray behind the keel
And waits. The mighty vessel's systems growl,
The course is set, the garbage is disgorged,
And off it flashes. Still Fett waits. The fleet
Disperses, yet he waits. He waits. At last
Amid the twirling junk an engine flares:
The target, Captain Solo, swerving off
At no great clip. Unseen, Fett lurks in back,
420 Perceiving that Anoat's nearby star
Is not the destination, but beyond
Lies Bespin and the city in the sky.
Thither the *Falcon* limped and thither Fett
Stealthily tracked her, 'til, all doubt dismissed,
His signal to Lord Vader claimed the prize.

On Bespin thus all courses now converged,
On Bespin, where the morn's magnificence

BESPIN

Was stacking layers of light, as through the gas
Shades shift and mingle: lilac, apricot,
430 Magenta, turquoise, flax, and amethyst,
The palette of the silent winds, rich hues,
Yet not so precious as those chemicals
Which in that airy planet coalesced,
Durilliam, rethen, clouzon-36,
And most of all tibanna, gaseous gold,
Rarest of all components of the drives
That knit the galaxy: for its dear sake
That city hung in orbit, like a tear
Inverted, flattened, tapering to a point,
440 A place of glossy opulence, of work,

CLOUD CITY

A small, smooth operation, little known,
Unregulated by the guilds, untaxed,
Neglected by the Empire. Happy he

Who lives carefree in such felicity,
Serene at sunset, vigorous at dawn,
Residing in a city in the clouds.
      One man there was who ruled that lofty town
With tact, protecting peace, lest miners irk
The idlers, idlers interrupt the rounds
450 Of serious sabacc, the gamblers' game
In which the giant bets would come and go:
LANDO
CALRISSIAN By that sad route his predecessor's ring
Had passed to him, staked in a frenzy: thus
A single card had reassigned a world.
No more the cocktail and the idle jest
Would make his fate, he'd sworn it; dignity
Seduced him: all the genius of a rogue
Was focused on the task of government.
There in his office, 'midst the daily grind
460 Of labor problems and supplies, he stood,
Lando Calrissian, whom the poets love,
A prince of rogues, mustachio'd and suave,
And at his side was Lobot, trusty tool.
Aye, there he stood and trembled as he faced
A formidable figure, robed in black,
Armored and gloved and helmeted and masked,
FETT AND
VADER Darth Vader, newly come to Bespin: this
That deadly shape of evil now declared:
      "Dispense with pleasantry, Calrissian. Here
470 My task is simple. We shall make a deal.
To Bespin comes a freighter, unaware
That we precede it; I shall seize the crew,
A Wookiee and a smuggler and a girl,
And Skywalker, a boy; and, once they're mine,
In recompense Cloud City shall be spared
VADER'S
DEAL And even get a treaty; do not doubt
My power exceeds my ships: in me behold
An agent of th' indwelling power that binds
All living things and balances your fate."
480   So spoke Lord Vader, and Calrissian's heart
Trembled, though smiles of admiration danced
Upon his lips: a leader must adapt.
Swift preparations place the stormtroopers

In ambush at the glossy dining hall,
To which the clever brain of Lobot clears
A route from Platform 327, whence

The task of guiding those unlucky guests
Falls to Calrissian. No more liquid tongue
Had charmed the Outer Rim, no suaver wink

490 Had won the trust of millionaires; how vague
The line between a statesman and a cheat!
Diplomatists are card sharps of the state,
They have their coins and sabers, flasks and staves,
The bluffer's grit, the caller's canny faith;
Yet premonitions lurk in Lando's eye,
The mask of Vader and the greed of Fett
Foreboding ill: uneasily he waits,
A host without a guest, 'til evening falls.

The windy sunset had begun to whip
500 Calrissian's cape of office, when came word
The freighter had appeared, her hull well marked
By rocky impacts and the scorch of war;
The Wing Guard's crimson cars escort her down.
Then Lando stands amazed, for what descends
But the old *Falcon*! Aye, the very ship

That he himself, in bygone days, once raced
Across the galaxy, 'til one grim night
Another's luck, a cunning card, prevailed
Upon Numidian Prime. He knew each plate,

510 Each landing jet: for steel endures, not flesh:
Our ships outlive us. Yet nostalgia fades
As down the gangplank lowers: down he steps,
The very swindler, aye, the pirate, Han,
His grin untouched by time, and, oh, what guts
To come to Bespin after what he'd pulled –
To Bespin and his doom: is Han the prize
Of Fett, of Vader? And – what have we here?
A girl, a woman, no, a princess stands
Behind him, with the Wookiee and a droid.

520 And thus the sly Calrissian, as he steps,
Ponders two courses in his teeming brain,

Whether to feign hostility and bile,
The better to forewarn them, or to clasp
His buddy's hand and reminisce, whose doom
Would not, in any case, be much delayed;
And anyway their lives were guaranteed.
Pondering all this, he picks the friendly path,
Making to strike him, bursting into smiles,
And, with a laugh, addressing Solo thus:

530   "Han Solo, you old swindler, welcome back
To civilization! Now a bath, a meal,
A tale, perhaps another bath, and then
Cloud City's at your service – for repairs
To this dear ship? Ah, Han, what have you done
To my poor *Falcon*, fastest hunk of junk

LANDO
REMINISCES

I ever knew? Recall that Kessel Run,
When through the churning Maelstrom, past the Maw,
As if intent on stubborn suicide,
You flew us – Beckett, old Chewbacca here,

540 And Qi'ra, hard as diamonds and as bright –
The cargo holds packed full and fit to blow
With ripe coaxium. Oh, those were the days;
And just last week, with youthful awe, some kid
Was talking of the feat, your Kessel Run
In sixteen parsecs; What (said I), just twelve!

THE KESSEL
RUN

And monsters – aye, a summa-verminoth,
With my own eyes – they lurked at every turn;
The days of high adventure. But an end
Must come to everything. See how my crews

550 Will fix her up, while I refresh your own."
    So Lando spoke, and kissed the gentle hand
Of Leia, whose distrust was like a wall;
Solo dislodged him with a laugh and spoke:
    "Indeed an end must come to everything
But your smooth speeches. Knew you'd not forget!
To suffer side by side, and then prevail,
Is friendship such as time can never dull.
But high adventure, if by that you mean
A price upon my head, half-crazy friends,

560 Th' Imperial fleet in ceaseless hot pursuit,

I fear I bring it with me. Nonetheless,

We'll soon be off, if experts can restore
The *Falcon*'s hyperdrive; we've come from Hoth,
That icicle, bound now for Tatooine
To pay back Jabba. Chewie you recall,
Leia you've met: beware, she likes a rogue.
But you and I must lift a heavy glass,
And see if leaders can still play sabacc."
    So spoke Han Solo, trusting Lando's smile,

570 For friends must trust each other; what is life
Without true friendship? Through the quiet streets
Th' Administrator leads them, guards dismissed,
Chatting with Leia, Han; Chewbacca stalks
Some distance back, and Threepio behind.
Tall were those hallways, straight and smooth, bright white,

As if the work of nature; portholes show
Soft purple twilight tracing lofty towers,
But inside, from cylindric chandeliers
And gentle fountains, luminosity

580 Diffuses through the geometric art,
Backlit with creamy or metallic shades,
Or white on white, abstract, a chain of moods.
They pass a pilot, legs unused to stone;
A lady in her litter, miners bent,
Three Ugnaught engineers, small solemn folk,
Doctors and dicers, merchants, managers;
And as they go Calrissian tells his tale:
    "How little my belovèd citizens
Perceive the politics that keep them safe!

590 Look how they prosper, though the Empire's shade
Threatens and darkens everything we've built.
Hard is the task of government; afar
All things seem simple, like a planet's port
From orbit, though disorder reigns below,
A maze of choices, sacrifices, loss,

With little praise, but blame in every eye.
Yet choice unmade is worse than a mistake.
Indeed the Empire looms, but just today
I've made a deal to keep this city safe."

600 So spoke Calrissian; Han applauds, amazed
At Lando's statesmanship; but Leia's mind
Senses a menace rising, indistinct,
Despite the bright, neat corridors, despite
Calrissian's smooth assurance; as they go
She suddenly perceives that they are three

LEIA'S Instead of four: C-3PO is gone,
UNEASE Lingering, perhaps, exclaiming at the art;
The Wing Guard has rejoined them; one bald man
(Lobot, although she'd not yet learned his name),
610 Equipped with cybernetic headgear, slips
In step with Lando. Whither are they bound?
She marvels at Han Solo's confidence.
The hallways seem too beautiful, too clean,
The art too easy, people too well dressed,
And where was Threepio? Not like that droid
To wander off! They reach their perfect rooms,
Where soon, refreshed but little reassured,
Again the Princess voices her mistrust;
But fatefully Han Solo interrupts,
620 For friends must trust each other; at the door
Stands smiling Lando with that Lobot; now
He leads the three — but where was Threepio? —
Along Cloud City's footways, 'til they reach
A dining hall. There Lobot stepped aside
And Lando dolefully unlatched the door.

A table set for seven stretched beneath
The inlaid ceiling arching far aloft,
A marble table, polished to a sheen;
Upon it bowls of crystal caught the light,
630 Replete with luscious fruit; chrome plates were set
THE DINING By silver cups. Upon the walls behind
HALL Hung masterpieces: here toward the left
The endless circlings of the Bespin moons,
Each finely picked; and there toward the right
Lord Figg, the founder, whom the Ugnaughts loved.
Tall were those chairs, and six were empty: but
There in the seventh, at the head, now sat
A formidable figure, robed in black,

VADER AWAITS

640   Armored and gloved and helmeted and masked,
Darth Vader. In the hallway at their back
His stormtroopers assemble, rifles cocked,
And, as he rises, to his elbow steps
Grim Boba Fett in Mandalorian helm.
      Then Solo, like a hero, made to fight,
The heavy pistol flashing to his fist:
Shooting at Vader two, three, four, five blasts

FIGHTING IS
USELESS

Along the table, right on target; yet
Lord Vader did but lift an iron hand,
Deflecting every laser to the side,

650   Then twitched his fingers: twirling through the air,
The blaster pistol flew to Vader's grip.
      Then Lando turned to Leia and to Han;
His eyes were empty and his face aghast;
All suavity had vanished; thus he spoke:
      "I had no choice: they'd come before you came.
I'm sorry it was I and it was you."
      To which Han Solo answered with a scowl:
      "I'm sorry you have lost your eloquence,
But doubt your sorrow's deeper than your friends'."

660   With that they stepped into the spacious hall
And Vader took his seat. There on his right
Was Boba Fett, Calrissian after him,
Then Lobot in his cybernetic gear;
On Vader's left was Leia, pale as death,
Then Han, then Chewie. Now the Sith lord spoke;

VADER
THE HOST

His voice was subtle and he would have smiled:
      "This invitation was too long delayed:
At last you join us, though you are but three;
But soon, I think, another may appear,

670   And then there shall be merriment indeed."

BOOK VII

CLOUD CITY

O ne virtue reigns supreme above the rest,
    One virtue, knitting body, mind, and soul,
    Which otherwise decouple and decay,
Trustworthiness, the will to write one's word
In deeds. What else is valor? Patroness

INVOCATION

Of my dark journey, trust me with the truth,
The truth however bitter: Luke's return
Into the teeth of Vader's trap, wherein
He learned at last the secret of his birth;

10

For you alone can summon his despair:
In me your cry shall echo, ere we part.
But first accompany my blind descent
Beneath th' Administrator's fortress, down

Through dim and rusty corridors, a maze
Of steel as brutal as the halls above
Were delicate: what dismal prisons there,
Chambers of torment, cells of solitude,
In which, at Vader's order, Han was caged,
And Princess Leia, brave Chewbacca too.

20   How far, poor Wookiee, far from lush Kashyyyk
You suffered from the sirens and the bulbs,

TORTURE OF
CHEWBACCA
Unending sirens, piercing to the brain,
Inaudible to human ears, like fire
That picks the tallest tree amid the storm
And leaves the rest unscathed: that searing light
Is gentler than th' excruciating glare
Those bulbs inflicted on your silvan eyes.
At last the torture ceases, unexplained;
They haul the trembling giant to a cell

30   Of quiet darkness. Soon – or was it days? –
The scrape and clack of metal, which the guards
Have kicked into the room, absorbs his care:
A single lamp illuminates the wreck
Of Threepio, cloven in pieces, limbs
Detached, head dangling from a torso scorched
By blaster fire, wires sticking from the stumps,
The staring eyes defunct. Chewbacca moans
But straightaway, unstinting with his skill,
Rebuilds the circuit board, and wire by wire

40   Rejigs the neck, the battery flooding back
To light the pupils and restore the voice
Which babbles of poor Threepio's ordeal:
    "Now, what is this strange door? Why, could that be
The voice of R2-D2? Best to check.

C-3PO
RESTORED
Hello, hello? Ah, what is this? Oh my!
Stormtroopers here? The captain must be told!
Forgive me, no, I don't wish to intrude,
Please, don't get up, I'll just – oh, I've been shot!"
    Such was the testimony of the droid,

50   Belated proof of their betrayal; yet
He vents his spleen on Chewie, since his head
Is screwed on backward! Flicking off the switch,
Chewbacca blocks the torrent of abuse,
Patiently turning to the severed limbs.

And so the Wookiee labored – not for long:

HAN AND LEIA
JOIN THEM

Soon the cell's twin doors yawn and soldiers shove
First Leia, then Han Solo to the floor,
Bolting the latch behind them. With a moan
Chewbacca bears his comrade to a bench,

60 For Han can hardly breathe: the Princess sinks
Beside his beaten body, strokes his cheek,
That cheek which heat and voltages have marked
Even as Luke on Dagobah foresaw.
Her voice revives him; coughing, he observes:
"Now here's a scrape, Your Worship, which no speech
Can get us out of. How my body aches,
And you two look no better, maybe worse.
Is this interrogation or some sport?
It's strange there were no questions, only pain,

70 Of which I fear I cannot take much more."
So Solo spoke; the Princess made reply:
"Alas, I'd guessed this city was our bane,
For peril lurks where everyone's a friend;
That bounty hunter must have tracked us here,
And here, I guess, we'll die; but savor now
These hours together, 'til we lose the taste
Of friendship and the world forever; tricks
Serve but to teach us true nobility."
So Leia answered; Solo clasped her hand:

80 How fair she was, unbroken even now,
The enemy of evil: wrath suffused
His honest heart to think her doom was near,
All thanks to Lando's treason. With a hiss
The cell door lifts: no stormtroopers intrude

LANDO
RETURNS

But rather Wing Guards, blaster pistols drawn,
And Lando too, limbs tense beneath his cape,
Which ripples as he paces back and forth;
Ere Han can curse him twice, Calrissian speaks:
"Enough! Shut up and listen. There's no choice

90 Except to do what must be done to live.
The deal was this: arrest you three for now
But free you later; Vader in exchange
Would spare us from destruction. Vader's word
Has marked you now as Boba Fett's reward,
Since Fett intends to sell you to the Hutt

For some vast sum. All this I heard amazed,
And challenged Vader, growling that our deal
Involved no bounty hunters; in reply,
His breath like gravel, Vader told me this:

.100 'Perhaps you feel, Calrissian, you've been wronged?
Unfortunate indeed would be the fate
Of such a city with my garrison.
No? That is well. The Wookiee and the girl
Must never leave this prison in the clouds;
The bounty hunter may escort his prize
To Jabba once young Skywalker is mine.'
And so I saw the deal was worsening fast –"

So Lando spoke; before he could go on,
Han's vigor, fed by anger, had returned

110 At mention of Luke's name; he found his feet
And slammed his fist into Calrissian's jaw.
Th' Administrator falls, the guards kick out
Han's legs, their vengeance looming; Lando's word
Alone spares Solo's life, who from the floor
Scowls up at the Administrator's face:

"Luke too? So that's the trap? And we're the bait!
Perfectly done, you've fixed us all real good,

HAN'S O faithful friend; to think we thought our deaths
ANGER Would satisfy that monster and his scum!

120 At least there's one to question Vader's plan:
This story has a hero, and it's you."

Thus Solo spat his scorn, through clenching teeth;
But Lando answered, not without remorse:

"A man must ponder his own problems first,
Then turn to those of others. It gets worse:
Lord Vader fears his quarry may escape,
Once caught, before he brings him to the goal.
Deep in the heart of our facilities
There lies an apparatus, where we lock

130 Unstable gasses, dangerous to shift,
CARBON- The carbon-freezer: whatsoever sinks
FREEZE Into its chamber rises petrified,
Encased in carbonite, perhaps alive
If living it descended; maybe not.
To it he'll lure this Skywalker; but, Han,

Wanting to test it first on living flesh,
They've picked you for the purpose. Here they come."

    So Lando spoke, as at the prison gate
A squad of stormtroopers appeared, who thence
140   Escort them to the hall of carbon-freeze,
Han stumbling, bound, with Leia at his side,
Chewbacca (whom the rifles never leave)
A step behind; Threepio, half-repaired,
Now dangles from the Wookiee's back. The pace
Is swift indeed: up from the cells they march,

FREEZING
CHAMBER   Up elevators built for giant loads,
Into a chamber dark as some deep trench
Lit from below by furnaces unseen.
As when rash mountaineers at last behold
150   The summit of a fiery cone and peep
Over the lip into a churning bowl
Of liquid rock below, their faces bright
Beneath, though foreheads vanish into gloom,
Just so the amber radiance of that hall
Lit all things from below, the tools, the steam.
A metal scaffold, circular and broad,
Enclosed the freezing pit; a platform bent
Some distance higher, whence the troopers watch
The worried Ugnaught engineers at work:
160   Some test the panels, some the countless ducts,
As others, at the center, raise and dip
A pair of giant tongs, with which to lift
The finished slabs of rigid carbonite.
Down from the platform to the scaffold walks
The chosen victim with his friends, aghast;
And soon Darth Vader joins them, flanked by Fett.
Then even as the Ugnaught engineers
Signaled that all was ready for their task,
Vader addressed Han Solo and them all:
170   "Indeed I grieve to see a guest depart
So soon; but do not worry: if you die
The Empire shall not fail to compensate
This worthy bounty hunter: thus your debts
Shall be repaid in full. Now put him in!"

At that the troopers grappled Han – in vain:

For Chewie, like a hero, made to fight,
Seizing the first, he hurled him to the floor,
Then seized the second like a chunk of meat;
But Vader checked the shot of Boba Fett,

180 And Solo's voice delivered this rebuke:
       "Chewbacca! Chewie! Stop it, what's the point?
What help for me is there in suicide?
Ten years we've roamed the heavens; you I trust
More than I trust myself. I've seldom begged

HAN ASKS
A FAVOR

A favor, but I need one now, old friend:
No longer can I be the Princess' guard,
So guard her for me: nothing more I ask."
       At once the Wookiee's anger ceased; he looks
To Princess Leia with a feeble moan;

190 And she, before more troopers seize on Han,
Leans up to kiss Han's mouth a final time,

PARTING OF
HAN AND LEIA

Too passionate to weep, too shocked to speak,
Except to stammer, as they drag him back,
"I love you." There above the freezing pit
They bind him on the pad; yet with his eyes
Intent on hers, he answers, "That I know."
What use are words compared to such a gaze?
As when a mother, after hours of pain,
Cradles the baby in her arms, each line

200 Of its damp features graven in her brain
Forever after, though it live or die,
Just so he watched her, just so she watched him.
       The metal pad descends; swiftly he sinks;
The Ugnaught captain flicks a single switch.
A raucous hiss of superheated gas,

FREEZING OF
HAN SOLO

Flash-frozen to a solid, fills the room;
Steam billows from the pit; the heavy tongs
Are lowered, clench, and slowly rise again,
Bearing the slab of carbonite, in which

210 Han's face is frozen, clenched in agony,
Palms pushed ahead (for so in vain he'd sought
To shield his face): now silent stands
A statue where a living man had sunk.
The slab is tilted, slamming to the floor:

Calrissian, stooping, checks the screen: Han lives
In perfect hibernation. Lando's eye
With effort rises to his helpless friend,
Noting the rigid hand that shook his own.
But even as he kneeled there, Vader spoke:
220   "This crude facility has proved of use.
So, bounty hunter, Captain Solo's yours.

THE DEAL
ALTERED
Calrissian, take the Wookiee to my ship
Along with Princess Leia. Yes, our deal
Has altered: pray I alter it no more.
Reset the chamber now for Skywalker,
It won't be long before the boy is here."
    So Vader spoke, and truly: even then
An officer brought word of Luke's approach:
A solitary X-wing in the sky.
230 So Vader waits in that horrendous hall;
But Leia and Chewbacca, under guard,
With Threepio protesting all the while,
Retrace their shuffling steps, which Lando steers,
As Fett escorts his trophy to his ship.

    Meanwhile the faithful son of Anakin,

LUKE
ARRIVES
Luke Skywalker, the Jedi's final hope,
Arrived at Bespin's vivid atmosphere.
As when a mother hawk, cruising aloft,
Whose chicks are chirping, not with appetite
240 But at the steady menace of a snake,
Will plummet straight toward the distant nest,
Just so Red Five shot past the tufted piles
Down to the city floating in the sky.
The sunset, long sustained, had daubed in mauve
The landing pad on which the X-wing rests.
No Wing Guard greets him, no one seems alive
Within th' Administrator's palace, which,
His saber sheathed, the blaster in his fist,
Luke enters with his loyal astromech.
250   The chirps of R2-D2 echo shrill
Within those bright, blank halls, though soon enough
An unseen footfall, 'round a distant bend,
Flattens him to the wall; and there Luke waits

With many courses weighing in his brain:
The Force, he knew, was with him: to what end

LUKE SEEKS
VADER

He would discover. Onward he proceeds,
Since now he recognizes, up ahead,
Despite the wafting warmth of paradise,
A wind of ill that left the air unswayed.

260   Again he pauses, silencing R2,
Peering around a corner to behold
Another silver street: two stormtroopers
Walk there behind two Wing Guards: these propel
A floating slab of stone, bizarrely carved:
A strange procession, headed by a man

FETT FIRES
AT LUKE

In Mandalorian armor red and green.
Luke lets them pass, then makes to follow. Shots
Explode beside him, forcing his retreat,
Four shots from Fett's fat carbine, aimed to miss

270   But meant to keep the boy on Vader's path.
With that the bounty hunter left. Close by
Those blasts were heard within the maze of streets,
For as the Princess and the Wookiee marched
At gunpoint, Leia's ears were pricked for Luke.
Their paths converge. The sharp lieutenant notes

LEIA'S
WARNING

A shadow on the wall – a man, a droid –
Ordering his troops to open fire; he grabs
The Princess as a shield, wherewith to reach
The safety of his master's shuttlecraft.

280   Yet Leia, struggling, hollers back to Luke:
    "Luke! Don't, it's Vader's trap, Luke! It's a trap!"
    So Leia called – in vain; they pass a gate
Which straightaway the officer secures.
Not far to go now. Yet Imperial power
Had failed to reckon with one factor, this:
Calrissian's pride: for while the troopers' guns
Were keeping Skywalker at bay, he'd lit
His wrist link, tapping Lobot's consciousness,
Sly Lobot's, whose sleek cybernetic gear

290   Revealed all odds: good Lobot never failed;
The time had come to vindicate the deal.

LOBOT'S
AMBUSH

So even as that company pulled away,
Chewie in chains, Threepio on his back,

Leia resisting, even as they neared
The hangar where Lord Vader's shuttle sat,
A squad of Wing Guards, blaster pistols drawn,
Sly Lobot at their head, with sudden step
Leap from their ambush at the Empire's troops.
As when, upon the grassland of Lothal,
300   A gang of thugs, despoilers of a tomb,
Piled high with plunder, settles by the fire,
But soon the stillness of encircling night
Discloses pairs of discontented eyes,
The giant Loth-wolves, hungry for redress,
So Lobot took that escort unawares
In bloodless ambush, plucking up their guns.
Lando commands the stormtroopers be jailed
With utmost secrecy; he takes three guns,
Handing them off to Leia. Once alone
310   He sets to work on Chewie's binders, pulls
The chafing cuffs apart, and tells his plan
For swift escape. Poor Lando, you yourself
Had failed to reckon with one factor, this:
A Wookiee's anger: like a steely vice
A WOOKIEE'S   Chewbacca's hands close tight around his neck,
ANGER   Choking and strangling; to his knees he falls;
And Princess Leia taunts him for them both:
    "Traitor, will you cheat justice even now?
Your eloquence is wasted on the wise.
320   Are we such fools, to strut a second time
LEIA'S WRATH   Into the torture chamber you've prepared?
Han lies a prisoner of the carbonite,
Luke seeks his doom, and you expect our trust?
At least there'll be one hypocrite the less!"
    Thus Leia in her fury. Lando's life
Would then have ended, had it not been you,
Magnanimous C-3PO, who hung
In jangling pieces on the Wookiee's back;
For you, with many a groan, addressed them thus:
330   "Oh, this is madness! Trust him! Trust the man
Who'll get us off this beastly cloud! Perhaps
C-3PO   He sold us once, perhaps he means it all;
INTERVENES   But if he sold us, why deceive us now?

Why free Chewbacca's hands, dismiss the guards,
Give us the guns? Is no one listening? No?"
So spoke C-3PO, and as they paused
They seemed to hear, from Lando's choking throat,
A whisper of Han's name. Then Chewie's grip
Relaxed a little; Lando strove to speak:
340   "There's time, still time, for us to rescue Han:
East Platform, Boba Fett is there, his ship –
But we must hurry, hurry to save Han!"
So Lando spoke, eyes pleading for the truth,
Which Leia, as her fury slackened, saw:
She bids Chewbacca cease, allots the guns,

RACE TO
SAVE HAN
And leads them, sprinting, off toward the East,
Calrissian wheezing from the Wookiee's grip.
Yet, as they ran, the strangest thing occurred:
Threepio, jostling and dislimbed, beheld
350   The good R2 (who'd lost the path of Luke)
Behind them; so th' interpreter rejoiced,
Informing his companion of their deeds,
Bemoaning his vicissitude. Now blasts
Of E-11s prove a fresh pursuit:
From passageway to passageway they fight,
As Lando covers Leia, Leia him,
And Chewie both; the spotless streets are scarred.
At last they reach the platform: through the gate
They hustle, Leia in the lead: red clouds
360   Delineate a spaceship's silhouette,
The Firespray's, prow pointed like the nose
Of some misshapen mask. Are they too late?

BOBA FETT
IS GONE
No sign of Han, no sign of Boba Fett.
Yet even as they watch, the spaceship lifts
Into the sunset, wheeling to depart
With Han stowed somewhere in the cargo hold.
The engines flare: he's gone. Then Leia's heart
Was filled with shame, with pity, with regret,
Her eyes not quite believing. From behind
370   The blaster bolts fly thick; she must retreat,
Back out the door, 'neath Chewie's covering fire,
Alongside Lando, who through twisting streets
Now leads the way toward the Falcon's bay.

As when mice scatter helpless in a maze,
Probing a route toward a distant scent,
Forlorn and baffled, 'til the leader's nose
Asserts a destination and they rush
Behind his squeak, on pattering feet, ahead,
Just so the party stuck to Lando's path.

380   Landing Pad 327 – yes, at last;
But at the gate Calrissian's code is blocked;
The city, he perceives, has been usurped.
So, while the prim C-3PO directs
Good R2's effort to bypass the lock,
Lando Calrissian plucks the comm, and speaks,
Addressing every listener in the state:
    "This is Calrissian: your attention, please!
The Empire's seized Cloud City. I advise
You leave before more forces can invade."

390   So Lando spoke, resigning from his post,
As leaders who love honor more than rank
Must do, when honor calls. Meanwhile R2
Was whirling, beeping angrily, the smoke
Fuming from deep within: C-3PO
Had steered him to a socket by mistake.

R2-D2'S   Again they flee down corridors of fear,
EXPLOITS Through bundled knots of muddled refugees,
The firefight still raging nonetheless.
Another gate: this time R2 selects

400 The right computer terminal, his beeps
Expressing some astonishment that – no,
Threepio cuts him off, bidding him lift
The door before they're slaughtered; R2 works
And cracks the code: was ever astromech
More canny? Through the rising gate they rush,
And none too soon: the stormtroopers behind
Pile on their salvoes, reinforced, inspired;
But R2 sheds a smokescreen, thick and white,
Impeding aim: Calrissian spins to shoot,

410 Covering the Wookiee as he gains the ship,
Then Leia; 'round about him lasers burst;

ESCAPE OF R2's aboard; Calrissian sprints behind;
THE *Falcon* The *Falcon* rises, stormtroopers' last shots

Still scattering sparks as Chewie's steady hand
Restores them to the safety of the sky.

But now the doom of Skywalker drew near,
Long planned and long delayed. Across the maze

**LUKE IS
DRAWN**

Luke picked his way toward that deadly power
He'd felt before, deep in the cave of dreams.

420   The echo of the city's exodus
Bustles behind him; silence waits ahead,
Down passageways, past iron gates that drop
As quickly as he crosses. Where's R2?
Direction has dissolved; he twice descends
Great elevators built for giant loads,
The mental menace swelling. Suddenly,
Hurtling aloft upon a pad, he stares
Around a chamber lit with amber light
Below his feet, which tread a metal grate.

430   Panels and ducts and weighty instruments
Surround a steaming pit; a platform bends
Some distance higher. There a shadow stands,
A sable silhouette against the gloom;
And from the shadow came that rasping breath

**VADER
SPEAKS**

None ever could forget. The shadow spoke:
"The Force is with you, son of Skywalker,
In which the darkness and the light unite.
But you are not a Jedi yet. 'Tis well,
For I am death to Jedi, though to you

440   I show the way to make your skill complete."
So spoke Darth Vader, hard and tall as stone.
As when the river moon of Al'doleem
Would hush to hear the echo of a gong
Struck in the distant monastery, mark
Of winter's mournful onset, deep and clear,
So Vader's awful silence filled the room.
In answer Skywalker ascends the stair,
Blaster discarded, saber in his grip,
Which quickly he extends; the sapphire flame

450   Flickers across his features as he speaks:
"If you are death to Jedi, I am life:
Before your master fell beneath your blade,

With mantic sentence framed by withered lips
He prophesied the Jedi must return.

LUKE'S DEFIANCE

In me you'll find a few surprises. Fight!"
    So spoke young Luke; it seemed his trembling hand
Was steadied by the weightless blade itself.
In answer Vader's lightsaber, blood-red,
Glowed forth. Then Luke attacks him, slashing first

460   To left – a feint – then looping to the right,
A blow with all his strength, with doubled fists;
But Vader parries with one hand, his wrist
Dealing a quick riposte, which Luke can block:
As in the swamp of Dagobah, he feels
Events unfolding like a woven fugue,

THE DUEL BEGINS

Chord answering chord; the voice of flame and steel
About him asks for answers, which he gives;
Yet they won't yield: another's hellish will
Has dominated and diminished them,

470   For here the music of the Force is bleak,
A hymn to Vader's darkness. Luke again
In desperation thrusts; the blade is turned;
He heaves it down from overhead, blue flame
Pressing the red, hilts nearly touching; back
The Sith lord flings him with a steely arm,
But from the floor Luke springs again, eyes locked
Upon the awful mask, blade straight: a lunge
Forces the shadow backward: with a shout
Luke rushes to renew his swift assault:

480   But every stroke is parried, every thrust
Is turned; and Vader chuckles at the boy:
    "In fighting me you fight your destiny,
As Obi-Wan himself knew well, who hid
An infant from the teachings of the Sith.
Enough of such defiance; shall I prove

VADER'S THREAT

The limit of your insolence? Behold!"
    Then with the ease of virtuosity
Darth Vader spun his wrist, gliding his blade
Beneath the blue, and flicked it from Luke's grip;

490   It clattered far afield. Then Luke, disarmed,
Rolled down the stair, but Vader followed fast,
The crimson saber forcing his retreat

Toward the pit of carbon-freeze. Luke trips
And tumbles with a holler of alarm.

**LUKE FALLS
AND LEAPS**

But ere the Sith can activate the switch
To flood that pit with carbonite, Luke leaps
Aloft into the tangle of the ducts
Above the pincers: as on Dagobah
The air itself propels him (so he felt) –

500 As quick and high a leap as Tarados
Or Tassu or blind Jarrus ever made,
So quick that Vader marks it not and gloats:
    "I find it all too easy. In the test
You prove much weaker than the Emperor thought.

**VADER'S
ADMIRATION**

But, wait, what's this? The boy has leapt away!
Impressive. Obi-Wan has taught you well.
Aye, most impressive – yet you lack a sword."
    With that Darth Vader rushed to the attack,
Slashing the ducts and adamantine pipes,

510 Which spew hot steam; Luke drops, but cannot fight,

**LUKE CALLS
HIS SWORD**

Helpless without his saber, which he calls:
    "O blade of light, o heart of crystal, come,
Defend me now again! No greater foe
Opposed you ever, not when you dispatched
Even the cruel Count Dooku: 'tis the Sith
Whom you yourself knew well on Mustafar!"
    No sooner had he spoken than the sword
Tumbled from some dark corner to his grip
To parry Vader's onslaught: now again

520 The sabers slash, riposte, reprise, and press,
Sparks scattering, blue and crimson, from the glides;
And Luke, sustained by incoherent hope,
Gave not an inch. Then Vader stood and spoke:
    "The Jedi way was passive fearlessness,
Though at my coming countless Jedi quailed;

**VADER
GOADS HIM**

Now you've controlled your fear. See, eager boy,
That's not enough for victory: free your wrath:
Against me only hatred can prevail."
    Just so Darth Vader spoke; nor was he wrong:

530 For hate was swelling in the boy, who thought
Of all the victims of Darth Vader's edge,
Uncounted or beloved: his father, Ben;

What mercy do the merciless deserve?
And victory seemed a thing within his reach.
Relentlessly he strikes: past Vader's blade
He somersaults, his lunges barely blocked,
LUKE'S Beating his foe toward the scaffold's lip
ATTACK And over: Vader, with a strangled cry,
Falling back into shadow, disappears.
540 Luke pauses, staring, shutting off his blade,
Detecting nothing of the sable foe.
Bravely he drops down after, fervor drained
From heart and limb as through the passageways
And steely corridors he stalks, to prove
His unexpected victory. Oh, alas,
What can restrain the recklessness of youth?
Doors open of themselves, and he goes in;
Lights switch on, and the daring boy proceeds.
But that was Vader's trap and second test:
550 He knew Luke's power, untamed and raw, might yet
Be turned to ill and evil agency,
For arrogance is easily ensnared.
No, Vader was not beaten: not far off
He feels young Skywalker's approach; he waits
There where Cloud City's workers would distill
VADER'S The planet's bounty of tibanna, stored
NEXT TRAP Within the vast reactor shaft, compressed
From that control room. Countless panels, gears,
Terminals, switches, intricately wired,
560 Suffused in blue fluorescence, stud the walls;
A giant window shows the blank abyss.
Into that hall the dauntless Luke now stepped,
The steely door behind him shutting tight.
A stillness reigns – his footfalls resonate –
A brittle stillness broken by a breath,
The rasp and suffocation of despair.
        Again, with saber lit, Luke stands on guard
Against Darth Vader. There the Sith lord looms
Motionless, 'til he lifts an iron hand,
570 Wresting with his indomitable will
A pipe from its attachment: through the air
The missile hurtles: Luke must spin aside

To slice it; but another soars: the Sith
Advances swiftly, even as Luke fights
The jetsam and debris, which in a whirl

LUKE
PELTED
Smite him amidst that desperate duel; he twists,
Parrying Vader's saber, swipes a crate,
Slashes a duct, turns double thrusts aside,
Knocked on the back by pieces of the lab,

580
Battered by hunks of steel: one passes past
To smash against the window, which explodes
Into the void beyond, sucking the air
And remnants of the room into the gulf.
Luke battles for his life against the wind,

LUKE
BLOWN OUT
But nothing can withstand it: like a leaf
Borne out to sea before the autumn blast
To sink amid the surging foam, so Luke
Was blown into that vast reactor shaft.
He tumbles, writhing, past a narrow path

590
That stuck into the emptiness, and grasps
Its edge with fingertips, willing a surge
Of strength to fling his legs to safety: there
His saber lies nearby, his father's blade,
Which, gasping hard, he clutches in his fist.
Along the narrow scaffolding Luke reels;
Below, the broad reactor shaft descends
Beyond the reach of sight, a yawning pit.
He staggers through a doorway: there inside
Vader awaits, whose ruthless swordsmanship,

600
The best in all the galaxy, is loosed

VADER'S
ONSLAUGHT
Upon the boy, remorseless, unrestrained,
His saber thrusts precise, his slashes swift,
Cutting the doorway and the rail beyond
To bits, his power the greater, Luke's the less:
Before the towering shadow and the mask
The boy is beaten backward step by step.
Too late he recollects wise Yoda's words
That counseled prudence, warning of the risk
Of facing Vader unprepared. He falls

610
Backward upon the path, his foe's red sword
Before his throat, the chasm black below.
And there Darth Vader warned him of his doom:

"Now you are beaten. I was beaten too,
On Mustafar, by Obi-Wan's bright blade,

VADER
URGES HIM

Before I wore the mask. But in the dark
I won my victory; Obi-Wan I've slain,
Who like a fool preferred to be destroyed.
Choose not the path of such futility.
There's no escape. From me accept your life."

620   In answer, Luke, through bruised and swollen eyes,
Looks for his chance, and plucks it: with a whirl
He springs to slash the shoulder of the foe,
Who, quick recovered, with a mighty sweep
Cleaves through the jutting sensory array
Between them, and then slides the crimson blade

LUKE'S HAND
IS LOST

'Neath Luke's, and spins his wrist: the fiery edge
Severs Luke's hand, which with his sword is sent
Into oblivion. With a cry Luke grasps
His empty limb, retreating to the tip,

630   The pinnacle above the precipice,
A crushed and lonely figure, whipped by wind.
Then once again there came Darth Vader's voice:
        "You do not realize your importance, Luke.
Your power is in its infancy. Join me,
Whom you may equal, whom you may surpass;
I will complete what Obi-Wan began.

VADER BIDS
LUKE JOIN

Together we may end the age of war,
Bring order to the restless galaxy.
You will not join? You do not guess the power

640   Of life lived far beyond the dread of death.
Let not the Jedi prejudice your soul
Against ambition, which aligns the wise
Beside the Force itself. Do I not know?
None knew the Jedi better: I was one,
Indeed I was the best. Did Obi-Wan
Not tell you of your father's destiny?"
        So Vader spoke; but Luke replied in pain:
        "I know that Anakin was best, not you;
And, what is better still, that he was good.

650   Aye, Ben and others told me you destroyed

ANAKIN
RECALLED

That prince of pilots, prince of duelists
By means of some foul trick, on Mustafar.

O father, if my dying voice can reach
To death, the hidden kingdom of the Force,
In which, perhaps, your steady soul persists,
See that I die in fighting for revenge!"
     So Luke replied, but Vader laughed, and spoke:
     "O son of Skywalker, you are deceived.
You father did not die on Mustafar.
660   Your wish is granted: he has heard your prayer.
I am your father, Anakin the Just,
LUKE'S FATHER   Enlightened by the dark, death's conqueror,
The Jedi's bane, and mighty in the Force,
Whose infant son Kenobi stole away.
You doubt me? Search your feelings for the truth!"
     Then Luke, like one who rises in the night
From half-forgotten visions, damp with sweat,
To find worse ruin – murder, suicide –
In his own home – Luke saw inside himself
670   A truth as horrible as stark, the truth
He could not face and yet could not deny.
His staring eyes shed tears of black despair,
LUKE'S DESPAIR   His mouth is twisted and his face is white,
The contradiction dies inside his throat.
But now Darth Vader gazed upon his son
And saw the eyes familiar to his dreams,
The eyes of that sweet, secret bride who bore
His offspring, whom the Jedi had betrayed –
Beholding Luke's shorn hand, and in his mind
680   He felt again how Dooku hewed his own.
To Sidious he'd sworn, should Luke not yield,
That he himself would see to his demise;
Yet now the saber trembled in his grip;
Toward the boy he clenched the other fist:
     "Your destiny, o son of Skywalker,
Was written in the Jedi's prophecy,
THE JEDI
PROPHECY   To which unto the bitter end they clung:
In riddles it foretold a Chosen One
Fated to bring a balance to the Force:
690   So now, my son, the Emperor has foreseen
You may destroy him, whom I must obey,
As I destroyed the Jedi. Join with me,

And after you and I shall rule the stars
As master and apprentice; father, son.
Luke, come with me, it is the only way."
    So Vader spoke, and all his will was bent
Upon persuasion, like a circling storm
That beats the sea high up the suffering shore.
But even as he spoke, Luke's final choice
₇₀₀ Was made: he had no weapon, no escape;
If this was fate, then fate must be defied;
LUKE'S CHOICE Between the path of death and path of wrath
He chose to die, though not at Vader's hand,
And, standing at the brink of the abyss,
With half a smile, he loosed his grip; he dropped.

    How brittle is the body of a man,
How weak, how light, how feeble, how infirm,
The puppet of a day, soon chucked aside,
Crude matter seeking dissolution; yet
₇₁₀ Inhabited by destiny, alive
Amidst a boundless universe of death
Until the very finish. So Luke fell,
Plummeting down into the blank abyss,
LUKE His speed increasing, 'til the yellow lights
PLUMMETS Streaked 'round him, and it seemed the shaft itself
Was hurtling up, he floating weightlessly,
Buffeted by a twirling hurricane.
No bottom rises up: that shaft was deep
In which the miners stored their precious gas.
₇₂₀ And yet Luke's death was still to be delayed:
A current in the air, an unseen stream,
Sucked him aside into a twisting pipe,
A valve that filtered refuse from the shaft.
LUKE IN As when a marble, spinning down a tower
THE PIPES Constructed to amuse a clever child,
Rattles and bounces 'round from spout to spout,
Circling and clattering, 'til it finds the end,
Just so Luke's body skidded through the pipes.
At last he stops; a sudden aperture
₇₃₀ Opens beneath him: down he tumbles: now
Below him drift the parti-colored clouds

Of amethyst and indigo, their tops
Still kindled by the sunset: aye, below
Is nothing, cloud and gas and whirlwind,
An infinite descent, a ceaseless drop

**LUKE ON
THE VANE**

Toward the planet. With his single hand
He snags a vane, clinging with just his knees;
But ere he stood to hoist his body back
The aperture was closing, clanging shut,

740

Leaving Luke dangling, utterly alone,
Lashed by the endless atmospheric gale,
His strength at last exhausted. Overhead
The underbelly of Cloud City stretched,
Impenetrable, like a sky of steel.
Yet still the son of Skywalker resists,
Calling in his despair upon old Ben;
But Ben can do no favors; Ben is dead,
And Master Yoda waits far, far away.
Yet even as Luke faced the final pit,

750

He felt a tiny tremor in his soul,
A single note of fearlessness amid

**LUKE CALLS
TO LEIA**

That symphony of ruin: Leia's face
Unbidden filled his memory and his mind,
Knitting his sinews; vividly the Force
Moved near her. Oh, and Leia heard the call,
Just as the old *Millennium Falcon* fled
Across the clouds in fear of swift pursuit;
His anguish rang and echoed in her mind;
So she addressed the brave Chewbacca thus:

760

  "Chewie, we must go back: I hear Luke's voice
And I can find him! Chewie, turn around,
He's there, he's calling, and it's not too late!"
    So Leia spoke; Chewbacca, growling down
Lando's objections, spun that ship about

**RESCUE OF
LUKE**

At once: a Wookiee's loyalty is real;
They speed back to the danger they had left.
And there, etched black against the last red line
Of Bespin's sunset, clinging underneath
The city's underbelly, there a man

770

Is barely to be seen: Leia directs
Their nimble course beneath him: Lando opes

The hatch, and down Luke drops, received and wrapped
In thermal blankets by Calrissian's hand.
    Then Chewie flees again: three TIEs give chase,
    Their cannons blasting as the hunt proceeds

THE
BLOCKADE

Up to the starlit reaches. There a ship
Lay moored, gargantuan *Executor*,
Lord Vader's flagship: thither he'd returned
Intent on victory. Well he felt young Luke,

780

His son, who, shivering, mutilated, lay
Within the *Falcon*, as she sought her course
For lightspeed from the planet: tractor beams
Were ready: Admiral Piett's engineers

HYPERDRIVE
SABOTAGED

Had slyly sabotaged her hyperdrive.
So even as Chewbacca punched it, now
The *Falcon* seemed to shiver, hanging there
Helpless in space; the Wookiee gives a howl
Of misery and frustration, clambers back
To start repairs. What else was there to do?

790

But 'cross the gulf of space came Vader's voice
Inside Luke's spirit: Jedi and the Sith
Could share their thought without the use of words
Afar; and to his son the father spoke:
    "You cannot hide or run from me, my son.
Fast comes the hour when we shall meet again.
Then you and I must join: so I foresee."
    To this young Skywalker could not reply;

DOOM
IS NIGH

He sensed his father's overwhelming might.
And to that might the *Falcon* seemed condemned:

800

Though Chewie hacked and begged and overhauled
The fizzled hyperdrive, the tractor beams
Would shortly seize the *Falcon*, troops arrest
Those fugitives at last; their doom was nigh;
And nothing Lando did, no switch, no gear,
Could bypass Piett's clever sabotage.
    But R2-D2, while his acumen
Was wasted on the fixing of his friend,

R2-D2'S
PROWESS

Had overheard the Wookiee's moans; he rolled
To where the freighter's hyperdrive was stowed:

810

One detail that computer had disclosed
Upon Cloud City: Piett's clever scheme;

And so that droid deployed his little arm,
Deep in the circuits of the creaking ship,
Twisting a single breaker: like a squirrel
That pauses, listens, measures, tenses, shoots
Into the forest air in one huge leap
From tree to tree, eluding every foe,
Just so, thanks to a trusty astromech,
The swift *Millennium Falcon*'s fevered flight
820   Broke through to hyperspace: the smudging stars
Yield to the velvet of that wrinkled zone
In which existence folds, whereby all worlds
Are reached across the infinite abyss.

    Aboard th' *Executor*, Lord Vader's mask
Beheld its disappearance. Filled with fear,
Its officers expect their master's wrath;
Yet Vader, skilled in prophecy, perceived
VADER SEES   In Luke's escapes some meaning unrevealed,
THEM GO   The action of th' indwelling power that binds
830   All living things and balances our fate:
Nor could the Sith themselves defy the Force.

    Dread spectre, cease: at last I must ascend
Back to the world above, to seek the balm
That heals the crippled and restores the blind;
'Tis not for you, fierce mistress of the dark,
To tell how, at that secret rendezvous
Of rebel ships by some uncharted star,
The proud *Millennium Falcon* was repaired,
Luke's mangled limb by patient care replaced
840   With artificial fingers; most of all
How Luke and Lando, Chewie and the droids,
PACT TO   Before the grieving Princess, steeped in woe,
RESCUE HAN With solemn pledges made their sacred pact
Against all desperate odds that no true friend
Would rest until Han Solo was reclaimed.

BOOK VIII

THE RESCUE OF HAN SOLO

Aye, only what must be can ever be,
A thousand proofs attest it; yet what droid
Could calculate the causes of a flower,
A lily on the water at the dawn

Of its first morning: temperature and seed,
The soil unseen, the weather, and the sun,
The hand outstretched, the ripple of the lake?
In beauty waits what little we can know,
And you are beauty, Muse: none other spoke

10 The Jedi's ancient prophecy: to you
With hand outstretched a poet must return
For certain knowledge. So Luke too returned

To where, among the tendrils and the fogs
Of slimy Dagobah, he'd learned to move
In step with life to music of the spheres,
To linger and to listen and to learn;
And there, not far from Yoda's homely hut,
Beside the X-wing, which R2 repairs,
He meditates in perfect solitude.

20 Then sleep, perhaps, or something deeper still,
Engulfed his vision, or unbound his gaze:

BEN'S For in the mist, approaching close, he saw
GHOST Before him, heard and witnessed with his mind,
A form of man, but insubstantial, pale,
Flickering, but still in sandy robes, concealed
Beneath a drooping hood; he cast it back,
And it was Ben, who, with a gentle voice
That echoed in the distant forest, spoke:
      "Come now, don't be surprised, young Luke, to meet
30 Old Ben, your friend, for everywhere I rest,
Forsaking love and hate, aligning thus
With only nature; Qui-Gon taught the way.
But what has brought you back to Dagobah?
Some deep emotion grips you; what is wrong?"
      So spoke Kenobi's ghost, taking a seat
Beside the youth, who answers with a sigh:
      "Alas, some doom attends me still, dear Ben:
I must persist past every loss alone.
Hither I had returned, a humbler man
40 Than when I'd disregarded Yoda's word,

LUKE'S Rushing to face my foe; I had returned
RETURN To learn completion of the incomplete,
The swirl of peace, the constancy of change,
To strengthen; yet I found the master's fist
Was feebler; like the slap of some slow tide
His age advanced; his precious words were few,
The final lessons falling from his eyes.
Just now, in yonder hut – oh, Ben, I weep
As I should not – just now the master lay,
50 With many a sigh, upon the tiny couch,
Fixing me with the perspicacious stare
That trained the generations. Soon he laughed

As best he could, and spoke these wingèd words:
'Ah, do I look so old to youthful eyes?

YODA'S INJUNCTION
Indeed I ought, for sickness, weakness, age
Unite to bid me rest, forever sleep,
And douse the flickering candle. 'Tis the way.
You know already, Luke, that which you need.
One deed alone remains now – only then,
60 When I am gone, a Jedi will you be,
The last of all the Jedi – only this:

DEATH OF YODA
Vader, whom you must face again, and shall.
Pass on then what you've learned; seek out your twin,
The other – oh – the other Skywalker.'
So Master Yoda spoke; the final words
Were gasped, as now that ancient body failed;
And even as I watched, and from my lids
The grateful tears had just begun to drop,
His body seemed to fade into the dark,
70 Like steam that rises, twists, and dissipates;
Only the little robe and stick remained.
Here long I've sat, a happy mourner, since
I knew he'd chosen nature as his grave,
Forsaking love and hate; and now I weigh
Those last few words: had Anakin two sons,

LUKE'S QUESTIONS
Had I a brother? Oh, reveal, I beg,
That secret, though no man is so discreet
As you, Kenobi, who, on Tatooine,
Alleged my father fell to Vader's blade."
80   So spoke the youth, and not without reproach;
Then ruefully the spectral form replied:
      "Forgive the lie, young Luke. What could I say?

BEN'S APOLOGY
That evil had consumed your father's heart
And twisted all his love to cruel despair?
Youth cannot bear such burdens. It's my fault,
But I have paid: when Anakin was turned
And took the name of Vader, that good man
Was murdered by himself, and nought remains
Of my fair comrade, best of friends, with whom
90 I battled in the Clone Wars, side by side.
Yet in two newborn babes the Jedi lived,
A brother and a sister, twins concealed

To save them from the horror on the throne;
Yourself I brought to Tatooine, to wait
And guard your childhood; as to the girl,
To no one may I ever tell her name."
　　So spoke the form of Obi-Wan, but Luke,
Grinning with sudden insight, answered thus:
　　"Alas, dear Ben, you may be gone, but still
100　You speak in riddles; though no match for me.
Listen, therefore, to how I guess her name:

LUKE'S The night is wondrous long; alone we wake
TALE While even Dagobah's grim monsters sleep,
And you, I think, were always fond of tales;
Here then is one of Tatooine, our home,
The latest tale, and, what is better, true.

　　"Han Solo – aye, the very one that flew
The *Falcon* from Mos Eisley with the droids –
Is my fast friend, and friendship's noble debts
110　Summoned me to the empty sands of home,
For there, as rumor had it, waited Han,
Claimed by a bounty hunter and displayed
As Jabba's palace trophy – aye, the Hutt,
That lord of gangsters, greedy and debauched –
Han Solo, still encased in carbonite.

PLANS To Tatooine, therefore, we slipped, we six
LAID Who'd sworn to save him, laying careful plans.
Then one by one the others took their leave,
Each to a role, while I remained behind,
120　Picking my way from Espa down hard miles
Of desert rock and salt, a lonely trek
Beneath the burden of a jet-black cloak.

JABBA'S At noon I saw my goal, the lonely towers
PALACE Of Jabba's palace, built not by the Hutt
But by those monks, the Order of B'omarr,
Whom Jabba's heathen malice had enslaved,
Four rounded towers of stone and blasted steel
Atop an outcrop. At the rusty gate
Ten meters tall and twenty meters wide,
130　As thick as any starship's fuselage,
I did not pause: it lifted of itself,

Thanks to the Force, my ally; as I went
Two startled sentries rushed to bar my path,
Gamorreans, hoggish thugs, in armor clad
And wielding vibro-axes. Wordlessly
I gestured at their throats, a simple trick;
They snort and choke and stagger to the side.
Onward I stepped, and down the curling stair
That sank into the gloom of Jabba's throne.

140 Yet ere my coming could disturb that scene,

BIB Old Bib Fortuna stopped me, Jabba's hand,
FORTUNA A red-eyed Twi'lek, dainty and debased,
Pink fleshy head-tails wrapped about his neck,
Who served his master well; Fortuna spoke:
  "'Skywalker, as I guess! Who else would dare
To pass the mighty Jabba's gate unasked?
Where are the guards? Here punishment is swift.'
  "But from beneath my cloak I made reply,
Gesturing with my finger to poor Bib:

150   "'Indeed I've come, and your delinquent guards
Have punishment enough. But for yourself,
Master Fortuna, look to your reward
And tell me how my name is not unknown.'
  "Just so I spoke, for thus my skillful hand

FORTUNA'S Was calling once again upon that power
TALE That may be wielded like a club or cloth
To steer the feebleminded back and forth;
And Bib Fortuna, like a child inspired
To introduce an uncle to his toys,

160 Naming the figures and the stacks of blocks,
Breathlessly furnishes the latest news:
  "'Dear Jedi, listen, I'll tell everything.
Two days ago, at dusk, there came a knock,
The gatekeeper reporting just two droids,

R2-D2 AND An astromech and an interpreter,
C-3PO Who brought, they said, a message for the Hutt –
And also, said the astromech, a gift.
Amazed – for this was recklessness indeed,
Or had they never heard about the Hutt? –

170 I led the way to Jabba's awful throne.
No friend to interruptions, still my lord

Allowed a hologram, which showed yourself,
Dear Jedi, and your flitting image spoke:
'Greetings, Exalted One, from Solo's friend,
Luke Skywalker. How potent is your name!

LUKE'S
MESSAGE

And potent too, I guess, your anger bent
On Captain Solo. Soon I shall appear
And bargain, if I may, for Solo's life.'
(I must admit, at this the whole court laughed.)

180 'For bargains' (you continued) 'wisely made
May spare much trouble and unpleasantness.
Accept a token of goodwill: these droids,
Hardworking, loyal; may they serve you well.'
Such was your hologram: that brassy droid
Was ludicrously startled at the gift.
But since that hour he stands at Jabba's side,
Translating at his mighty master's will;
The other, somewhat feisty, serves the drinks.
   "'Yet those were not the final visitors:

190 A bounty hunter walked in yesterday,
Heralding his arrival with a blast,
Grim Boushh, whom even Boba Fett respects,

BOUSHH
ARRIVES

Croaking beneath his mask, and in one hand
He tugged the chain about Chewbacca's neck –
Chewbacca, who with Solo had conspired
To swindle and defraud my patient lord,
The Wookiee, not so terrifying now,
Mewling in chains, the sport of all the court!
Then Boushh, like one despising death itself,

200 Bargained for twice the bounty, fifty grand,
Flaunting a thermal detonator primed

BOUSHH'S
PLOY

To blow the court to pieces: all despaired,
Save Fett, but Jabba chortled his esteem
For such invention, offering thirty-five.
   "'Then all rejoiced, for Boushh and Boba Fett
Had triumphed where so many failed before;
The feast was long renewed, and all drank deep,
Quaffing the potent spotchka by the cask –
Or all but Boushh. Then Jabba, 'midst the glee,

210 Softly instructed me to set his couch
Behind a curtain and to pass the word

Among his favorites. Soon the frolic fades
As drunken sleep encroaches; all is still;
In silence we await we know not what.
On tiptoe through the darkness and the snores
There slipped a stealthy shadow: that was Boushh;
On tiptoe he approached the throne-room wall
Where hung great Jabba's cherished work of art,
Han Solo, still encased in carbonite.

220 Some time Boushh gazed upon that frozen face,
Then stepped to the controls. At once the stone
Began to whirr, to trickle light, to glow,

BOUSHH FREES
SOLO
Yielding its prisoner, Solo, from the tomb,
Who tumbled, trembling, to the floor to clutch
His sightless eyes, which only time would heal.
He touched the mask and shuddered, whispering this:
    "'O stranger, do I live, and do I breathe?
I cannot see, but from your steely snout
I guess you are Ubese – aye, Boushh perhaps,

230 Or Boushh's kin, no fools, who know a deal.
In this rock prison I was trapped, deprived

SOLO'S SPEECH
Of love and friendship, just as I'd set forth
To settle debts with Jabba: do not sell
My feeble carcass to the Hutt, I beg,
For he is vengeful: take the cash instead,
So you, Ubese, may profit, I depart
To seek the love that set my spirit free.'
    "'So spoke the swindler, eager even then
To bilk the mighty Jabba; in reply

240 The bounty hunter seemed to shake; he touched
The shameless Solo's stubble, croaking thus:
'Poor man, you lie already at the heart
Of Jabba's palace: here for many months
You've hung, the jest of jesters, who'll soon
Ten times repay the pain of their abuse.
But come, the night is passing: flee with me,
But do not seek your love: she came for you.'

BOUSHH'S
SECRET
So spoke the bounty hunter, tugging off
The steely helmet, showing no Ubese:

250 It was a woman rather, soft of cheek,
Save where the tears, which trickled as she spoke,

Had run beneath the mask. She kissed his mouth.
But then the mighty Jabba, still concealed
Behind the curtain, no more could resist
The comedy of that rash tryst; at last
He bellowed such a laugh as woke the fort,
Prompting a storm and chatter of guffaws.

HAN AND LEIA
SEIZED

Guards seized the smuggler, bantha-fodder soon,
But Jabba took a fancy to the girl
260   Who fills the place of that poor dancer, her
Who lately fed the rancor's famished maw.'
      "So spoke Fortuna, eager to fulfill
The duty which my powers had imposed.
At my behest he led me down the stair.
Deep to the cloister's heart it turned; the light
Fell from tall wells in columns thick with dust.
There the poor monks had used to gather, sunk
In peaceful chant and meditative gloom;
There now a scene of vast carnality

270   Was playing, Jabba's court, the denizens

JABBA'S
COURT

Of every vice: the heartless music rocked
The palace as bold Rebo's band took flight
And Snootles at the mic sang long and loud
Of Jabba's feats of enmity and crime.
The plump Askajian, Yarna, led the dance,
Fueled by the spotchka: every race was there,
Quarren, Yuvernian, Whiphid, Ishi Tib,
The Nikto and the Weequay and the Gran,
Amani, Jawas, aye, and countless more;
280   There was the frog-dog pet, Buboicullaar,
And Crumb the jester, whose harsh cackle soared
Above the mingling babble of the mob.
There too was Fett, aloof and prudent, clad
In Mandalorian armor, beskar-faced;
There, ringed with snarling guards, the dais stood
Where stretched the fatness of the Hutt himself,
Slug-like, three thousand pounds in bulk, asleep,
His eyes of amber shut amid the roar.
There too, now chained, humiliated, lay
290   My comrade, Leia, stuck at Jabba's side.
She was the first to note the quiet tread

Upon the stair, as Bib Fortuna brought
Myself, the mystery figure, to the throne.
Fortuna then, still captivated, woke
Great Jabba, met those massy amber eyes,
And spoke, as all the startled court looked on:
   "'O Jabba, here's a worthy visitor,
Luke Skywalker, a noble Jedi Knight:
He sent those useful droids, and now he brings
300   More presents. We must listen to his words.'
   "So spoke Fortuna, and the Hutt's contempt
Flung him aside into the dust and shade,
Huge nostrils flaring, with a growl of wrath:
   "'Weak-minded fool, 'tis but a Jedi trick

JABBA'S
CONTEMPT

To prove what half this filthy planet knows:
These gorgs, on which I snack, have twice the brains
Of my own servants. What, a Jedi Knight?
Cretin, where is his lightsaber? Nay, look,
He seeks to charm me too, this eager boy,
310   Who knows but fables of the ancient Knights,
And nothing of the Hutts, who are immune.
Shall I, who faced the mighty Jedi, bow
Before a beardless beggar? What is this?'"

   – But here the shade of Obi-Wan broke in,
Astonished at a detail of the tale:
   "But surely, Luke, you did not dare to face
The court of Jabba weaponless? What trick
Concealed a blaster or your lightsaber?
It's true about the Hutts, who are immune."
320   To this young Skywalker, with half a smile:
   "Ah, Ben, have patience; only recollect
That down into the depths of Bespin's gas
My lightsaber had tumbled, your great gift,
Then when Darth Vader nearly took my life
Or, worse, my honor, madman that I was
To face him unprepared – but I'll go on.

   "Such then was Jabba's boasting. There I stood
Before his throne with pity in my eyes,
And quietly I offered this reply:

330

LUKE'S
BARGAIN

"'Great Jabba, is it thus indeed you treat
The message of a Jedi? Oh, beware,
And do not underestimate this power
That stands before your throne. Restore my friends,
The Wookiee and the woman and old Han,
Bargaining wisely: in one hand I bring
Prosperity and profit and delight;
The other holds destruction. Choose yourself.'
        "Just so I spoke, and Jabba's cold response
Was translated for all by Threepio:

340

        "'There'll be no bargain: what are jewels and gold,
Whatever ransom you dare name, beside
My joy in Solo's slavery? Age, alas,
Provides no keener pleasure than revenge.
There'll be no bargain; ponder now my choice.'
        "At this the solid floor beneath my feet

LUKE FALLS
INTO A PIT

Opened; I tumbled; one Gamorrean guard,
Teetering along the lip with many a shriek,
Tipped after, down a twisting slide, to land
In some vast grotto, cool beneath the hill.

350

Shaking away the shock, I stared about.
The dimness showed a floor of broken bones,
Some gnawed, some shattered, walls of smoothest rock,
A massive gate of steel; from far above
The court grinned down upon us, hapless pair,
Haggling already, hooting out the odds.
I wondered if I must confront the guard
As gladiator, battling hand to hand;
But then the massive gate began to lift.
The plump Gamorrean dashed this way and that

360

But found the slide too steep to reascend,
The walls too smooth, the window bars too strong;
And now the gate had risen. From beyond
A pair of tiny eyes emerged, blood-red
With ravenous fury, and a deafening roar:

THE RANCOR

It was a rancor, huge, five meters tall,
Its hide like armor and its limbs like trees,
Its stench immense, its muscle infinite;
Between those tiny eyes a monstrous mouth
Disclosed huge teeth like yellow scythes; the claws

370 Upon its reaching fingers plucked the guard,
Who, squealing piteously, was hoisted, crushed,
Bitten in half and swallowed. From above
Jabba's grim chuckle and the courtiers' cheer
Were all his eulogy. The rancor turned

FACING
THE RANCOR Its half-trained mind on me now; back I dashed
To find and wield a heavy femur bone.
But there was no escape: the fingers wrapped
About my waist: I too was hoisted, crushed;
But ere the slavering mouth and teeth could chomp

380 I planted that huge bone between its jaws.
The rancor, writhing, howling at the pain,
Released me and I tumbled through its legs,
Along the grotto, 'neath the ponderous gate,
Toward a narrow door. The femur snapped,
The monster turned. I raised the narrow door
To find thick bars of iron; from beyond
The rancor's trainer pushed me back to meet
The second onslaught. Far above I saw
Leia's pale gaze; she wrestled with her chain,

390 But what could save me? Crashing step by step,
The rancor stomped beneath the ponderous gate,
Pure fury seething from its famished mouth.
But Yoda's pupil did not hesitate
As from the sandy floor I plucked a skull,
Aiming for one red button on the wall,
The gate controls: I did not try, I did,
Nailing the button, sending down the gate,
Full fifty tons, upon the rancor's head,
Crushing the cranium, cleaving through the brain.

400 As when the snows are heavy and the sun

DEATH OF
THE RANCOR Beats down upon the patient peak, which sheds
An avalanche to churn the trembling wood
And settle in a valley, where men seek
In vain for any whisper of the dead,
Just so the rancor lay beneath the gate,
Bewildered, dying, dead. But Leia's joy
Was lost amid the awful wave of rage
From Jabba and his minions: years he'd fed
That behemoth his foes, their every shriek

410 Fresh proof of his dominion; now it lay
As mortal as its meals, the trainer's tears
Shed vainly for the prodigy of yore.

JABBA'S   But Jabba was a creature of revenge.
RAGE   Back to the throne, hands bound behind our backs,
First I, then Solo and Chewbacca too
Were dragged like beasts; there mighty Jabba spoke,
Well translated for all by Threepio:
        "'This outrage must be paid for. What was planned
Is mild indeed compared to what's in store.

420 Dread no delay, this instant we depart
THE SARLACC For where it opens in the vast Dune Sea,
The Great Pit of Carkoon, eternal nest
Of th' everlasting Sarlacc; in its gut
A thousand years of agony await,
A thousand years as it digests your flesh,
With no release, but time enough to curse
The name of Jabba and regret his pet.'
        "To this, again with pity, I replied:
        "'Alas, you heap mistake upon mistake;

430 Thus pride itself oft overthrows the proud,
LUKE'S   Cast down by that indwelling power that binds
WARNING   All living things and balances our fate.
This error, mighty Jabba, is the end.'
        "Just so I spoke, before the heartless thugs
Dragged me behind my friends to face our doom."

        – Now here again Kenobi interrupts,
As dread, or something like it, fills the shade:
        "Alas, poor Luke, that all your planning failed!
The droids enslaved, the Princess' scheme exposed,

440 Chewbacca and Han Solo and yourself
Doomed to the foulest fate – but do go on!"
        So, with a smile, young Skywalker resumes:

        "With no delay we journey to the waste:
JABBA'S   The lord of gangsters and the heinous court
BARGE   Embark upon his private pleasure barge,
The bronze *Khetanna* with her sails of blood,
Floating above the dunes; beside her zip

Two skiffs, the Sarlacc's victims and their guards
Upon the first, escorted by the next.
450   As when the clacking needles stitch the wool
In twisting patterns purled above the rest,
A handiwork untouchable by time,
Until a grandson struts before the eye
Of its creator, shimmering in the light,
Just so the twisting dunes of Tatooine
Caught the bright glare across the wide Dune Sea
Whose ruddy waves, unrippling, glittered gold.
     "On Jabba's barge (as afterward I heard)
Unspeakable carousal never ceased,
460   The dancing and the cocktails and the glee;
At Jabba's side C-3PO, appalled,
Took in the frightful scene; from deck to deck
Devoted R2-D2 served the drinks.
But Leia, shackled still to Jabba's flesh,
Sought for a porthole, looking for the skiff
On which we stood, the three of us, in chains
Among five brutal Weequay buccaneers
And one tall, silent guard, his face concealed.
There Han was squinting straight into the sun,
470   And with his cynic's chuckle offered this:
     "'The blind begin to see: that big dark blur
Is blurry still but lighter; must I live
To witness my demise? It's no great thing
HAN AND LUKE   For you to perish, junior, in the sand,
Since you grew up here; aye, it's natural;
But, for myself, I miss the carbonite.'
     "To this I had to answer with a grin:
     "'Wasn't this always how it went with us?
I'd rather be afraid if all were well.
480   Relax, while you hung lifeless on the wall,
Much was foreseen, much plotted; place your trust
In one you thought a traitor and a fraud.'
     "Just so I spoke; before I could explain
We'd reached our destination, dread Carkoon.
Two heartless pirates seize me, cut my bonds,
And prod me with their axes to the plank
Which stretches 'cross the site of our demise.

"Amid the level desert was a gash
Whose sides ran steeply to a lightless hole:

490
THE PIT OF
CARKOON

That was the Sarlacc's nest, a creature foul
Beyond all reckoning; thirty thousand years
Had brought the titan to maturity,
And here it waited, feeding on the scraps
Of Jabba's court. That lightless hole, its throat,
Was ringed with fearsome teeth, bent inward, hooked
To stop escape; from deep inside its craw
Thick tentacles extended 'round the pit;
It squawked with hunger, sensing it would feed.
Even the pirates shivered with disgust.

500
JABBA'S
TAUNTS

　　"Onto the plank I ventured; from the barge,
Translating for the Hutt, whose entourage
Had paused to feast their eyes upon the scene,
The woeful voice of Threepio was heard:
　　"'O victims of the Sarlacc, may your deaths
Be honorable; yet Jabba offers this,
If any wish to beg for mercy, now
He'll condescend to listen to your pleas.'
　　"So spoke C-3PO, and even then
The giant bulk of Jabba on the barge

510

Was watching – Leia too, who'd dragged her chain
To view the nightmare. Solo bade the droid
Inform the Hutt, that wormy piece of filth,
He'd get no pleasure of the sort; but I
Ruefully answered as I walked the plank:
　　"'Jabba, the day of doom has come at last.'
　　"Just so I answered Jabba from the edge,
Winked at the silent guard, and raised my hand
Against the glare; and so the fight began,
So long foreseen, long plotted: 'twas my sign

520
THE BATTLE
BEGINS

To R2-D2, where that loyal droid
Was watching from the main deck of the barge.
At once he furnished me, from secret stash,
This blade of emerald, work of my own hand,
The lightsaber I'd forged the ancient way,
Its kyber crystal eager for the war:
Across the sky it shot, above the pit,
From barge to skiff, tracing a graceful arc

To me: I'd leapt straight up into the air,
Rebounding from the plank in somersaults
530   To fall upon our enemies: the sword
Dropped to my waiting fingers, there to hiss
And slay a Weequay, slicing through his axe;
Another tried to dodge, but dodged too far,
Into the railing, over, down to die,
Clawing the sand, slipping into the maw;
A third, more prudent, aimed for Solo's chest,
But ere the blaster flashed, a vibro-axe
Had clipped him, wielded by a foe unguessed,
The silent guard, who tore his helmet off,
540   Lando Calrissian, with his eager laugh,

LANDO
REVEALED
So long disguised, but desperate to expunge
The stain of that betrayal in the clouds.
I fought the rest as Lando leapt to free
Chewbacca and Han Solo, seize the skiff,
And steer for freedom. No, it was too soon
To triumph: launching from the great bronze barge,
Where uproar gripped the crowd and crew, he came,

FETT ENTERS
THE BATTLE
Proud Boba Fett in Mandalorian helm,
His jetpack flaring, landing on the skiff.
550   But ere he could discharge the EE-3,
His trusty carbine, from the hip, my blade
Slashed through the famous barrel: so Fett's doom
Seemed near; but from the bronze *Khetanna*'s deck
The guards had opened fire and hardly missed
My head, for I could barely block the bolts;
Then Boba aimed his whip of fibercord,
A rope unbreakable, around my chest,
Pinning my arms, my saber useless, save
To redirect the blaster bolts at Fett,
560   Who stumbled, freeing me. The Wookiee ripped
Han's binders off, while Lando, fist to fist,
Wrestled a weapon from the last Weequay;
The desperate figures grappled at the rail

LANDO
CLINGS
Which buckled, bent and softened by the blasts;
They topple, tumble, Lando barely clings
To one thin cord, his enemy devoured,
Begging assistance, dangling over death.

"Yet now the other skiff banked 'round the barge,
Crammed with fresh forces, cannon blasting hot.

570

I saw it coming it, charged it, leapt aloft

LUKE
ATTACKS

Onto its prow, my saber slashing fast
To block, deflect the salvoes. Boba Fett
Had found his feet: the rockets on his wrist
Were aimed at me, to blow the skiff itself
Straight down into the Sarlacc's gaping mouth.
But Chewie saw Fett's strategy and roared,
Commanding Han to turn; but Han was blind,

FALL OF
BOBA FETT

And as Han panicked, spinning, axe in hand,
The butt end smacked the jetpack on Fett's back,

580

Which flared unbidden, sent him tumbling up
To crack against the bronze *Khetanna*'s hull:
In vain he clung, in vain he bellowed, howled,
In vain he sought for purchase as he slid
Off the ship's lip and down the steep decline,
Across the toothy throat into the depths.
The monstrous stomach claimed him with a belch.
    "Meanwhile, on the *Khetanna*, Jabba's wrath
Was roaring orders at the startled court;
His grim Gamorrean guards were sent on deck

590

To load the heavy gun and shell the skiffs;

LEIA
ATTACKS

The band throbbed on. But Leia saw her chance,
Seizing the crime lord's microphone, she wrecks
The cabin circuits, shorting out the lights.
Then panic, madness seized them, all but her,
Who hauled her heavy chain behind the Hutt,
Looping it 'round his fleshy neck. She pulled,
Catching his gullet ere the tiny hands
Can break the stranglehold of steel; she pulled
With every ounce of strength; the chain bit deep,

600

That chain that others wore before, turned now
Upon the master, whom no courtier saved;
The huge tongue lolled, the spittle scattered wide,
The tail, like some disgusting serpent, shook,

DEATH OF
JABBA

And still she pulled, 'til with a final gush
Of filthy air great Jabba breathed his last:
The massy amber eyes lay frozen wide.

"Then Leia called for Artoo, but the droid
Was there already, rolling to her side;
His slender arm sawed through the rusty chain;
610 And then they parted, he to save his friend,
Who stretched nearby, the jester's victim; Crumb
Was zapped away by Artoo; then the pair
Fled through the rolling tumult of the barge,
Dropping to safety in the ruddy sand.
But Princess Leia rushed up to the deck.

"There pirates, thugs, and guards were aiming free
At Lando as he dangled from the cord;

RESCUE OF
LANDO

The skiff was listing: Lando dropped, but Han,
His vision slowly clearing, reached him down
620 The vibro-axe; Calrissian climbed; again
The lasers sizzled 'round them: Chewie snagged
Han's feet as he too staggered off the skiff.
Then Lando, inch by inch, clawed up the slope
Of slippery granules, 'mid the blaster bolts,
'Til from the maw a tentacle leapt up
To wrap around his leg; Calrissian screamed
As down it dragged him. Chewie's fist passed down
A blaster to Han Solo, who took aim.
Then Lando in astonishment declared:

630 "'Between the fates below me and above,
I'll gladly be a target for the blind!
But, Han, a little higher, just a bit,
A little more – that's it, now fire away!'

"So spoke Calrissian, trusting Solo's eye,
For friends must trust each other; Solo shot
And nailed the tentacle, which dropped its grip.
Then inch by inch Calrissian climbed aboard
The listing skiff, where Solo hugged him close.

"Meanwhile the other hovered, cleared of foes
640 By my bright lightsaber: but now I looked
Toward the barge, where now the heavy gun

LUKE ON
THE BARGE

Was wheeling on my friends. At once I jumped
From skiff to barge, and not without the Force,
Into the thick of battle with my foes;
These I soon scattered, some cut down, some knocked

Into the Sarlacc's mouth, the blaster bolts
Deflected at the shooters by my blade.
There Leia met me, and our eyes were locked
With love untrammeled by desire: I saw
650 Her will to victory, she my Jedi skill;
But more: I heard some whisper of the Force.
She hailed me, fighting still; I gladly spoke:
      "'O Leia, come, we must destroy the ship,

LUKE AND LEIA Pointing the giant weapon at the deck;
We'll blow the Hutt sky-high; 'tis only just;
But where are Artoo and C-3PO?'
      "To this the Princess answered as she ran:
      "'The droids are safe, they tumbled overboard
Upon the other side; the Hutt is dead,
660 Whom I myself, with these bare hands, have slain.
But all his court must perish. Hurry up
And figure out some way we can escape!'
      "In answer I took up a hefty sheet
That governed the *Khetanna*'s blood-red sails;

LEIA AIMS But Leia, spinning in the gunner's chair,
THE GUN Pointed the cannon at the deck itself,
Where now the courtiers, peeking from below,
Were gawking at the carnage. So she aimed,
Cranking the power to max, then ran to me;
670 So from afar, and not without the Force,
I pressed the gun's great trigger; she grabbed hold,
And so we swung across the vast abyss,
Descending on the skiff, which Lando steered

THE SEVEN To where the droids were waiting. 'Cross the dunes
ESCAPE We six, with Solo as the seventh, sped
Toward Mos Espa and the greater war.
      "Behind, the roaring cannon had discharged,
Holing the metal hull from stem to stern,
Ripping the fuel tanks, which in turn blew up
680 In swelling balls of opalescent flame:
The proud *Khetanna* buckled, Jabba's corpse
Burning along with that all that hideous court

END OF THE Of slavers and assassins: few survived,
KHETANNA For Jabba's day of doom had come at last.
As when a bolt of lightning, swiftly forged

As clouds collide, with awful thundercrack
Obliterates an ancient tree, its stump
A monument to nature's righteous power,
Just so the ruddy sand beside that place,
690   The Great Pit of Carkoon, eternal nest
Of th' everlasting Sarlacc, shall display
The proud *Khetanna*'s broken, blackened wreck.

    "So, Ben, you see, no riddle yet remains.
Myself I've felt how vividly the Force

THE RIDDLE
SOLVED

Moves near her, aye, in battle and in peace:
Leia's my sister – Leia is my twin!"
    So spoke young Luke, his crystal eyes alight,
Envisioning the Princess' gaze, who'd proved
A firm companion on the lonely path
700   That spread before his feet. Ben's voice replied:
    "Your insight serves you well, Luke. None must know!
Bury your feelings: now the hour is late,
And shortly you will face the lord of lies,
Before whose throne all love is suicide,
There to confront your father once again."
    So spoke the stately shade of Obi-Wan;
In turn Luke raised his saber, lit the blade:

LUKE'S
NEW SABER

A plasma edge of green at once extends,
Firing the woods with beryl and with teal.
710   Then gravely Skywalker addressed that sword:
    "Are you then, heart of crystal, what shall slay
My father? Have I only forged a tool
Of murder and revenge? Was Yoda's wish
That I should stain my soul with parricide?"
    So spoke the son of Skywalker; to him
The Jedi Master's spirit made reply:
    "Go forth to seek what you alone can find,

BEN'S
BLESSING

Your destiny. But in what lies ahead
You fight, young Luke, for things beyond your ken,
720   The past, the future; as to Obi-Wan,
There is no present, no today, no now,
But in my mind the galaxy extends,
The fate of every planet in the scale:
The Core itself, old worlds of Coruscant,

Caamas, Corellia, Duro, Tangenine,
Eufornis, Kuat, Chandrila, Brentaal,
Dowut and Ganthel, Plexis, Corulag,
Tinnel, Anaxes, Hosnia, Balosar;
The Mid Rim too, Trandosha and Naboo,
730   And Bothawui, Naator, Phorsa Gedd,
Ithor, Coyerti, Haidoral, Kashyyyk,
Shu-Torun, Takodana, Malastare,
And many more; and then the Outer Rim,
The frontier planets, Kessel and Lothal,
Ryloth, Nal Hutta, Sullust, Dathomir,
Mon Calamari, Bith, and Tatooine,
Cantonica and Carlac, Ord Mantell;
Even the distant regions from beyond
That maze of stellar storms and vast black holes,
740   Ilum and Csilla and remote Jakku
And blue Ahch-To in utter solitude:
All these, young Luke, await the last attack,
The battle of the darkness and the light
So long foretold; the saber is your tool,
It serves you only: make your destiny;
And may the Force be with you as you go."

BOOK IX

ENDOR

T o claim a place among the valiant dead
    Whose names adorn the corridor of fame,
    Forever echoing, incorruptible –
Such is the sweet ambition of the spring;
But when the light begins to fade, when leaves
Of brittle autumn rattle, which must fly,
Mere mortal goals suffice, a humbler grave
Unshod by marble, whose inscription fades,
Provided some brave feat, perhaps unsung,
Perhaps unknown, but worth the price of life,
Lies buried also. Glorious sentinel,
None know them now, the Bothan spies who fell
So far from battle, in a lonely war,

INVOCATION

10

Or none but you, past whom forgetfulness
Can never skulk or sneak: describe at last
How Mothma, prudent, patient through the years,

THE BOTHAN
SPIES

Received their information and the news
Of their demise, a network wrapped and rolled
Into the Emperor's prisons, or cut down

20 Upon the lowly streets of Coruscant
Or Bothawui; so they paid the price
Of victory's distant possibility.
She shed no tears: instead she set to work
With just a trusted few – Cracken, Madine –

A SECOND
DEATH STAR

To test, corroborate, and verify
The looming truth: a second Death Star, vast,
Indomitable, yet still incomplete,
The Emperor's answer to their insolence,
Orbiting distant Endor's forest moon.

30 As when a glass, slipping from careless hands,
Shatters and pieces tinkle 'round the floor
On which a mother's children love to skip,
And so she plucks the shards, not missing one,
To reassemble with unsparing care,
Just so Mon Mothma tallied the receipts,
Treasure untold, the Empire's hidden wealth
Pouring into the project, memos, grants,
Officers' pleas for time, for men, rebuffed
Most coldly by Lord Vader's ruthlessness,

40 A project incomplete, if not for long:
She weighs the choices but a moment, turns,
And summons Admiral Ackbar and the fleet.
        Deep in those districts blank between the stars
Its vessels lurked, intent on lightning raids,
Enticing and eluding all pursuit,

MASSING OF
THE FLEET

Each cell expecting Ackbar's rendezvous.
Squadron to squadron now, and ship to ship,
They relay cryptic orders to escape
To Sullust, stealthily, but vigilant

50 Lest the Imperials track a single jump:
There day by day they gather, eight corvettes,
Five frigates, sixteen GR-75s,
The seven Dorneans and the Spectres' *Ghost*,

Four slim Corellian gunships, ten X4s;
The B-wing squadrons, Blade and Blue and Gray,
And five of A-wings too, the Greens not least,
And Y-wing bombers also, U-wings sleek,
And X-wings of Corona, Yellow, Red,
With Wedge Antilles flashing in the lead;
60 After them streaks the Calamari fleet,
The MC80s, giant in their strength,
Dappled in black and green, in red and white,
Peers of the Star Destroyers, city ships,
The *Independence* and the *Liberty*,
Defiance and *Nautilian* and *Home One*,
With seven more, sworn ever to sustain
The war 'til blue Mon Cala should be free.
As when a hermit, by the water's edge,
Ceases to brood upon his wrongs, and plucks
70 A pack of crusts from its familiar pouch,
And from all corners of the pond they turn,
The swift and silent mallards, while his heart
Is softened by their greedy appetite,
Just so the rebels gathered for the war.
        Thus the armada lay at Sullust, massed
MOTHMA'S For battle on a field unspecified;
BRIEFING But Mothma briefed the admiral straightaway,
And straightaway they planned the target's doom
With Crix Madine, then summoned all the rest
80 Aboard the vast *Home One*, old Ackbar's flag,
The stubborn captains of the rebel cause:
Cracken was there, Syndulla, Delto, Nantz;
Antilles and the squadron leaders too;
Forell and Massa, Tantor and Veertag;
Calrissian, brilliant victor of Taanab;
And General Solo, rescued from the Hutt
By Leia and the Wookiee: there he sat
Alongside Skywalker, whose solemn glance
Was drifting to the Princess' eager face.
90 When all had found their places, Mothma spoke:
        "The Emperor's error calls for swift attack.
His power has built a second Death Star, vast,
Orbiting distant Endor's forest moon,

Indomitable, yet still incomplete
And unprotected, weaponless, his fleet
Spread through the galaxy in hopeless quest
Of rebel raiders; but the great mistake
Is this: upon that battle station sits
The emperor Palpatine himself. We strike
100   To kill the tyrant and decide the war.
For this the nameless Bothans gave their lives."
      So spoke Mon Mothma, torn by grief and hope;
And Admiral Ackbar now picks up the tale.

ADMIRAL
ACKBAR

That was a veteran warrior, Raddus' peer,
The sworn avenger of his martyred king,
Lee-Char of sacred memory; with a flick
Of claw-tipped fingers Ackbar activates
A glowing hologram of Endor's moon,
'Round which the Death Star orbits, incomplete.
110   With many a croak the Calamari speaks:
      "Here is our target, weaponless, but screened
By this defense, a thick magnetic shield
Projected from the surface of the moon,
Invisible, impassable, immune
To all bombardment. Once the shield is down,
Our cruisers, ranged in a perimeter,
Shall hinder all escape, while fighters lance
Into the superstructure, knocking out
The main reactor. Ah, perhaps you ask
120   What man could be so crazy as to lead
His squadrons through the heart of that machine?
He stands among you here, his name renowned,
General Calrissian, victor of Taanab."
      So spoke old Admiral Ackbar; murmurs rise
Of approbation: Lando was the man
For daring, and a fire was in his eye.
But Solo stood and spoke these wingèd words:
      "How much I've missed inside the carbonite!
The kid I used to rescue twice a week
130   Is now some kind of Jedi; Lando, you,
Who spent less time in sleep than at sabacc,

SOLO OFFERS
THE *FALCON*

Are now – well, what? What's this about Taanab?
Ah well, a better pilot, save myself

And maybe Chewie, never skimmed the stars.
One thing, I think, is lacking: will that cape
Be tucked into an A-wing cockpit? No!
Take the *Millennium Falcon*, peerless ship,
Which you yourself, in bygone days, once raced
Across the galaxy: you know each plate,
140   Each landing jet. I only ask one thing:
Your promise that she won't pick up a scratch."

    So spoke Han Solo, shaking Lando's hand,
Who stammers his confusion: so what ship
Will Solo take? But here spoke Crix Madine:
    "One thing, Calrissian, I will ask as well:
Do not forget the thick magnetic shield

**THE STRIKE
TEAM**   Projected from the surface of the moon;
For all your valor and your recklessness
Are useless if the shield still stands. Your friend
150   Has sworn to sabotage it, sneaking down
Upon a stolen cargo shuttle: there
He'll lead our bold commandos, blowing up
The generator. Aye, it's no small risk,
But friends must trust each other, and the Force.
But who'll make up the stolen shuttle's crew?"

    No sooner had he spoken, Crix Madine,
Than Luke and Leia sprang to volunteer,
And tall Chewbacca also, and the droids,
The one alarmed, the other duty-bent.
160   But Leia, as the officers dispersed,
Had placed her gentle hand upon Luke's arm;

**LUKE'S
RIDDLE**   He answered ere the question left her lips:
    "Yes, Leia, I have tidings, strange indeed,
From Dagobah. The hour is late: all things
Draw swiftly to a reckoning. Let's be gone
And leave my news until a quiet hour."

    Thus Luke, and Leia let the riddle be;
Luke often spoke in riddles, since the day
He'd ventured off alone to Dagobah.
170   How much that farmer boy had changed, who now
Moved mostly in th' indwelling power that binds
All living things and balances our fate!
But duty called her: through the vast *Home One*

They made their way, soon clad in camouflage
And bearing rifles. In the hangar bay
The strike team had assembled, picked by Han,
Delighted now as Luke and Leia join.

SHUTTLE
TYDIRIUM

There sat the pale *Tydirium*, humble craft,
A three-winged shuttle, *Lambda*-class, weird sight
180 Among the rebel fighters. Solo climbs
The gangplank, where the last explosive charge
Is being loaded. Up the others go
To take their seats – though tall Chewbacca's legs
Can barely fit the chair. To space they launch,
Wheeling among the busy rebel ships,
Those cruisers, frigates, starfighters, corvettes
Dependent on a single shuttle's crew.
To distant Endor Chewie plots a course,
And then Han Solo punched it: off they leap
190 Past constellations, through the gentle swirl
Of hyperspace, to regions little known,
Rehearsing, as they wait, their stealthy strike.

    Upon the very edge of charted space,
Before Bakura and the wilderness,

ENDOR

It stretched, the Modell sector, barely mapped,
Dappled and daubed by florid nebulas;
Well had the cunning mind of Palpatine
Selected its remoteness; no spies skulk
Where cities lack, no lawless smugglers roam
200 Where laws are never made; there nature ruled
Unchecked, unbridled: there the final stroke
Was taking shape in perfect secrecy.
There swung the planet Endor's lurid gas,
Cyan and silver, pink and purple, looped
By nine bright satellites; and on the ninth
A forest moon, the grandest of them all,
The Empire's clever engineers had raised
A shield projector 'mid the towering trees,
To insulate the Death Star as it grew.
210 That was the forest moon, which Han beholds
As out from hyperspace *Tydirium* streaks.

How vividly both Han and Luke recall
The *Falcon*'s visit to the first Death Star
As now toward the second, incomplete
But rigged already with its mighty dish,
They venture, where it looms above the moon;
Around it swarms of freighters and their loads
Are twirling, safe inside the unseen shield.
Between them and the pale *Tydirium*'s course
220   Lie two small warships, but the third in front
They know too well: the vast *Executor*,
The flagship, fifteen times the size and length
Of any Star Destroyer. Thence it came,

CHEWIE'S CODE   A weary voice requesting course and code.
None breathe as Chewie hurries to transmit
The stolen cypher; yet no answer comes.
Then, as they wait, Luke senses from afar
A menace on the vast *Executor*,
An icy turbulence, Darth Vader's will;
230   He felt him and was felt: aboard that ship
The deadly Sith lord suddenly discerned

VADER SENSES LUKE   His son, and, skilled in prophecy, perceived
In Luke's approach some meaning unrevealed.
Yet when he'd pondered and assessed the fact,
He bade his captains clear the shuttle's course;
But straightaway he sought his barren cell,
And there, before his master's hologram,
As though before an awful idol, knelt;
Then, breathing deep, the sable pupil spoke:
240   "O Sidious, my master, thee I name
In my perplexity, to thee alone

VADER AND SIDIOUS   I turn: long centuries in the dark we lurked,
But thou alone hast won the Sith's desire.
Long have I sought for Skywalker, my son,
Whom thou didst bid me gather to thee here;
Only his stubbornness, his will to die,
Forestalled our plan, on Bespin. Much I feared
The power of prophecy, for which this boy
Perhaps was chosen; but thy wisdom spoke,
250   Foretelling but the triumph of the Sith:

The boy himself, thou didst predict, would come
To me; and now the very thing is done.
For as I stalked the vast *Executor*,
My ship, I unmistakeably discerned
His presence on a shuttle: through the shield
It seems a rebel force hath passed, to strike
The generator on the forest moon."
    So Vader, kneeling, spoke, his rasping breath
Reverent and slow. At this the Emperor paused,
260 Pondering his pupil, weighing every word.
But then the master of the Sith replied:
    "Thy feeble son, Lord Vader, findeth strength;
'Tis strange, therefore, 'tis strange that in thy soul
His presence rippled, leaving mine unmoved.

SIDIOUS IS
CONFIDENT

In this thy heart, I hope, is steady? Good.
For only thou and I, aligned in full,
May turn him now, an asset to our cause.
Bring him before the adamantine throne:
There pity for his father shall undo
270 All equanimity, and by such rage
The turn toward the dark will be complete.
Dismiss thy empty fear of prophecy,
For all proceeds as I have long foreseen.
The Jedi, being dead, cannot return;
We stand beside the rebels' open grave."
    So spoke Lord Sidious; beneath his hood
The crimson eyes were laughing, though the mouth
Was twisted in an ecstasy of hate.
That dark apprentice, Vader, kneeling, bowed,
280 His reverence like a wave, and made his way
Toward a shuttle and the forest moon.

    Meanwhile the pale *Tydirium*, cleared to pass
The Death Star's shield, had softly nestled down

THE STRIKE
TEAM LANDS

Within the forest; soon the silent crew
And strike team, in their camouflage, had crept
Halfway toward the generator's door,
Han Solo in the lead, then Leia, Luke,
Chewbacca with his bowcaster, the droids,
And ten commandos slinking close behind.

290   'Midst the staccato of the distant birds
And secret pulse of crickets, mammoth trees,
'Round which ten men could barely fasten hands,
Rise from enormous roots toward the sky,
So high that eyes grow dizzy that behold
The lofty canopy. They fill their lungs
With earthy tangs and luscious oxygen.
The ferns enclose them, and the mossy logs
Absorb their steps. Then first to spot the foe
Was Solo, signaling for stillness: there,
300 Not far ahead, bright white against the green,
A pair of biker scouts was lounging, bored,
Their speeders oiled, the woods unchangeable.
Then Solo, as he summoned Chewie's aid,

BIKER
SCOUTS

Pondered two courses in his teeming brain,
Whether to lead his strike force roundabout,
Or rather take the sentries out himself,
For time was passing fast: tomorrow's dawn
Would greet the fleet and Lando's swift assault.
Pondering all this, he chose to take them out,
310 And scrambled, with the Wookiee, down a bank.
As when a mouse, the soul of caution, flits
From leg to leg among the chairs, intent
Upon a morsel carelessly disowned,
Of no great worth to others, but to her
The cure for famine and the taste of bliss,
Just so the stealthy Solo, blaster drawn,
Covered by Chewie's fearsome bowcaster,
Crept 'round the trees, behind the sentries' backs.
      Now those who live by luck know every creak
320 Of fortune's wheel, its lurches, its ascents;
As Han stepped out his luck collapsed: a twig
Snapped, and the troopers, with a shout of shock,

A TWIG

Spun 'round: one slapped Han's blaster to the side,
Then punched him down; the other dashed for help,
Jumping upon a waiting speeder bike,
Accelerating through the trees. Alas,
He'd failed to reckon with one factor, this:
A Wookiee's bowcaster, whose orange bolts
Laid low that speeder in a burst of flame.

330   Yet, even as Han wrestled with the scout,
    The rebels up the bank observed two more
    Running for speeders: Luke and Leia rush
    To leap upon the wrestling trooper's ride:

LUKE AND LEIA
GIVE CHASE
    In front, she jams the comms, Luke holding tight,
    Then twists her wrist and launches on the chase,
    Accelerating at fantastic speed: the trunks
    Flash past along the shortcut she selects,
    Banking around great boulders, under logs,
    Teeth clenched against th' asphyxiating wind.

340   Ahead, her nervous targets hesitate
    To break their necks in such velocity,
    So soon she overtakes the hindmost. Luke,
    As Leia slams her bike against the foe's,
    Jumps as they scrape, hurling the trooper off
    To crack against a tree: the bike is Luke's;
    He pulls behind the Princess in the race.
    But this last scout was clever: 'round he swept
    To pass a spot where other bikers lurked.
    So two more join the deadly steeplechase,

350   Pursuing Luke and Leia, blasting quick,
    Singeing Luke's speeder; with a cry he calls
    For Leia to ride down the one in front,
    He'll take the others: so he slams the brakes,
    Feeling the shock as back between their bikes
    He hurtles: then pursuers are pursued:
    They try to shake him, but the forest maze
    Lies open to his instinct: straight he shoots

A DESPERATE
RACE
    And wings one target, which, off-balance, skids
    Into a tree, a wreck of flame and steel.

360   The second cannot shake him: soon the pair
    Are jostling, grinding, elbows brushing, locked,
    Intent on murder at stupendous speed:
    Racing toward a massive trunk, both doomed
    If neither jumps; too late the scout looks up,
    So Luke must hurl himself into the air.
    Aye, then the Force was with him: as a cat
    In falling finds its feet, so Luke rebounds
    From where he'd tumbled, only to behold
    His foe, still blasting, wheeling to the charge.

370 As when a bat comes whistling at a ball,
The ball that fatherly affection sets
Upon a stick, an easy target, such
As children's hands can hardly fail to hit,
Just so the speeder, blasting, swung at Luke;
But from his belt Luke drew his shining sword,
That blade of emerald, work of his own hand,
Deflecting every bolt into the trees,
And, as the speeder passed him, with a slash
Too swift for human eyes to track, he lopped
380 The nose, the steering vanes: a dozen times
The trooper, screaming, spun before the crash.

**LUKE
PREVAILS** Then quiet filled the woods: the nervous birds
Had fled the whine and echo of the chase;
No sign or sound of Leia haunts the leaves.
So back along the route he picked his way
To Han and Chewie and the loyal droids.

Now, all the while, the Princess, in pursuit
Of that last scout, lest all surprise be lost,
Had clung no less intently to her goal:
390 In her the rhythm of the Force beat strong.

**LEIA'S
CHASE** As when, in those incalculable depths
Beneath Naboo, a monstrous vertebrate,
Th' opee sea killer, which the Gungans name
The Gooberfish, will stalk its passing prey,
Riding the current, matching course, then strike,
Attaching with its giant, gummy tongue,
Just so the Princess, late of Alderaan,
Adhered to that pale target in the trees.
Alas, he cannot shake her, nor outpace
400 Her daring: when at last she overtakes,
He fumbles for his pistol, overjoyed
To shoot and see the rebel speeder swerve
And fling the girl aside into the ferns;
But heedless victory leads to swift defeat:
A fallen tree, its roots a timber trap,
Enfolds him, unavoidable as death:
Th' explosion echoes in the Princess' ears
As from the scene of consciousness she slips.

How many hours she'd lain there, helmet lost,
410 She cannot guess; her coiling braids are loose;
The sun, perhaps, was falling. Everywhere

LEIA
AWAKES
Those mammoth trees recede, whose arch of leaves
Sieves the white light; the ambient warmth, diffused,
Save where its incandescent pools were poured,
Tempers the coolness of the forest floor.
Nameless, unseen, infrequent voices call,
Critter to distant critter, shrill, forlorn,
From sinking branch or prickly underbrush.
The air is rich with nourishment; a stream
420 Tinkles down secret stones not distant, where
The earth is hidden by the drooping ferns,
Some tiny, some the height of apple trees.
Groaning, she staggers upward, unaware
That she is watched, 'til, as she reels about,
Despairing of direction in the maze,
Abruptly she perceives a pair of eyes
Watching her from a distance, on a log.
Now Leia was no stranger to the strange,
For every species passed her parents' door;
430 Her schooling had been spent among the stars;
But these are eyes she's never met before,

THE EWOK
Eyes large as medals in a tiny face,
Polished like stone, no pupil visible,
Ruddy as roots fresh dug from rusty earth.
Their owner was a furry creature, small
But bright, two-footed, hair a matted brown;
Wearing upon its head a cap of hide
That clothed the upper body; in its fist
It held upright a stone-tipped spear of wood.
440 Stock still it stood, amid the shifting shade
Which seemed to show its modulating thought,
Stock-still and wary as its woodland world.
She gestures, and the weapon snaps to point
A flinty edge; yet Leia's unafraid:
She senses nothing evil, and she sits,
Offering to share a wafer from her pouch.
The courteous furry face approaches, sniffs,
And eats it, nestling in a mossy spot,

Sharp spear discarded, ruddy eyes alight.
450   There then began a conversation such
As Endor never heard, extensive, odd:
For neither understood the other's words
Yet each perceived the meaning: Leia told
Her tale of the *Tydirium* and the chase,
The friends she'd lost, the enemies she'd slain;
The Ewok – such was that small species' name –
Answered with bold adventures in the hunt;
For eloquence is but the love of truth,
And both rejoiced in love of truth itself.

460   Yet even as they speak, the Ewok starts,
Scrambling to reach a lookout, motionless,
His weapon static in a rigid fist.
He sniffs; the branches hush the breeze; he sniffs.
As when a Jedi temple, long decayed,
Would stand in silhouette against the sky
On Vrogas Vas, or Tython, where the hills
Were cut with figures of a fallen age,
Just so the Ewok's silhouette was etched
A SNIPER   Against the shifting greenery. With a flash
470   A laser cracks the concentrated air:
The log between them splinters with a hiss;
The Princess and her ally drop and roll
Beneath a fern, poor cover, but concealed.
Peeping to spot the sniper, Leia shoots;
The Ewok tumbles off and disappears.
Her blaster barking, as her unseen foe
Answers and that slow, deadly duel proceeds
Beneath the canopy of leaves: she's pinned.

      My heart, I know, is with the rebel cause:
480   In vain they thirst for immortality
Who bully, taunt, imprison, or oppress
TROOPERS'   The poets, vessels of a deathless truth.
VIRTUES   But valor knows no loyalty: he lies
Who says that stormtroopers lacked courage, they
Who'd pile their bodies on the prior wave,
Disdaining safety, rushing to assault
Some rebel cell's impregnable redoubt:
No shining vision of a better world,

A galaxy not shackled, stirred their souls,
490   But simple duty and integrity;
And neither were they stupid: sent to scour
The forest for the wreckage of the chase,

LEIA A
PRISONER

That pair of scouts ensnared her: from above,
One pinned her, blaster hot behind a tree;
The other, careful as a cat, had looped
Behind her. Fixed upon the hidden shots,
She's taken unawares, and must give in,
Menaced with execution. One is sent
To fetch his speeder, as the other plants
500   The blaster tip between her shoulder blades,
Chucking her weapon off into the trees.
        Leia, your tale was nearly at an end
In cold Imperial vengeance; nonetheless
The Force was with you, and a newfound friend:

WICKET'S
RESCUE

For Wicket (such was that brave Ewok's name)
Had not forsaken you at all: below
He lurked, beneath the log, cooly intent
On rescue: now he loosed the battle cry
Which Ewoks, since the origin of trees,
510   Had loosed upon their foes, a gargling call,
And hacked the trooper's ankle with his spear.
The trooper staggers, waving; Leia strikes,
Spinning to smash him with a stick; he falls;
She strikes again, then plucks his blaster, spins
And nails the other's fleeting speeder bike,
Hitting it once, twice, thrice; it crashes, burns.
Atop the log the Ewok climbs, to dance
Their double victory, joyful as a child:
Bitter, however petty, was the feud
520   Of Wicket's people with the biker scouts.
        Then through the tangled wilderness they rush,
The Ewok leading, Leia at his heels;

A SWIFT
JOURNEY

He knows each hollow, precipice, and slope,
Each jagged stone, each root: his pattering feet
Are planted with the favor of the trees.
As when the armored clans of Mandalore
Would launch their mighty jetpacks, taking wing,
Ere cataclysm wrecked a broken world,

That warrior race, stepping from cloud to cloud,
530   Just so the nimble Ewok leapt along
The intricacies of the forest floor.
They rest beside a stream, then rush again;
The shadows deepen. Soon they reach a rope
Cunningly stowed; she wills her muscles up
Some fifty feet, to reach a little porch
Of corded branches plaited 'round the tree,
Propped from beneath, secured by heavy cord.
Then from its holster Wicket plucks a horn,
Blowing the note of his return: they cross
540   A lowered drawbridge to another perch,
Then swing across a gulf upon a vine.

    And so it was that Princess Leia came
To Bright Tree Village, nestled on the trunks,
Safe from the gorax' claws. There Chirpa ruled,

THE EWOK VILLAGE Not counted least of Endor's potentates,
Together with the council, whose decrees
Wise Logray kept in union with the stars.
Two hundred souls dwelt there together, joined
In happy federation, clan by clan,
550   Their huts thatched thick and warm. To Wicket's home
She follows, where she scrubs the grime of war,
Letting her long dark hair flow down her back,
Accepting newer garments, swiftly sewn;
She puzzles, nonetheless, at why the hut
Is bare, save for some grandmothers, who cluck
In comfort at the circle of the hearth.
As though in answer Wicket takes her hand
And leads her out toward the village square,
Where three thick trunks rose close together, fused
560   By one great floor, poles woven tight: there stood
The elders' council hut and Chirpa's hall;
There were the Ewoks wont to gather, there

A JOYOUS SACRIFICE With eager whoops and whistles now they worked
Amid the throbbing of a dogged drum,
Preparing a delightful sacrifice,
The pious youth, the newborn and the aged,
Mothers and fathers, widows, bachelors,

The hunters and the gatherers of herbs,
The chief, the Elders, and the cautious priest.
570   But Wicket starts, amazed, for in their midst
A strange new wooden throne is raised: there sits
A golden man, perhaps a mighty god,
To whom wise Logray, in his condor crown,
Offers in homage one short silver stick.
But Leia's pleasure at the joyous scene
Is shattered as the victims are displayed:
No animals, no birds are these, but friends,
Luke and Han Solo, Chewie and R2,
Bound by the wrists and ankles under logs
580   Aslant across four fires as yet unlit;
But Solo now, while Ewoks strike a match
Beside his bonfire, busily rebukes
The golden figure on the throne of wood:
    "Now, Threepio, this has gone far enough!
Speak up, since only you, it seems, can talk
The lingo of these fuzzy carnivores:

SOLO'S   Call off this little festival, before
REBUKE   We're cooked like juicy mutton! Oh, hello?
Does no one listen to a general's word?
590   This mission's been one long disaster, since
I broke that blasted twig, since Luke brought back
The Princess' helmet, and I vowed to find
Her body or herself, leaving the team
To wait above the bunker. Off we crept,
Along the racecourse of that crazy chase.
Then Chewie was the first to pay no heed
To my stern warnings, when across our path
We met a carcass draped upon a stake:
Ah yes, perhaps that's normal on Kashyyyk,
600   No trap, no, just a carcass on a stake.
Well, who could guess? Head over heels we fly,
Hoist in a net ten feet above the ferns,
A droid's leg in my ribs. So, I announced,

THEIR   We must be careful climbing down – in vain!
ADVENTURES   No sooner are we up than this good droid,
This astromech, this gizmo, saws us free,
Dumping us in a pile, myself beneath

A Wookiee's weight. Alright, says I, we're off,
Escaping from whatever set this trap.
610 No sooner had I spoken than a crowd
Of these plush heathens, growling, crests the bush,
Armed to the teeth, suspicious (shall we say)
Of such intruders. Aye, well, from the pile,
You finally stirred, that golden armor bright,
Discoursing on the grammar of their tongue,
Their distant dialect. Says I, 'We'll fight!';
But heedlessly you chattered to the crowd,
And next – but why go on, except to prove
The folly of this forest? – next the growls
620 Shift to a reverent chant, a solemn hymn,
Directed at our brass interpreter;
And you inform us you are now a god.
Fine choice, says I, a fine theology;
We'll blast the critters and inform the world.
But Luke (since Jedi love a joke, I guess)
Decides we shall surrender, giving up
The guns, the saber, and the bowcaster,
Submitting to their superstitious scheme,
Insulted, bound, and jostled – all but you,
630 Whom half the tribe has carried on its back,
SOLO'S Enthroned, no less, while we await the pyre.
PLEA Well now, Lord Goldenrod, may I suggest,
As humbly as a simple mortal can,
That you exert your holy influence,
And save us ere we're roasted to a crisp?"
    So spoke Han Solo, as the fiery brand
Is passed beneath his kindling, which combusts;
In answer poor C-3PO objects:
    "Your pardon, General Solo, but your plan
640 Is quite improper: programming forbids
THREEPIO'S That ever I impersonate a god.
RELUCTANCE Moreover, is it decent or polite
To seek to abrogate a sacred feast
Held in my honor? Am I such a guest?"
    At this the Princess, pushing past her guide,
Most sternly bids th' interpreter obey;
But such is custom: though the god himself

Demands delay, the ritual proceeds,
With fresher pilings of the driest wood.
650   In vain the Wookiee wrestles with his bonds,
In vain the smuggler huffs the rising flame;
But Skywalker calls out across the drums:
    "Now, Threepio, we may try something else.
Inform the chief and shaman that your wrath
Is kindling hotter than the pyre itself,
And magic shall be loosed upon their heads."
    So spoke Luke Skywalker, and shut his eyes,
Breathing a silent summons: through the air
The wooden throne, Threepio clutching tight,
660   First rises slowly of itself, then twirls
Faster and faster, higher, higher still,

DIVINE
ANGER

Above the Ewoks' terror and remorse:
They cast themselves upon their faces, down,
The pious youth, the newborn and the aged,
Mothers and fathers, widows, bachelors,
The hunters and the gatherers of herbs,
The chief, the Elders, and the cautious priest;
The drums have ceased; the chant, the solemn hymn
Returns, redoubled from two hundred throats,
670   Directed at the floating throne above,
With pledges of obedience; from the spits
They rush to free the Wookiee, droid, and men,
Until at last the awful chair descends,
Its occupant astounded at his powers.

    A different, gentler banquet soon is set,
With seats of honor laid for Luke and Han,
For Chewie, most of all for Wicket's friend;
Over the feast the deity presides.
Then there began a story oft retold
680   In Bright Tree Village by the Ewok bards,

THREEPIO'S
ACCOUNT

And soon across all Endor (though the best
Was still to be achieved): all through the night
The god himself, in dialect divine,
Informed them of what heroes had arrived:
The tall man flew among the moons themselves
On some great bird; the giant also flew,

And he alone was blessed with proper fur;
The smaller man, so serious, was sworn
To battle evil and maintain the right;
690   The lady was the bitterest foe alive
Of biker scouts, for they had burned her moon;
The little steel one was the god's best friend.
Now they had come to Endor, since the scouts
Were building some great evil in the air,
The sphere; but when that sphere was finished, then
The prince of evil, Vader, who had slain
The smaller man's great-grandfather, would rule
The stars themselves, and punish every race,
Even the harmless – aye, those most of all;
700   At dawn, upon the morrow, in the sky
The enemies of Vader would appear
On giant birds, far up, to burn the sphere:
Its sole protection lay not far away
Inside the bunker where the walkers stalked.

     So Threepio explained, as through the night,
Shivering and gasping at such daring deeds,
The spellbound clans sat listening in the hut,
The Elders silent 'til the god had ceased.
Then straightaway they rise, as one: the drum
710   Beats singly, and Chief Chirpa pledges this:
The heroes shall be counted with the tribe.
At that the feast redoubles, long sustained;
But Chirpa, 'midst the revelry, consults
The bravest hunters, Teebo, Asha Fahn,
CHIRPA'S   With Logray too, whose caution he requires.
COUNCIL   They weigh the chances and the consequence,
But soon agree, and soon dispatch their best
As holy heralds to the tribes nearby,
Proclaiming truce, requiring to be heard.

720   Meanwhile, as Chewie, R2, even Han
Indulged their woodland fame, Luke slipped aside
To seek the cool advice of solitude.
Tall torches float amid the misty night;
LUKE   He found a spot where wooden walkways met,
SLIPS OFF   Searching his spirit, roaming, sensing still

What had been felt upon the shuttlecraft,
The menace, Vader's malice: thus he knew
His father too had reached the forest moon
And sensed Luke also, waiting for his son.

730   The hour was late: he must depart: all things
Drew swiftly to a reckoning: he must go.
One duty still remained: she must be told.
     No sooner had Luke named her in his thought
Than she appeared, wrapped in the Ewok cloth;
He thinks of R2-D2's hologram,

LEIA JOINS
LUKE   Her supplication; well he recollects
Her fierceness on the Death Star and her touch
When Ben was dead; but now her eyes are sad,
As though she felt the breath of destiny.

740   She halts before him, calling him by name:
     "O Luke, what's wrong? What deadly shadow sways

LEIA'S
CONCERN   About your shoulders? Why, your brow is pale.
What worry, what bewilderment is this
Which loyal friends and comrades may assuage?"
     So spoke the Princess, shuddering at the sight;
To her young Skywalker made this reply:
     "If only, dearest Leia, that could be!
But grief, and not bewilderment, torments
My spirit, for I hesitate at last:

750   Not distant now the deadly shadow stands,
Beneath the shield projector, feeling me
As I feel him: Darth Vader. He awaits.

LUKE'S
FEARS   How then can you and Han destroy the dish?
If I am with you, there is no surprise:
I am the only weakness in your plan.
But listen first, before I go: I swore
To solve a riddle when the moment came.
Leia, you told me once that you were born
Not to the regnant queen of Alderaan

760   But to another: have you ever known
Her name, her people? What can you recall?"
     At this the Princess starts, but answers true:
     "Little enough, alas, for she was dead
Before I left the blanket of my birth;
Yet even so, strange visions sometimes come,

LEIA'S
MOTHER

When duty leaves me leisure to reflect,
Like dimmest memories of a woman's face,
Smiling, but sad, as though she must depart,
Her dark eyes rich with beauty; then I wish

770

I knew her, whether she were real or no.
But why is that your question? Oh, poor Luke,
I see you weep: you were an orphan too,
Since your great father fell on Mustafar,
Anakin Skywalker, whose name resounds."
    To that Luke answered with a rueful smile,
Taking her hand, extinguishing a tear:
    "Oh, Leia, could you only see yourself!
Her dark eyes rich with beauty – they are yours;
In you I greet her valor and her grief.

780

My father did not die on Mustafar,
My father lives, beneath a name of dread:

LUKE'S
FATHER

Darth Vader is my father, Leia, who
Destroyed the Jedi, and whose power defers
To nothing but the horror on the throne.
No, it is true, for Vader swore himself,
And then on Tatooine Ben's ghost agreed.
The fact is hard, but this is harder still:
If I should perish, Leia, none but you
Shall prove the hidden heiress of my power:

790

For in my blood the Force is strong indeed:
My father wields it as a tool of death;
In me it heaves and surges, hardly tamed;
My sister feels it, though she names it not,

LUKE'S
SISTER

My comrade and my sister and my twin,
Daughter of Anakin, of Vader, you
Whose ceaseless fire oft reignites my own."
    So Skywalker declared, his eyes suffused;
But no more now she shuddered: she perceived
The present and the future and the past,

800

Answering the hero with these wingèd words:
    "So, brother! Now I know what I have felt.
That Vader is my father I accept,

LEIA BIDS
LUKE FLEE

But not that he should take my brother's life.
You go to face him – why? If he discerns
Your spirit here on Endor, oh, escape!

Flee from the moon, the sector, far beyond
The distant edges of the stellar map,
Returning once the Emperor is destroyed.
Shall I be robbed of family once again

810 And gain a brother but to mourn his loss?"
     So Leia spoke, and sorrow overcame
Her steely virtue: well she understood
She pled in vain; she staggered to a knee.

LUKE'S
INTENTION But Luke, lifting her gently, added this:
    "I go to face him and to bring him back.
My father will not hand me to the Sith.
He is not wholly evil, and the good
That served the Council and maintained the right
Endures within his soul: so I foresee;

820 But if I journey only to my doom,
As Anakin's not Vader's son I go.
Farewell, dear sister! Trust the living Force,
In which all things arise and fall away."
    So spoke the son of Skywalker, and kissed
Her forehead, turning; Leia grasped his hand,
Stung by the bitter prick of parting; Luke
Was gone, vanishing silent in the mist
That drifted like a river past the porch;
She steps toward the firelight and Han.

830 Aye, there Han stood, before the council hut,
LEIA AND HAN Witness of their farewell; cruel jealousy
Was gnawing at his lower lip; he sulks
To think that she relies on Luke, not him.
But Leia, in the midst of her despair,
Laughed at his vanity, his eager love;
She kissed his mouth, and shook away her tears,
And, smiling proudly, answered Solo thus:
    "Indeed my love for Luke is like a rock;
For he's my brother, who now seeks his death

840 For all our sakes, and will not be denied.
But you I love as sailors love the sea."
    Just so she spoke and sank into his arms.
As when the wroshyr forests of Kashyyyk
Would bend before its fearful hurricane,
The Mrawzim, twirling seeds and cones aloft

To distant cliffs, so Han and Leia's hearts
Twirled through the night of Endor – so it felt.
But soon they sought their comrades by the fire,
Preparing for a strike before the dawn,
850   When Endor's groves, sweet haunts of silvan peace,
Would host hot battle and the screech of war;
But meanwhile Luke was stepping to his doom.

BOOK X

THE CHOICE OF VADER

T here is the shining sun, and there the shade,
    The hope and the despair of all who live;
    Life parts them, yet they stretch across th' abyss,
'Til lastly, at the end, in death, they meet;

The universe itself, the spread of space,
Shall someday cease, when time is gathered up,
Without a future and without a past;
To this the very constellations tend.
Such is the pure enigma of the Force:
10 There stand the Jedi, learning each from each;
There stand the Sith, th' eternal enemy;
There is your sacred spring, from which I sipped

In youth, o Muse of stark infinity,
Receiving from your own soft hand this staff
Inscribed to me alone. O goddess, hear
My final prayer for victory: now conclude
The battle of the darkness and the light,
The fate of Luke, the fate of Palpatine,
The fate of Empire, and Darth Vader's choice,

20 Telling how through the tunnel of the mist,
Out from the deepest shadow of the ferns,
Before the sudden dawn could seize the sky,
A single silent figure, clad in black,
Came stepping to the fortress and the base,
Past AT-AT walkers, bunkers, speeder bikes,
The searchlights and the sandbags and the wire,
Advancing with his lightsaber outstretched,

LUKE Surrendering; there the troopers bound his hands,
SURRENDERS Their captain baffled at his steady gaze;

30 They lead him to Lord Vader, who by chance
Had landed to inspect the Death Star's shield.
He takes the weapon, bids the captain scour
The towering trees for further terrorists:
Alone he'll sift this rebel; off they march.
        Together thus the father and the son
Conversed within a silent corridor;

VADER AND But first Darth Vader lit the emerald blade,
LUKE Exulting in its elegance, his breath
Like wind amid the branches; and he spoke:

40   "Here is a noble lightsaber, your work;
Already many foes have felt its edge.
Your power was once untamed and raw, my son,
But now your skills are perfect, as foreseen
By him before whose face the future bends,
The Emperor, whom you shortly shall obey;
Already he awaits; to him we go."
        So spoke Darth Vader, pointing to the door;
Instead the son of Skywalker, his eyes
The brighter in the darkness, made reply:

50   "I know there is a face behind the mask,
The face of Anakin; to him I speak;

LUKE'S As Anakin's not Vader's son I come.
APPEAL My father will not hand me to the Sith

To kneel before the throne: I sense the strife,
The conflict. Search your feelings for the truth,
The truth for which, when over the abyss
I dangled, you held back the final blow.
The path of hate can only come to this,
The murder of your son. I will not turn,
60   I will not stumble and I will not fall;
So come with me, it is the only way."
      Thus Luke, and all his youthful will was bent
Upon persuasion; but Darth Vader paused
To ponder. Just as when the summer wind
Flutters the ivory forests of japor
On Tatooine, when widows' aching bones
Foretell a storm, just so the boy's fresh power
Recalled a trinket which his hands had carved,
An amulet of white japor, his gift
70   To her, the amulet she'd ever worn
About her neck on Coruscant, and soon,
Too soon, around her fingers (so they said),
When down the tearful streets of old Naboo,
Her deathless beauty decked with precious flowers,
Upon the bier she'd rolled toward the tomb,
Doomed to an end unnecessary. Now
Darth Vader shut the emerald blade and spoke:
      "My son, if destiny destroys you, I
Must serve that destiny. The name you speak
80   Is empty, as Kenobi learned too late,
Old fool, who spoke of turning back; in me
The dark side triumphs in a different name,
The dark side which, I see, you do not grasp.
I must obey my master: 'tis the Rule,
The ultimate solution of the Force,
In which all things arise and fall away
Save us, the sages, for whom life itself
LUKE
REBUFFED   Is clay to mold, to fashion, or to crush.
The dream of Obi-Wan is finished: come,
90   A final teacher will complete the art
Of Vader's son, so mighty in the Force."
      So Vader spoke in answer, leading Luke
Toward his shuttle, which, as dawn broke forth
Above the curvature of Endor, launched

Toward the battle station in the sky.
Thus even as the rebel fleet approached,
Racing the velvet lanes of hyperspace

TO THE
DEATH STAR
From Sullust, bent upon the Death Star's death,
Luke reached that giant project, incomplete,

100 Its sphere still swelling, ceaselessly increased
By droids and bustling vessels with their freight.
They dock in one of many hundred bays,
The Emperor's own, close by his puissant seat.

THE ROYAL
GUARDS
There, as the gangplank sank, the Royal Guards
Were waiting, six grim figures, each arrayed
In rippling robes of blood-red crimson, masked
And helmeted in crimson; in their hands
Were pikes, beneath their mantles vibroswords;
Stock still they stood, their loyalty unchecked

110 By mercy or remorse, and all men shook
Before the chasm of their vacant gaze;
Stock-still they stood, 'til Vader and his son
Strode down the gangplank, guarded every step
Toward the power and dread of Palpatine.
　　　Atop the tallest of the needle towers
Studding the Death Star's crust, it overlooked
The vastness of that artificial moon,

THE THRONE
ROOM
His lofty throne room, reached by turbolift.
The scarlet escort halts before the door.

120 Vader and Luke, with fateful step, go in
Together, crossing, by a narrow bridge,
A gulf that plunges past the reach of sight
Into the Death Star's core; vast panes reveal
The distant systems over which his will
Already reigned; a catwalk hugs the wall;
A staircase climbs toward the awful throne.
There on a spreading dais was his chair,
Turned back to face the emptiness; thereon
A figure wrapped in robes of sable sits;

130 Beside it, on the lofty walls, arise
Twin statues hewn from hardest crystal, picked

THE
FOUNDERS
To show the nameless founder, he who first,
Deep in the age of lightlessness, had quit
The feeble Jedi Order, he who penned

A secret scripture, shifting to the dark,
Rejecting Jedi pieties for deeds,
Acceptance for ambition, joy for hate,
Order for rage, contentment for despair,
And peace for ceaseless battle; with him went
His pupils, dubbed the Sith, whom in the wars
The Jedi barely vanquished. Only one
Arose from lonely ashes to restore
His Order, instituting its stark Rule,
Which since that day, a thousand years, had held,
Darth Bane: down from the second statue blaze
That second founder's dazzling eyes of stone,
His iron armor and his scowl inscribed
With curses tempered in forgotten tongues.
Such were the statues, witnesses sublime
Above the court of Sidious the Cruel.
   Now Vader and his prisoner climb the stair;
The adamantine throne begins to turn,
'Til Luke, upon the dais, meets at last
His enemy, the master of the Sith,
The Emperor, Sidious or Palpatine,
In whom the dark side flickered like a flame:
With crimson eyes 'neath flesh as pale as death,
His voice malevolence itself, his will
Flicking the binders off Luke's wrists afar,
He spoke, pretending to a noble tone:
   "Welcome, young Skywalker. The hour is late,
And you are long expected. Guards, begone.
I do not dread the anger of a guest,
A new apprentice, though he lingers yet
In error, thinking to resist his hate,
The way of rage unshackled, and to split
His father from his father's destiny.
Alas, the young are hopeful! Does he doubt
The dark side must consume whoever starts
Down its relentless path, himself not least?
Is this his saber? Vader, give it here;
Ah yes, how like the blade of Anakin,
Which sliced the neck of Dooku, while I sat
High in the war-torn sky of Coruscant

140

150

DARTH
SIDIOUS

160

SIDIOUS'
WELCOME

170

And watched their final combat; 'tis the Rule.
Ah yes, a Jedi's blade; but now we bid
Farewell to Jedi and that prophecy
To which unto the bitter end they clung:
In riddles it foretold a Chosen One
180   Fated to bring a balance to the Force
And overthrow the Sith forever. Him,
Your father, in their folly, they declared
The one elect; and he, to my delight,
Proved but the instrument of their demise.
But now you come, o son of Anakin,
And so at last the Jedi are no more."
     Thus in his gloating spoke Darth Sidious;
But now in answer, stainless as the breeze,
The voice of young Luke Skywalker replied:
190   "You are mistaken. Though the hour is late,
I will not stumble and I will not fall:
In me the ancient Jedi stand restored
And we reclaim our own, who was the best
With sword, with word, with every mindful art:
The Force flowed through him as through channels carved
By ancient waters, and I am his son.
But if in truth my father will not turn,

LUKE'S
DEFIANCE   Then death, the hidden kingdom of the Force,
In which the darkness and the light unite,
200   Shall soon enfold us, and Your Highness too."
     So spoke the fearless son of Anakin;
The master, though, was laughing, and his mouth
Was twisting in an ecstasy of hate;
Then, pointing at the stars, the Emperor spoke:
     "My careful plans, it seems, are overlooked
In their perfection. Oh, perhaps you mean
The imminent arrival of your fleet?

SIDIOUS'
PLANS   From here we may enjoy its last attack
In utter safety. It was I myself
210   Who let them learn my Death Star's secret flaw,
The shield projector on the forest moon,
Where, even as we speak, your hopeless band
Is battling with a legion of my troops,

The very finest, merciless, elite;
But since the vast deflector shield still stands
I fear our entertainment may be short."
　　　Just so the master spoke, and gave a laugh;

THE REBEL
FLEET

And even then the rebel fleet appeared,
Which Luke and Vader, through the glass, beheld,

220　A fearsome vision which the Force conferred:
The fighters first, swift A-wings in the lead,
And X-wings locking S-foils to attack,
The B-wing and the Y-wing bombers too,
And at their head the *Falcon*, racing quick
Toward the Death Star's thick magnetic shield
Projected from the surface of the moon
(Still standing, though Calrissian knew it not);
Behind them streak the frigates and corvettes,
The transports and the Dorneans and the *Ghost*,

230　With four Corellian gunships, ten X4s;
Then Admiral Ackbar's Calamari fleet,
The MC80s, giant in their strength,
Who range themselves in a perimeter.
Beneath their turbolasers, fighters lance
Toward the monstrous Death Star and their doom.
But then, to Luke, it seemed a miracle:
For now those fighters broke off their attack,

LANDO
BREAKS OFF

Banking away before they struck the shield:
Aye, that was Lando's doing, and Nien Nunb's,

240　His canny copilot, who told his chief
The comms were blocked, and Lando in a flash
Deduced the Empire knew of the attack
And banked away; yet ere the rebel fleet
Could heave to, jibing, tacking back to jump,
The scans pick up an interdiction field
That hinders all escape, immense in scope.
Then Ackbar knew it was the Emperor's trap,
Ordering evasive action; from afar
He notes new vessels curving 'round the moon,

250　The Star Destroyer fleet, full forty ships,

THE STAR
DESTROYERS

Black wedges stark against the sun's ascent,
And in their midst the vast *Executor*,

The flagship, fifteen times the size and length
Of any Star Destroyer. Luke, appalled,
Must listen to the glee of Palpatine:
　　"The final battle! But its heroes fall
Unsung, unmourned, for history little notes

SIDIOUS'
GLEE
A rebel's failure: history's in my fist.
Soon Mothma and old Ackbar shall rejoin

260
Organa and the Calamari king
As equals in futility. But come,
What thought is this? The Jedi Padawan
Ignores my battle and regards the sword
Upon my chair. But I am weaponless,
What checks him? Let the Jedi strike me down
In deadly anger; surely that is just,
And also, dare I say, the only hope
For friends who fight while others stand and watch."
　　Just so the master spoke, whose matchless mind

270
Perceived that Luke was starting down that path
From which, as Vader knew, there's no return:
Soon would the reckless boy be in his grip.
Then, with a grunt, the Emperor pressed the comm,

DEATH STAR
CAN FIRE
Instructing his vast battle station's crew
To fire at will. Aye, then the son must watch
And find that Death Star was no helpless hulk,
No fantasy, no project half-complete,
But fully operational, its dish
Directly pointed at the rebel fleet.

280
Already was the labor well begun
Of using that great weapon: target lock,
The final pause, the final safety check,
Ignition of the kyber cores, which yield
Eight hypermatter beams, a livid green
As lucid as a pulsar, whining through
Eight tributaries, 'til the focal point
Perfects the bright, apocalyptic ray.

DEATH OF
THE *LIBERTY*
Then first of all the rebel ships to die
Was *Liberty*: the superlaser struck

290
The hull amidships: instantly she blows,
Stupendously exploding, pulverised,
Her baffled escorts staggered at the shock;

Yet while the rebels reel, a second blast

Is readied as the unforgiving dish
Takes aim at sleek *Nautilian*, which again,
Pinpointed by the livid pulse of green,
Is smashed to pieces, blasted into bits;
And all the while the master's clever smile
Was spreading, as he goaded Luke afresh:

300 "It seems there is a limit, after all,
To what a pack of farmers can achieve
Against an Empire. Perfect, matchless power
Now crowns at last the labor of the Sith.
Alas, your friends have failed, your fleet is lost,
Th' Alliance dies, upon the moon, in space,
On every petty planet in my grip,
And death will seem a blessing to their heirs.

But what is this, the spirit of revenge?
The breath of anger? Good! Now strike me down

310 Like a true Skywalker, as hatred swells
Within: all of them, all the Tuskens, all,
He sabered, slaughtering, hacking, 'til that camp
Was strewn with limbs of old and young alike:
Aye, Anakin recounted it himself
To Palpatine, his mentor, ere the mask
Was settled by my hand across his face.
Now you yourself are stepping on the path;
What mercy do the merciless deserve?"
     Just so he spoke, Darth Sidious the Cruel,

320 And, even as he spoke, the boy, enraged,
Spun 'round, his hand outstretched to catch the sword

That hurtled to his fist; it glowed; the blow
Was angled at the neck of Palpatine.
But just as when another Knight's keen edge
Had sought to slice that master, Windu's blade
Upon that day of reckoning, but the blow
Had broken on the blade of Anakin,
Just so Luke's stroke was thwarted by the sword
Of crimson red that danced in Vader's grip:

330 Right at the master's throat the sabers met,
Sparks scattering from the blades of father, son;
And loud the Emperor cackled: well he knew

The stronger would prevail and claim the place
Beside his throne; and Vader must obey.

THE BATTLE IN SPACE

Meanwhile the regal dais' lofty panes
That looked upon the roil of battle, show
The Calamari cruisers wheeling back
At Ackbar's order, seeking to escape
The Interdictors, lest they wither quick

340 Before the Death Star's blasts; but Lando called
Across the comm link, as the *Falcon* flew
Against vast swarms of TIE fighters unleashed
Upon the rebel fleet; thus Lando spoke:
    "No, Admiral, no withdrawal, no retreat!
We'll never get another shot at this,
It's now or never! Press your swift attack
Against the Star Destroyer fleet, point-blank;

LANDO'S FAITH

We'll last far longer fighting ship to ship
Than here against that Death Star! We need time

350 For Han's commandos: Han will break the shield
Upon the moon, I know it. How? Just this:
Good friends must trust each other, and the Force.
But if this is our final battlefield
We'll take some Star Destroyers as we go!"
    So spoke Calrissian, racing to attack,
And Ackbar saw the wisdom of his words:
His cruisers soon engage at point-blank range,
Advancing past the Death Star's field of fire.

    Yet Han's commandos on the Endor moon

360 Were far indeed from any such success:
How can a thousand soldiers not prevail
Against fifteen? The Emperor's finest troops,
His proudest legion, laid the careful trap,
Letting them infiltrate the generator: there,
Before their bombs could sabotage the shield,

HAN AND LEIA PRISONERS

Chewie and Han and Leia faced arrest,
The strike team too; the droids alone remain
With Ewoks, overlooking that bleak scene
Of rebels crouching by the bunker doors,

370 Hands on their heads as stormtroopers await
The word to finish off the rebel scum.

Your tale then, Han, was nearly at an end
In wretched execution; nonetheless
Your luck was with you: from the hill above,
Where the thick ferns swept round a jutting rock,
A golden figure gleamed beneath a beam
With shrill announcements for the enemy:
　　　"Hello, hello! I say, you troopers, here!
Oh, were you looking for me? Over here!
380　　My counterpart and I give up! Come here!"
　　　So spoke C-3PO, and never droid
Was braver, snatching victory from defeat:

**THE EWOKS
ARRIVE**

The Ewoks knew but little of that tongue:
They only saw the golden god himself,
Alone, defying every biker scout
In their own language; from the underbrush,
As up toward R2 and Threepio
The stormtroopers came climbing, now the growls
Had shifted to a reverent chant, grim hymns
390　　Resounding through the forest, hymns of war
From many thousand throats: the tribes had marched
'Neath treaties such as never Endor knew,
In singular alliance: now the cry
Which Ewoks, since the origin of trees,
Had loosed upon their foes, a gargling call,
Echoes from trunk to trunk, from branch to branch:
A sacred war begins beneath the leaves.
As when upon the prairie of Jaresh
A scruffy-looking herdsman of the nerf,
400　　Half-witted, too complacent in his pride,
Neglects his beasts, 'til, startled from a nap,
He trembles at the patter of their feet
Ascending to crescendo, to stampede,
And tumbles from the hammock in despair,
Just so those startled stormtroopers took fright
At hymns of battle and the horns of war.

**BATTLE IN
THE WOODS**

Then from a hundred ambushes they rose,
The Ewoks, sons of Endor, with their god:
A volley first of arrows tipped with flint
410　　Assails the troopers; many find a mark.
Disorder checks the infantry's advance:

The little woodland savages had come!
At once the AT-STs rev to life,
Blasting the underbrush; the armored squads
Disperse, with cruel intent, among the ferns
While officers and engineers retreat
Inside the solid bunker, blast doors shut.
The rebels, freed, pursue the foe too slow,
Barred from the bunker; rather, digging in
420   With captured blasters by the gate, they strafe
The speeder bikes that whistle through the fray.
        Ah, how that forest rang, as hand-to-hand,
In mad melee, the Ewoks first prevail:
Some swing upon the vines, impacting hard,
Then wield the clubs and hatchets; some drop rocks

EWOK   From hang gliders that drift between the trunks,
TACTICS   On AT-STs or on speeder bikes;
Some seek to snare the chickenwalkers' legs,
Lifting a weighty rope, secured, alas,
430   Too lightly, since its draggers soon are dragged
Behind the metal monsters; with the sling
The hunters smite more targets from afar.
        But now the legion, shedding its surprise,
Regains the upper hand: the marksmen pick
The squealing critters from the branches, charge
To scatter and surprise them from behind;

IMPERIAL   The AT-STs, with their thudding guns,
RESPONSE   Explode the secret nests of ambuscade,
Blasting hot canyons through the forest floor,
440   Indomitable, armored, resolute:
No catapult can down them, cedar clubs
In vain attempt to stub the iron feet.
        And yet that legion, so invincible,
Had failed to reckon with one factor, this:
A Wookiee's ingenuity. While Han
And Leia held the bunker, Chewie prowled
The forest, climbing with two furry friends

CHEWIE'S   Into a perch from which a swinging vine
PLOY   Was poised for just the moment to attack.
450   How long they waited, while the war below

Was boiling, and the beaten warriors fled!
At last an AT-ST ambled past,
Incognizant, intent on homicide,
And then the Wookiee and the Ewoks struck,
Swinging upon their vine above its head,
Dropping atop it; Chewie rips the hatch
And down he climbs, the Ewoks in the lead
Befuddling the bewildered pilots, whom
The Wookiee plucks and launches from the roof.
460 Then proud Chewbacca studies the controls,
The mortar and the thudding double guns,
And picks a route across the fearful fray.

So surged the forest battle to and fro,
But meanwhile at the bunker Leia called
For R2 on the comm, who straightaway
Proceeded to his duty, since those doors
Would yield to naught but his cryptography.
R2-D2 AT Down through the forest paths he rolled, his friend
THE BUNKER Tottering behind in fine anxiety;
470 That gate was sore defended by Han's gun
And Leia's courage: stormtrooper platoons
Were pressing ever forward down the glen,
For if one fell, two occupied his place.
Then R2-D2 at the terminal
Plugged in, his circuits beeping with success;
But even as the gate began to budge
A trooper's E-11 nailed the droid,
Who screeches back in smoking ruin, mourned
By Threepio and Leia; Han takes charge,
480 Dashing to hotwire those controls himself,
His not infrequent task since days of youth;
But luck has nothing for him now: the door
Redoubles, thicker still, impregnable.
Then Leia, in her inward thought, despaired,
But silently addressed herself to Luke,
Calling upon his spirit far away:
LEIA WISHES "Oh, brother, how we miss your saber's light!
FOR LUKE Here is the final ruin of our cause,

The shield undamaged and the fleet undone.
490 Alas that you should venture to your death!
Where is the Force to rescue us at last?"
So Leia spoke in sorrow and despair,
A vision rising in her teeming brain:
The face of Luke, his features dark with rage,
Half lit, half overshadowed as he fought
The somber shape of Vader, far above,
High in the sky of Endor's eager morn,
Within the Death Star throne room, to and fro
Before the laughter of the lord of lies,
500 Along the dais, up and down the stair.

VADER DUELS LUKE As when two champions of combatant packs
Dispute a lonely carcass in the hills,
Snarling defiance, twisting through the air,
Teeth ripping, muzzles spattered, stained in red,
So Vader and his rival, stroke for stroke:
Battled: the sabers cut and parry, cut
Two-handed, quick as crashes in the sky,
Clashing and crackling, weaving through the gloom,
The upstart still advancing, Vader pressed,
510 'Til from the staircase lip Luke spun and kicked
The sable figure backward: through the air
Above the stairs grim Vader tumbled, saved
By mastery of the Force, as nimble still
As in that fateful duel on Mustafar;
The crimson weapon pulses in his grip;
The throne room rings with Sidious' delight.
But Luke, his shoulders heaving, shook his head,
Like some deep sleeper shuddering in a dream;
Clenching his teeth, he shut the shining blade,
520 Renouncing such a battle, such a foe,

LUKE WILL NOT FIGHT Vanishing into shade as love and hate
Fought back and forth across that still fair face;
But Vader would not cease: the silent hall
Communicates the lesson and the threat
Inside Luke's spirit: Jedi and the Sith
Could share their thought without the use of words
Afar; and to his son the father spoke:

"If Obi-Wan has taught you well, my son,
You know you cannot so defer the choice.

530
For friendship's sake you did not hesitate

**VADER
GOADS HIM**
To die on Bespin; now you hope the same
Will save them, and elect to be destroyed.
Is that the limit of your loyalty?
A selfish death is this, a feeble end.
Your comrades' lives depend upon the dark,
On you, the Emperor's servant and my son."
So spoke Lord Vader; Skywalker replied,
Communicating also voicelessly:
"I will not fight you, father. Hidden things

540
I see: by your own thoughts you are betrayed.

**LUKE
RESISTS**
I hear what your dark master does not know,
The conflict and the ceaseless war within,
The battle of the darkness and the light:
Your saber shall not deal the final blow."
So spoke Luke Skywalker, and in his mind
He saw his sister, heiress of his power,
Crouched at the bunker gate on Endor's moon,
Her helmet shed, her shoulder wounded, yet
The blaster pistol jerking in her fist,

550
The light of hopeless valor in her eye.
But Vader, who of all the Jedi felt
The Force most keenly, saw what Luke had seen,
The Princess' pride, her stark ferocity,
And instantly he knew the secret truth,
The crown of old Kenobi's cunning fraud:
Not once but twice the father had been robbed.
But with a laugh of triumph he exclaimed:
"What war, what conflict? Did I hesitate
To slay Jocasta, Ferren, Cin, or Koth,

560
Or Shaak Ti or Ahsoka or Malreaux,
Or Obi-Wan himself? If thoughts betray

**VADER SEES
LEIA**
The thinker, what if in your vision sits
A comrade and a sister and a twin?
Indeed Kenobi was no fool to hide
The children of the pupil he betrayed;
But now the old man's failure is complete.

So let my son elect to be destroyed,
Perhaps there is another Skywalker,
My daughter, who will turn toward the dark!"

570   So Vader spoke, and then the soul of Luke
Surrendered to his anger and his hate,
All love for Leia twisted into rage

LUKE'S FURY   Against the threat of her corruption, fused
With long despair: on Vader from behind
His blazing saber fell, uncheckable
By any but that prince of duelists
And barely parried. Like a storm of hail
That hurls itself upon the helpless crops,
Smashing the winter's hope, a deafening beat

580   Against the roof, the windows, death to beasts
Or man or woman caught upon the plain,
Just so the boy, his son, possessed at last
By will to an implacable revenge,

VADER FALLS   Pursued him, hacking, slaughtering, 'til at length
As Sidious descended to behold
His new disciple's triumph, Vader fell,
Still fighting, stumbling back beside th' abyss.
But Luke, relentless in his enmity,
Attacked, and spun his wrist: the emerald edge

590   Hewed Vader's hand, which with his sword is sent
Into oblivion. Coughing, Vader grasps
The empty limb, a mass of twisted wire:
The very wrist which once, in that grim duel
On Geonosis, Dooku hewed, the Sith
Whom he himself, at Sidious' behest,
Had slaughtered in revenge, and so his steps
In that cruel hour had started down the path
From which, as Vader knew, there's no return.
But now he too lay beaten; once again

600   Before the loser's throat the victor's blade
Floats, pausing; for Luke's face was deathly pale;
What mercy do the merciless deserve?
Yet in the empty wrist Luke saw his own
On windy Bespin: over the abyss
He'd dangled but not felt the final blow.
He hesitates; he stares; he does not strike.

Instead he turns toward that lord of lies
Descending from behind, and shuts his sword;
With shining eyes he speaks these final words:

610

LUKE IS
A JEDI

    "The path of hate can only come to this,
The murder of my father. You have failed,
Your Highness. Like my father was before,
Great Anakin, whose name in me resounds,
Behold, I am at last a Jedi, sworn
To battle evil and maintain the right,
The last of all the Jedi; here I stand:
I will not stumble and I will not fall;
Your doom approaches: so I prophesy."

620

    So spoke the son of Skywalker, and then
The tide of battle in the forest turned.
For even as the Princess and her love,
Besieged, encircled by the bunker doors,
Were beaten, wounded, taken in defeat
By two tall AT-STs and three squads,
Ready for the inevitable end,
To Leia, oh, it seemed a miracle:
One AT-ST stood behind the next,
Taking a bead with double cannons, paused,
Then blew its peer to screaming smithereens,

630

CHEWIE'S
AT-ST

Turning to rake the infantry, who flee.
The hatch is opened and a Wookiee's roar
Salutes them – Chewie, boasting of his prize.
The swashbuckler and Princess shout with joy.
Yet, though they're saved, the mission still remains;
And how to breach a bunker's solid door?
But then Han Solo recollects again
The old man's very words: the winding path
To victory often takes us through the shade.
Among the dead he finds a pilot's garb;

640

Disguised, he climbs the walker: on the comm
He calls the nervous captain of the base
With news of triumph from the forest floor,
Requesting three more squads to reinforce.
Thus Han; the rebels lay their ambuscade,
And, when the blast door opens of itself,
Releasing reinforcements, then they strike,

Taking their prisoners; Captain Solo sprints
Inside with five brave men to blow the shield.
Along the metal corridors they rush,
650   Reaching the shield's reactor, to attach
Ten deadly charges on the glowing nodes;
THE SHIELD   The bomb is armed; they dash; it detonates,
DESTROYED   The roar resounding through the shaken woods:
Tall flames engulf the bunker and the base,
The shield projector shattered; from afar
The Ewoks heard it, through the thick of war,
And turned on their pursuers with a cheer.

Thus on the planet; meanwhile, far aloft,
The battle in the zone above the moon
660   Was raging: Admiral Ackbar's own *Home One*
And other MC80s broke the line,
Their mighty broadsides sweeping through the foe,
BATTLE OF   The frigates chipping in, the quick corvettes
ENDOR   Lancing ahead, while seething swarms of TIEs,
TIE fighters, bombers, Interceptors too,
Twist 'round the rebel cruisers, stalking, stalked
By A-wings, X-wings; now a B-wing blasts
A foe, itself destroyed; a Y-wing burns,
But not before its twin torpedoes launch,
670   Impacting on a Star Destroyer's prow.
Vast batteries hammer at the rebel fleet
From countless ships which long had paralyzed
The galaxy's clear heavens, *Harbinger*,
The *Devastator* and the *Vigilance*;
Together their TIE Interceptors roll
Into the reckless dogfights, through the fleet;
But there the swarming squadrons were assailed
By Red's undaunted X-wings, Wedge's pride,
The Blues' bright B-wings, and that dazzling ship
680   That seems to strike from everywhere at once,
Lando's *Millennium Falcon*: with a cry
General Calrissian shifts the swift attack
Against the Star Destroyer fleet itself:
Corona strikes the *Subjugator*; Grays
Behind good Horton wreck the *Vehement*;
And Crynyd's Greens, who yielded place to none,

Smite the *Executor*, itself assailed
From every vector as old Ackbar called
For concentration on the giant's shields:
690 A cheer – her bridge deflectors have been hit,
And Arvel Crynyd's A-wing, fighting close,
Before the TIEs can finish him, nose-dives

WRECK OF
THE EXECUTOR
Into her bridge, which, dying, he destroys.
The gyros shatter and the steering fails
As that enormous flagship, rudderless,
Keels to the Death Star's surface and impacts.
As when a fire, which tipsy travelers tend
Ineptly, burns the roots beneath the earth,
Running unseen to reach a nearby fir
700 Which soon is but a solid stack of flame,
Just so the vast *Executor* ignites,
Plowing her bow into the station's side.
But even as old Ackbar joined the cheer
He heard the voice of Lando on the comm:
"The shield is down! He did it! Good old Han!
All fighters, follow me! We'll finish off
Our mission and the Death Star! Follow me!"
So spoke Calrissian, and the *Falcon* swerved
Into the superstructure, Wedge in tow.

710 Upon that Death Star stood Darth Sidious,
The master, the anointed of the Rule,
Oblivious of the battle, poised and fixed
Before the fallen father and the son,
Surprised indeed that Luke should spurn the dark.

SIDIOUS VS.
LUKE
With crimson eyes 'neath flesh as pale as death,
His voice like poison in the ears, he spoke:
"You will not stumble and you will not fall;
So be it, Jedi. You have made your choice.
One final lesson only will I teach,
720 The price that must be paid for pretty words
And useless gestures: here is all your love
And loyalty, compassion, honor, truth:
Now join the Jedi as you meet the Sith."
Just so he spoke, and from his fingertips
The searing lightning, branching blue and white,
Flew through the crackling air to strike at Luke,

FORCE
LIGHTNING

Blasting him back, convulsing every limb,
Sizzling along his chest, his head, his neck,
The weapon and the horror of the dark;
730 And so had mighty Windu been destroyed
Upon that day of infamy when first
The face of Vader's master was revealed
On Coruscant, while Padmé still took breath,
And for her sake he'd made his choice. Now Luke
Lay twisting at the edge of the abyss;
But Vader slowly rises, gasping hard,
Cradling his empty limb, to see her son
Screaming in pain, the potent master's laugh
Increasing to an ecstasy of hate.
740 And now again spoke Sidious the Cruel:
     "What other ending, boy, did you expect?
Your feeble skills are nothing next to mine.
Relish your prophecy, the just reward
Of all defiance: in the truth you find
Your pain and then, young Skywalker, you die!"
     Just so he spoke, the white and withered hands
Blazing with electricity, Luke's scream

LUKE'S PLEA
TO VADER

Unending as the dancing lightning grips
His very teeth; he struggles for a word:
750 "Oh, father, here I am, the only son
Of her, whoever she once was, the bride
You must have loved, the woman you adored;
Farewell, my father, Anakin the Just!"
     Just so Luke spoke, and as his body bucked
Tortured by evil, victim of his faith
That by fresh valor sins might be undone
Or what is long since fallen raised again,

VADER'S
CHOICE

His foolish faith, meeting his just reward,
The last of Jedi – Vader made his choice,
760 And turned toward the laughing lord of lies,
Taking the wary prophet unawares,
Lifting him in his arms. The Emperor shrieks,
Too late perceiving where the peril lies:
His lightning swings to ravage Vader's chest,
The respirator and the durasteel
That knit the limbs, the muscles, and the joints,

Scorching the circuits; yet Darth Vader's grip
Was more than muscle, circuitry, and steel:
For even as the lightning took his life
770 He staggered with his burden to the lip,
The precipice, and with a last vast heave
He let his master drop into th' abyss.
   Down fell the Sith, down fell Darth Sidious,
END OF To perish, screeching, at the very core
SIDIOUS Of that vast Death Star; up from distant depths
A wind of ruin blew, a wind of doom,
A withering wind of evil and of hate,
Blew upward, blew away; then all was still.
At last the son of Skywalker arose,
780 Dragging his senseless father to the door
Toward the shuttle, whence the guards had fled
In panic as the vast *Executor*
Impacted and the mighty Death Star quaked.

   But now Calrissian and the *Falcon* swerved
Into the superstructure, Wedge in tow,
Santage and Norra hurtling right behind,
Six brave TIE Interceptors in pursuit,
Down shafts of steel, down tightening corridors,
Toward the vast reactor at the heart:
790 Now left, now right the *Falcon* pirouettes,
LANDO AND The Interceptors blasting at the stern,
WEDGE Though Norra and Keir Santage draw some off.
At last it looms ahead, the kyber core,
In one enormous chamber; Lando calls
To Wedge to blow the regulator, aims
The *Falcon* at the very heart of power.
Then Wedge Antilles did not miss his mark,
THE KYBER Torpedoes blasting through the northern tower;
CORE But Lando loosed the *Falcon*'s armament,
800 Concussion missiles, cannons, at the core,
Wheeling in desperation to escape
The fury of annihilating fire.
As when a flower, pride of the forest floor,
Opens a fragrant pair of leaves, its dew
Seducing some poor insect to its doom,

Which must soon flit away or be devoured,
Just so the *Falcon*, swiftest hunk of junk
That Lando ever knew, was sorely pressed,
Back up the tightening corridors, the shafts,
810   Racing against the surging wave of flame
In which her last pursuers met their end.
Nien Nunb, they say, would afterward attest
They never should have made it; blazing sheets
Engulf them, cook them, 'til against all odds
The blistering horror of inferno yields
To open stars, the safety of the void.
There rebel and Imperial vessels wait

END OF THE
DEATH STAR   To watch the vast apocalypse, white fire
Splitting the giant battle station's side,
820   A massive flash, the potent wrath of suns
Erupting as the crystal kyber core,
Jewel of the strongest stars, disintegrates
The terror of an empire: at a stroke
The shackles of a galaxy fall free.
As when the fitted portal of a tomb
Is inched aside, and searing sunlight creeps
Across the timeless mummy and its shroud,
Which crumbles at the softest breath of air,
Just so the deadly will of Sidious
830   Was dissipated. Such is destiny.

    Among the drifting wreckage, shattered droids
And corpses, chunks of fuselage, debris
Hung Vader's battered shuttle, spinning blind,

LUKE AND
ANAKIN   Which Luke, half-crippled still, had barely flown
Straight through the tumult and the maze of flame.
Beside his father's maimed and broken form
He crouched to hear a breathless whisper drop:
It bade Luke lift the helmet and the mask
To free his vision; anguished, Luke replied:
840   "But, if I break the armor, you will die;
I came to face you and to bring you back!"
    So spoke the noble son of Skywalker,

THE HELMET
LIFTED   Weeping; but soon he acted; well he knew
That nothing now could stop his father's end.

The heavy helm is lifted from the head,
White scalp exposed, which searing lava scarred
With livid marks and deep, on Mustafar;
Red eyes blink slowly as Luke's fingers shift
The breathing tubes to free the withered mouth.

850 Then Skywalker at last discerned his son
Uncolored by the malice of the Sith,
The last of all the Jedi and the best;
His voice was human and his eyes were clear:
    "Oh, son of Padmé, Leia's brother, Luke,
You did not stumble and you did not fall.
Behold the man you saved, for you were right:
I was not wholly evil; was I good?

ANAKIN'S   What was I but the child of prophecy,
FAREWELL   Slayer of Jedi, slayer of the Sith,

860 Fated to bring a balance to the Force?
I have become what I was born to be.
Now bring my body to the Endor moon
And light the pyre on which I travel hence,
Accepting death at last, going to meet
The shades of Yoda and of Obi-Wan,
Who showed me first th' indwelling power that binds
All living things and balances our fate.
Then greet your sister: tell her you were right."
    Just so he spoke at last, shutting his eyes,

870 Passing beyond us, Anakin the Just,
The Chosen One, so mighty in the Force.
The awful mask fell clattering to the floor,
And down the shuttle slipped toward the moon.

    There we may cease, my angel; other tongues
May sing the celebrations of the free
Upon Naboo, in Bespin's tinted sky,
On Coruscant and countless other worlds,
Not least in Endor's forest. There they dance:
A New Republic rises from the ash

880 Of Empire and that war among the stars
They fought so long ago, so far away.

▽△▽△▽△▽△▽△▽△▽△▽△▽△▽△▽△▽△▽△▽△▽△

ACKNOWLEDGMENTS

I would like to thank my wife, Luba, who married a penniless poet; my sons, Caius and Silvan, who rekindled my love of *Star Wars* and listened to the poem as it grew; my parents, Marg and Jim, and my brother, Dave, who have always believed in me; Miriam Sargeant, Rick Desclouds, Doug Taylor, Margaret Poetschke, Alessandro Barchiesi, Natasha Peponi, and Richard Martin: seven teachers who greatly influenced my life; Chris Grundke, Mark Alonge, Alex McLean, Paul McGilvery, Timothy Steele, and Eli Arsenault, who read part or all of the text; my aunt Cath Mitchell, for sage advice; Richard Stursberg, who raised a benevolent eyebrow at this project; my brilliant, indefatigable agent, Hilary McMahon of Westwood; at Lucasfilm, Jennifer Heddle, Kelsey Sharpe, and Leland Chee for their patience and many insightful solutions; at Abrams, the aesthetic expertise of Diane Shaw and Shawn Dahl, the efficiency of Rachael Marks, and the eagle eyes of Annalea Manalili, Katherine Furman, and Christopher Cerasi; Jessica Benhar, whose illustrations so beautifully complement my words; Jamison Stoltz and Connor Leonard, my editors at Abrams, for their faith in the book and their leadership through the thick of a pandemic; the tireless and selfless contributors to Wookieepedia; and, last but not least, Mr. George Lucas, to whom many generations are already indebted.

▽△▽△▽△▽△▽△▽△▽△▽△▽△▽△▽△▽△▽△▽△▽